THE
VINYL
UNDERGROUND

THE VINYL UNDERGROUND

ROB RUFUS

Mendota Heights, Minnesota

First Edition
First Printing, 2020

Book design by Jake Slavik
Cover design by Jake Slavik
Cover images by Glovatskiy/Shutterstock, MaxFrost/Shutterstock, PhotoStockImage/Shutterstock

Excerpt on page 9 from *DISPATCHES* by Michael Herr, copyright © 1977 by Michael Herr. Used by permission of Alfred A. Knopf, an imprint of the Knopf Doubleday Publishing Group, a division of Penguin Random House LLC. All rights reserved.

Excerpt on page 83 from *Johnny Got His Gun* by Dalton Trumbo, copyright © 2007 by Kensington Publishing Corp.

Excerpt on page 181 from *Dance The Eagle to Sleep* by Marge Piercy, copyright © 2012 by PM Press. www.pmpress.org.

Flux, an imprint of North Star Editions, Inc.

Library of Congress Cataloging-in-Publication Data
Names: Rufus, Rob, author.
Title: The Vinyl Underground / Rob Rufus.
Description: First edition. | Mendota Heights, Minnesota : Flux, 2020. | Audience: Grades 10-12. | Summary: In small-town Florida in 1968, four teens who bond over music and their objection to the Vietnam War decide to take a stand against the U.S. government and violent racism.
Identifiers: LCCN 2019054675 (print) | LCCN 2019054676 (ebook) | ISBN 9781635830507 (paperback) | ISBN 9781635830514 (ebook)
Subjects: CYAC: Friendship—Fiction. | Music—Fiction. | Draft—Fiction. | Vietnam War, 1961-1975—Protest movements—Fiction. | Racism—Fiction. | Florida—History—20th century—Fiction.
Classification: LCC PZ7.1.R8435 Vin 2020 (print) | LCC PZ7.1.R8435 (ebook) | DDC [Fic]—dc23
LC record available at https://lccn.loc.gov/2019054675
LC ebook record available at https://lccn.loc.gov/2019054676

Flux
North Star Editions, Inc.
2297 Waters Drive
Mendota Heights, MN 55120
www.fluxnow.com

Printed in the United States of America

For Elizabeth Asuka Fragosa.
Because you're more American than rock-n-roll,
and a million other reasons.

&

For (USMC Sgt.) Robert J. Rufus, my father and
inspiration. Because I wish I could write you the
homecoming from Saigon that you deserved.

AMERICA
1965–1973

The government drafted unwilling American kids into the Vietnam War. It was an unjust conflict fueled by lies, racism, fear, and misinformation. Most of those drafted were fresh out of high school. 648,500 were forced to fight, regardless of moral or political opposition.

Over 17,725 draftees died in a strange land.

People of every age, race, creed, and orientation were left mourning. Their outrage spurred new types of resistance for a new generation. Some chose the Free Love Movement. Others chose to fight back. All were grassroots revolts led solely by the youth of America.

SIDE

A

"Vietnam was what we had instead of happy childhoods."
—Michael Herr

ONE

EVE OF DESTRUCTION 1968

"Free Love" is bullshit. Nothing is free.

But I was too distracted to see it that summer. My brother was, too. All those new rock-n-roll records were too good for our own good. They hypnotized us, man. They psychedelicized us; they baptized us in the shiny and ever-changing sounds of '67. They made it easy for heavy topics to sink to the bottom of our consciousness.

Whenever I'd mention the war to Bruce, he'd change the subject by dragging me into his bedroom to play me whatever his new favorite record was—The Grass Roots, The Yardbirds, maybe Otis Redding's live LP—it was always something different, something righteous as hell and truly exciting.

"Why talk about the future when we can listen to it?" he'd say.

Whether he meant our future on the radio or that of our country, I'll never know. Because that was before he shipped out. Before the beaches emptied and the school bells rang and the Summer of Love got divorced.

Now it was winter. Now it was cold.

Now it was a new world.

Now it was New Year's Eve and my brother was dead and the sky was a gray slab of granite. I stood at the window of his bedroom, looking out at that dead sky. It seemed to stretch bigger than the whole wide world, hard and indifferent, a lot like the God who had organized this shitshow in the first place.

The gloom of winter didn't mesh with North Florida, and our neighborhood looked strange beneath it. The Southern homes with their bright pastel panels, the willows and red-berried hollies—in this new world their colors were dull.

I imagined the strange cold front had occurred in homage to Bruce, as if the atmosphere itself was in mourning. I visualized his last breath leaving his body and soaring up into the heavy sky of Vietnam and over the black waves of the Pacific, across the deserts and cities and plains until it finally reached Cordelia Island, Florida—a cloud made up of nothing, a cold front that blew him home.

I shivered and turned away from the window.

Dad said I spent too much time in Bruce's bedroom, and I knew he was probably right. But it was the only place I still felt like myself. Ever since Bruce died, the rest of the world made me feel like a jack-o'-lantern—hollow and out of season with an unconvincing smile. But in his room, I could turn the music up loud enough to drown my new world out.

I could live in those old songs for a while, like we used to. So I walked across the room to his record collection, which consisted of seventy-seven LPs and over three hundred 45rpm singles. Bruce stored the LPs in milk crates and organized the singles on his shelf by genre—pop, soul, rock-n-roll, folk, girl groups, Brit rock—labeling each with a thin strip of duct tape.

I took a single from a small stack that I'd tucked in the corner of the shelf. It was the only unlabeled group of vinyl. The others sat exactly as they had when Bruce shipped out. Same with all his things—wrestling trophies still sparkled on the dresser and pictures of girlfriends still hung beside his bed. Bruce's bitchin' 409 Bel Air still sat imprisoned in the garage, guilty of a crime that it didn't commit.

That was my parents' thing—keeping what little remained of Bruce *exactly* as it was. They worked as meticulously as museum curators, tending to everything but his stereo—a Marantz SLT 12-U turntable, which was fancy looking and had a tonearm that protracted straight from the cradle. This unusual design flagged it as an object of concern: dormant but dangerous, like a neighborhood stray or an old stick of dynamite. So my parents never touched it. They left that job to me.

I flipped on the stereo. The speakers *popped* into consciousness. I placed the adapter onto the center of the turntable so it would fit the bigger hole of the 7" vinyl. I turned the speed to 45rpm, and then took the single out of the sleeve.

-COLUMBIA 45RPM-

WE GOTTA GET OUT OF THIS PLACE
(MANN—WEIL)
THE ANIMALS
A MICKIE MOST PRODUCTION

I sat it on the turntable. Then I reached back into the dust sleeve and pulled out an envelope. Inside the envelope was a piece of paper folded twice down, three times over. I opened it up, smoothing it on my thigh. I held it before me like I was about to give some kinda proclamation. Then, with the other hand, I put the needle on the record. The vinyl crackled, and the song began.

Eric Burdon crooned above the walking bass line as I read the words my brother wrote me all those months ago.

Listen to: "We Gotta Get Out of This Place," by The Animals
How's the weather, Raspy Ronnie?
Hope your summer's been righteous. Believe it or not, little brother, boot camp isn't as tough as I figured it'd be. Hell, Paris Island is a laugh compared to Dad's wrestling practice workouts!
I think some of the boys in here with me came outta the womb with itchy trigger fingers. But I guess I should feel lucky to be surrounded by psycho killers like this, am I right? I know it's only been two weeks, but

"Ronnie!" Dad called from downstairs.

I sat the note on the speaker and dropped the volume to a whisper. I opened the door.

"Yeah?" I yelled back.

"Your mother says come set the table."

"OK."

I flipped the turntable off and slid the needle arm back into the cradle. The Animals made a silent cool-down spin, then stopped. I picked up the record, then slid it gently into the dust sleeve.

I didn't bother finishing the letter. I already knew what it said. I knew what all of his letters said. So I folded it into the envelope, slid it into the dust jacket, and put it back in the unlabeled stack at the end of the shelf.

Then I switched off the lamp and walked out, shutting the door behind me. It was New Year's Eve and my brother was dead and I went down to set the table.

———

Pork loin. Red potatoes. Green beans. Biscuits.

It's what Momma made for dinner every New Year's Eve. We passed the steaming plates around after Dad said grace. He was sitting at the head of the table, drinking a bottle of Jax. Momma and I sat facing each other. The end of the table was empty, as was the high chair—Roy, my two-year-old baby brother, was in his playpen, chewing on some toy or other. Wolfman, our cockapoo, was asleep in the backyard.

The absence of dog and toddler allowed me a thankful moment of silence. I enjoyed the sounds of dishes clanking, knives cutting, and teeth chomp-chomping . . . enjoyed it while it lasted, anyway. Silence never lasted long at our dinner table.

"Hey Ronnie," Dad said, "guess how many bodies our boys bagged this year."

"I dunno."

"Cronkite said we killed *a hundred and forty thousand* of

those bastards," he pronounced, slapping his heavy hand on the table like a punctuation mark.

"Can you believe the Packers won this afternoon?" I asked, changing the subject. "The radio said it was *negative* forty-eight on the field. Imagine playing in that—"

"I wonder how many Bruce got," Dad mused, not speaking to anyone in particular. "They had ten times the KIAs, so he musta killed at least ten of 'em, mathematically speaking . . . plus, when you factor in how *athletic* he was, his natural reflexes, he must've got twenty or more—at least twenty."

"Can we talk about something more pleasant?" Momma asked.

Dad blinked himself back to Earth. He nodded to her and smiled. "Hey Ronnie, whadda' ya say you have a beer with your old man, since it's New Year's Eve and all?"

"Yeah?"

"Just this once," he said. He looked at Momma and winked.

"OK. Sure."

Momma went into the kitchen and returned with two bottles of cheapo male bonding. She handed him a fresh bottle of Jax and gave me the other.

"To you, my boy," Dad said, "though you won't be a boy much longer. We're so proud of ya, Ronnie, and all the glory your future holds."

I blushed. We clinked our bottles together. I gulped down a mouthful greedily.

"*Easy,*" Dad said, "don't rush. The taste'll grow on you."

I guess he assumed it was my first beer.

"Jeez, I hope so," I said, and took another long swig.

"That blazer looks good on you, honey," Momma said. "Any reason you're all spruced up? Is there a special girl we should know about?"

Before I could respond, there was a knock at the front door. Momma went to answer it. I chugged the rest of the bottle, then let out a baritone belch.

"Well hello, Milo," I heard her say as she opened the door.

Milo Novak was my best pal, partner in crime, and next-door neighbor. It was only he and his mom in the house now; his older brother had just moved to Miami, and his dad—one of the thousands of troops killed in Korea—was an eternal resident of the same boneyard my poor brother resided in.

"Happy New Year, Mrs. Bingham!" Milo yelled in his squeaky voice.

"Happy New Year," she said, shaking her head at his tiny frame. "You've gotten so thin! It's not healthy for a boy your age."

"I have an overactive metabolism," he said, adjusting his thick glasses as he followed Momma into the dining room.

"Happy New Year, Milo," Dad said.

"Same to you, Coach. Hey, wait a minute, is that a *beer* I see Ronnie drinking? You expect me to show up at Rachel Harris's party with a *drunkard* on my arm?"

"Afraid so," Dad grinned.

"Well," he sighed comically, "if I gotta I gotta, but I *don't* gotta like it."

Milo made his eyebrows go up and down like Groucho

Marx, and both my parents laughed. I hated when he did that. But he loved to yuck it up with adults, and the dumber his jokes were the more they seemed to enjoy them.

"May I be excused, Momma?"

She nodded. I got up from the table.

"You knuckleheads be safe," Dad said. "I don't wanna hear about any jackassery tonight, you understand?"

Milo and I nodded in unison.

"And you're sleeping over at Milo's?" Momma asked.

"If that's still OK."

"Just get over here and give your Momma some sugar, first."

I laughed and went around the table. I wrapped my arms around her petite frame. She hugged me with desperate purpose, and kissed me on the cheek.

"It's a *new year*, sweetie," she whispered.

I nodded, knowing full well what she meant. In our family, grief and healing were spoken of in code, if they were spoken of at all.

Mothers can be sweet enough to break your heart, I thought.

Then I let her go and turned away.

———

Live oaks loomed on each side of the street, enveloping us in a canopy of Spanish moss. Milo and I hustled down the gravel road as the shadows turned the gray sky a shade closer to black.

There were no sidewalks in Cordelia Island. I never did think to ask why. I never did think to ask a lot of things, like why Cordelia Island was called an *island*—because it wasn't, not really. The town was on an inlet south of Jacksonville. There were beaches on the east and the south ends of town, and a marshland to the north. But most of the town—our neighborhood included—was miles away from the sand.

"Sorry I interrupted dinner," Milo said.

"Don't be," I said. "I was glad. If I had to listen to my dad anymore, I woulda taken a butter knife to my wrists."

"Poetic," he grinned. "He died how he lived—slow and dull."

"Shut up," I laughed.

We turned right onto Elwood, and the wind caught me off guard. I shivered as we walked against it, wishing I'd grabbed Bruce's bomber jacket instead of my stupid twill blazer.

"Coach wearin' ya out again?" Milo asked. By now, he knew the perpetual topic of conversation at the Bingham dinner table.

"It's all he talks about. *Vietnam. Vietnam. Vietnam.* He was listing off body-counts like they were baseball statistics."

"Once a marine always a marine, I guess."

"Yeah, I guess."

"On this particular evening," he said, "I may've joined in with him. We're finally *kicking ass* over there. If things keep up this way, maybe . . . I dunno, maybe this war will be over sooner than later. It's sure lookin' like ol' Big Ears Johnson is gonna pull the troops out before we graduate. If he does, then we've got no draft to worry about. I've really got my fingers crossed this time. Toes, too."

I shrugged in response. Milo nodded.

Silence was the only way to let the subject of Vietnam drop.

We continued on to the party, our fists buried deep in our pockets and shoulders clenched from the chill. A few blocks later, we saw Rachel's place—a big Southern home with a bright-red door and an immaculate veranda. A dozen cars and bicycles were parked in the driveway and on the lawn.

"I can't believe her parents let her have a party," I said.

"They didn't. They're still visiting family in Tuscaloosa. Not sure how she convinced them to let her come home early. Must be a late Christmas miracle."

"God bless us, everyone," I scoffed.

Then Milo stopped walking. I stopped, too. He looked at me.

"Hold up," he said, "I gotta talk to you about some stuff."

"Like what?"

"Best Friend Shit."

"Yeah," I said, "OK."

"OK," he said softly, "are *you* OK?"

I looked down at my loafers. I wasn't quite sure how to answer.

"I think so," I finally mumbled.

"I just don't want you to be hurting more than you've gotta be, man. I mean with the draft goin' on, and school, the everyday shit hurts enough."

"Bruce's death doesn't hurt the way it did," I admitted, "or maybe I've just gotten used to it. Now I just feel numb all the time."

"Numb," he mused. "Well shit, that's an easy fix."

He clapped his small hand on my shoulder, and we continued toward the house. He led me down the side of the Harris residence, past the porch, and up against the trash cans, out of sight. He pulled a poorly rolled joint from his jacket.

"We've just gotta get you *double numb*, that's all."

"You think that'll work?" I asked.

"For a few hours, maybe."

"Cool." I nodded and took a matchbook from my pocket. I handed it to Milo. The wind blew the first match out.

Suddenly, muffled rock music shook the house, signifying that the party had kicked into gear. Two matches later, the joint stayed lit.

Milo took a long toke, working his eyebrows over his frames in that stupid Groucho Marx way that I hated. But I laughed in spite of myself.

"*Shhhhhh,*" he hissed as he exhaled.

But then he began coughing loudly, which made me laugh harder. He put his finger to his lips, choking down his coughs as he handed me the joint.

I hit it with purpose, inhaling until the back of my throat caught fire and my eyes dried up. I held the smoke inside like that, there with the quiet pain. As I exhaled, the wind picked back up. The smoke whisked away like a tiny tornado and the tip of the joint blew out.

"It's almost 1968," Milo said with wonder.

"I know. It's the eve of destruction."

"Nah, man, it's the Year of the Monkey."

"The what?" I asked, clearing my throat.

"Every twelfth year is the Year of the Monkey. The monkey represents cleverness. It's, like, a year for smart people to thrive."

"What's that mean?"

"That we're fucked," he said. "Majorly, majorly fucked."

And we laughed and we laughed and we laughed and we coughed and we laughed and we laughed and we laughed.

————

The deeper into the night we went, the more crowded the party became.

The wrestling team claimed the kitchen, and their lettermen jackets looked comically out of place with the décor. A pink stove and pink refrigerator sat tactfully on the pink tile floor; but so did the keg, which trumped any shade of emasculation. Milo and I could've hung out in there, but I knew I'd make the others uncomfortable (when your dad's the coach, your presence is always suspect.)

So we posted up in the living room, where most everyone else had gathered. The cigarette smoke was thick and dreamlike, drifting through bodies and conversations, filling up pockets of empty space. The coffee table and furniture had been moved, save the TV and an armoire cabinet displaying Rachel's mother's collection of carnival glass. The room had been transformed into an unsanctioned dance hall, complete with a live rock-n-roll band.

They called themselves The Kryptiks—the band was comprised of three shaggy-haired juniors and a skinny sophomore on vocals. As they burned through the familiar tunes of 1967, I had to admit they were pretty good for a bunch of underclassmen.

Their bassist stood next to the TV, which Rachel had left on. Big bands in tuxedos boogied on the muted screen while The Kryptiks played a garagey interpretation of The Hollies' tune, "Carrie Anne." I leaned against the green floral wallpaper and watched the other kids dance.

Milo had been right—*double numb* was better than numb. My head didn't feel as cloudy, which was kinda funny, since I was stoned. But my clarity came with heavy thoughts that left me with no urge to join the others on the dance floor.

My gut was full of beer and my head was full of smoke, but I was hyperaware that every boy on that dance floor would be reporting to his draft board in the coming months, same as me. I didn't understand how they danced around that fact, but they sure as hell found a way; they shimmied and shook around the new year like the hands of a clock that's attached to a time bomb.

"Hi, Ronnie," someone yelled above the music.

I turned to my right. Some majorettes giggled together and passed around a bottle of gin. They waved and giggled again.

Flirty giggling—I still wasn't used to the sound.

Girls had never been into me before my brother died. But now I had a bleak sort of fame at school—not popularity, but notoriety—and near strangers were eager to lick up every ounce of trickle-down grief they could get.

It's messed up, I know, but *girls were finally into me*. So instead of complaining, I cleared my throat and walked over.

"Hey y'all," I said, smiling.

"What?" Lena Jacobs, the one nearest me asked.

"*Hey*," I said, louder.

I was used to repeating myself. Complications from a tonsillectomy had left me with a scarred vocal cord, which meant my voice was raspier than other boys my age. Medically speaking, this wasn't a big deal. Socially speaking, it meant patiently accepting the fact that people couldn't tell what the fuck I was saying.

"You look real pretty tonight."

She smiled a bright-red candy smile, and her friends giggled again.

She sure did look pretty. They all did. They had knowing eyes and delicate smiles, and bodies that only an old-timey poet could properly wax lyrical about.

The band began hammering out Jefferson Airplane's "Somebody to Love."

"Ask her to dance," one of her friends dared me.

But before I could respond, I heard a familiar rumble from the kitchen.

"*Ramrod! Ramrod! Ramrod! Ramrod!*"

I smiled as the boys in the kitchen chanted louder.

"*Ramrod! Ramrod! Ramrod! Ramrod!*"

The girls smiled, too.

We all knew that chant. The entire school knew it. The entire *town* knew it. We heard it at every football game, every wrestling tournament, and every pep rally. It was the overture of Lewis "Ramrod" Gibbons, our reigning athletic superstar and my brother's best friend.

Bruce and Lewis had been running buddies off and on the court, and they stole the show at every sporting event they participated in. They functioned like opposite sides of the same coin—when Bruce was picked for quarterback, Lewis was picked for fullback. When Lewis qualified for the heavyweight division, my brother wrestled at 155. They procured trophy after trophy for our school, like they were a two-man wrecking crew.

"Excuse me a second," I said.

Lena shrugged, and turned back to her friends.

I moved down the hallway, stumbling more than I expected. I passed the oversized dining room, aka make-out central, and then moved beneath the harsh lights of the kitchen.

The chants had died by the time I got there. Lewis stood in line for the keg, shaking hands with the guys from the team. The outline of muscle was visible under the sleeves of his jacket, giving him the look of an out-of-work superhero.

"Ramrod," I sang, waving as I entered the room.

He smiled when he saw me. His smile was incredibly confident, big and toothy and undeniable. It was the grin of a winner. He should've been offered an athletic scholarship on that smile alone.

I cut in line beside him.

"Happy New Year," I said.

"That'd be nice, wouldn't it?"

"Yeah man, it would."

The line moved forward. We were up. Lewis filled two plastic cups with beer. He handed the first one to me.

"Your daddy tell ya he wants me to help coach the team?"

"What?" I asked. "And not wrestle? But you're the best—"

"I can keep wrestling 'til my birthday. But he said once I turn nineteen it wouldn't be fair to the competition."

"Since when does he care about what's fair to the competition?"

"Beats me. It's my own fault, anyways. Flunking last year screwed everything up, and now I just—"

"Ronnie Bingham," Lena hollered, rushing into the kitchen, "you *better* come dance with me!"

I spilt half my beer on the bubblegum tile when she grabbed my arm.

"If you don't," Lewis grinned, "I will."

He smiled at Lena. Her eyes became hearts.

"Come on," I said to her.

I let her guide me back down the hall. As we got closer to the music, I registered the song: "Never My Love" by The Association. The Kryptiks' guitarist handled the riff, which sounded surprisingly righteous in the absence of an organ. We walked to the center of the room, and were encircled by swaying bodies and drunken drama and nervous teenage tongues.

I gripped Lena's hips. She arched her arms around my neck, and laid her head on my shoulder. Her tits pressed right up against me as we started to sway. I memorized the feeling, closed my eyes, and got lost in the music.

"You know," she whispered, "I keep thinkin' about how hard Christmas must have been for you, Ronnie. Like, without Bruce there."

She pulled her body closer against me.

"Um, yeah," I said clumsily, struggling to concentrate. "It was a drag—"

Suddenly, the Kryptiks stopped playing. A squeal of feedback shot from the microphone, and we all turned toward it. Our host, Rachel Harris, stood at the mic. Her paper party hat drooped down at a sad angle.

"*Shh,*" she yelled, "I need to hear the TV to know when the countdown starts! Shut! Up!"

We shut up. I gazed at the television. Guy Lombardo was doing his standard New Year's Big Band Bash. He held up his hand to count down with his viewers at home.

"OK!" Rachel yelled. "Here we go! *Nine! Eight!*"

The crowd joined in.

"*Seven! Six!*"

"*Five!*" Lena yelled into my ear.

"*Four!*" the make-out couples yelled from the dining room.

"*Three!*" the wrestlers yelled from the kitchen.

"*Two!*" The Kryptiks' front man yelled into the mic.

"One." I mumbled flatly, to no one at all.

"HAPPY NEW YEAR!"

Lena planted one on me. Her tongue slid into my mouth as Rachel's champagne cork popped. The band kicked into a funky version of "Auld Lang Syne."

"Happy New Year," she grinned.

"Happy New Year," I repeated unconvincingly.

"Are you OK?"

"Yeah." I shrugged. "Just kinda wish people would quit askin' me that."

She considered it for a moment, and then her expression changed. "This scene's bumming you out, I can tell. How 'bout we go somewhere more private?"

I nodded.

The band transitioned into "A Whiter Shade of Pale," with the guitarist once again handling the organ line. The crowd started dancing—slower now, pausing only to pull swigs off the champagne bottle as it made its way around the room. Lena led me through the dance floor, and then started up the stairs. I sluggishly followed.

I glanced down from the staircase and took a long look at those carefree kids. Through the haze, I could see Lewis standing by himself at the window. He wasn't dancing or watching the band. He wasn't talking to anyone. He just stared out that window and sipped his beer.

"Come on, Ronnie," Lena called. "Let's ring in 1968 right."

I kept moving up the stairs.

The dancers kept dancing. The drinkers kept drinking.

The band kept rocking and rolling.

Lewis stood alone at the window, peering into the unknown dark.

————

Dawn. Barely.

I walked home alone with my shirt untucked and my jacket pulled tight against the morning cool. My head felt like a cracked jelly jar, and it leaked onto the ground with every hungover step

I took. I didn't remember how the night ended, or much of the blur before the black, but I woke up half-naked in Rachel's little brother's bedroom, tangled in a set of Lone Ranger sheets. Lena was nowhere to be found, and I figured Milo had gone home at some point or another.

His mom worked the night shift, so she wouldn't know I stayed out. Still, I walked faster. I was eager to crawl into my own bed and sleep off the night for the rest of the day.

I turned onto my street and cut through Milo's yard, into mine.

One of Momma's yellow ribbons had come loose from our holly tree and blown into a hedge. It was snagged on a thorn branch, flapping aimlessly in the breeze. I untangled the ribbon and carried it back to the tree.

I crouched down to tie the ribbon, but then suddenly let my knees plant themselves down on the cold ground. I looked up at my house. My eyes were drawn to a loose shingle beating softly in the wind. That shingle had been holding on for dear life since I could remember. I looked at my window, then Bruce's, then down at the garage where his car was stored. I looked at Milo's house and then down the block, which led to the next and the next. I looked out at the streets of America, and felt tears sting at my reddened eyes.

"I can't go," I whispered. "I can't go to Vietnam."

I didn't pray—I hadn't once since Bruce died—but I came as close as I could let myself, and wished upon that shingle for President Johnson to end the war before I was old enough for the draft. The thought didn't go any further—all I could do was wait and give peace a chance, as they'd come to say.

So I turned back to the tree, and wrapped the ribbon around it as if it would tether me there to my front lawn, where my parents were close and everything was safe—felt safe—for that moment, anyway. Then I sighed, tied a knot, and let the ribbon go into the wind.

That's when I noticed someone watching me.

I stood up and turned to the Criswells' old place, which had been vacant for nearly a month. A girl was standing on the veranda.

Her hair was long and straight and blacker than a funeral veil. It was striking against her frilly blue nightgown. But the jacket she wore smothered the girlishness of her pajamas like a boot heel to a match; the jacket was black leather with silver buckles, just like Marlon Brando's motorcycle jacket in *The Wild One*.

She stood there cloaked in leather, smoking a cigarette, looking at me.

I threw her a tentative wave.

She turned her head and exhaled coolly. The wind lifted her hair like a marauder's flag, concealing everything but the smoke.

When she turned back to me, she didn't wave. But she nodded. Once.

She flicked her cigarette into the yard.

I stood there watching it die in the tall grass as she walked inside.

#

THE URGE TO SUBMERGE

My brother's jacket was a size too big on me and was the bitter shade of bad coffee. The wool collar was matted and smelled like the cigarette smoke of strangers from faraway lands. U-S-M-C ran down the zipper flap.

The government had shipped it to the house a few weeks after Bruce died. It came in the same package as his dog tags and his gloriously useless medals. There weren't any patches on the jacket (his eyes had likely been X-ed out before he had a chance to sew any on), and I was glad.

I wore the jacket daily. Other athletes would have been hassled for not sporting their lettermen jacket, and I knew it was for Bruce—not for me—that my teammates made an exception.

I was wearing the bomber jacket as Dad drove me to school. He looked sleepy, grumpier than usual—that was the general mood at school the first day back from a break. I'd be the only one in the building that was happy Christmas was over, but I found school's reliably repressive routine a great comfort in this cold new world.

Dad waved at a crossing guard as we rounded the next block.

I leaned back in my seat and counted the plastic yard Santas left out past their expiration. He pulled up to the edge of Cordelia High's vast courtyard. He stopped, but left the car running.

"Have a good day," he grumbled.

"You too, Dad. See ya at practice."

I grabbed my things and got out. Dad pulled the car around to the employee lot as I strolled through the grass, past a cluster of students chatting under a large willow tree. I waved hello but didn't stop to chat. My feet kept moving forward.

Our school was two stories of scholarly brown brick. It stretched the length of the football field, which ran parallel to the building, and boasted a relatively modern design, including a veranda outside of the auditorium and a slanted awning that extended over the front of the building.

"Bingham, my man!" hollered a wrestler smoking beneath it.

I smiled at him as I went inside.

The front concourse was packed. My ears rang with post-holi*daze* chitter-chatter as I looked around for Milo, but it was too chaotic to single anyone out. The first day of the semester was always a mess.

Then the bell rang, and I joined the tide of students flooding the halls. I walked beneath a large, abrasive banner hanging from the railing of the second-floor balcony. It showed a crude drawing of a shark fin with discarded bird feathers gliding above it. In thick black print, it read

SHARKS NOT RESPONSIBLE FOR RUFFLED FEATHERS
CREAM THE PELICANS THIS SATURDAY!

I groaned, exhausted by the thought of that match. I didn't get my kicks from confrontation, especially on the mat. I wasn't very competitive. Unlike my father and brother, physical domination never filled me with pride. That's not to say I wasn't good at it; I was a solid wrestler and could've been a real contender if I put in the effort. But that was my fatal hang-up as an athlete: I never fought as hard as I could—or should.

Why fight when you don't have to?

I found it simpler to ease up and let the current of the crowd do the work. That morning it pushed me forward, farther into the hall. Underclassmen bumped into each other as they checked door numbers and schedules. But I knew where I was headed—Room 112, by the gym. So I took my time, amused by the confusion.

Then I saw something I didn't expect: a mane of long, black hair flowing down a black leather jacket. The image disappeared into the crowd a moment later, a motorcycle mirage. I shrugged and entered Room 112.

The classroom was the same as all the others, besides the theme of the décor. Pictures of dead presidents lined all four walls. *Mr. Donahue* was written on the blackboard in chalk. A map of Southeast Asia was tacked up beside it.

Great. Another 'Nam addict.

I snagged a desk in back. The girl beside me had her face

crammed into the pages of a *TEEN Magazine*. I scanned the cover stories as I got situated.

KEEP OFF THE GRASS—Pot shot at Marijuana

ARE LEFTIES MORE LOVEABLE?—Studies Say Yes

ANATOMY OF A HIPPIE—The Urge to Submerge

THE YOUNG RASCALS—An Interview

She sensed me staring and snapped her magazine shut.

"Hey," I smiled, "I'm Ronnie."

"What?"

"*I'm Ronnie,*" I said, a little louder.

"Oh," she said. "Hi, I'm Jamie."

She turned back to her magazine, but then looked over to me.

"You don't happen to be left handed, do you?" Her tone was hopeful.

Before I could say no, a tall, bald man in a bright-blue blazer scrambled into the room. His posture was hunched, jittery. He looked truly excited to be teaching this subject, which made me nervous as hell. Benji Cutis, one of our beloved class clowns, *gulped* comically loud, sending a wave of chuckles through the room.

The teacher sat some papers on his desk, then turned to us.

"Ladies, gentlemen, welcome to Government Two. I'm Mr. Donahue. Now, I know some of you may still be on a *mental* vacation, but I expect that problem to rectify itself as soon as we—"

The intercom above the door hummed to life.

"Hello students," Principal Yonker said through the speaker.

"Welcome back. Before we get to the morning announcements, let us stand for the Pledge of Allegiance."

The entire class stood up.

We faced the flag above the window. The morning light gave it an ethereal glow. We covered our hearts, our eyes fixed on the flag. Every kid in the building stood the same way: half-awake and barely conscious of our actions, let alone their meaning. Then we mumbled the unkeepable promise of our fathers, once again.

"IPLEDGEALLEGIANCE
TOTHEFLAGOFTHEUNITEDSTATESOFAMERICA
ANDTOTHEREPUBLICFORWHICHITSTANDS
ONENATIONUNDERGOD
INDIVISABLE
WITHLIBERTY
ANDJUSTICE
FOR—"

———

"All I know is *this*: if Bill says she's a gook, she's a fucking gook."

It was the first thing I heard when I entered the locker room, and I instantly knew who said it. Stink Wilson's voice was as loud and grating as mine was hoarse and subdued.

Stink wrestled 165, but his imposing nature made him seem twenty pounds heavier. He had a face to match his voice, all raw zits and meanness. Kids like him weren't usually popular, but he possessed an asset more powerful than looks or charm—*horror*. Sophomore year, there were rumors he stabbed a colored boy in Old Town. I thought the rumor was bullshit, but wasn't eager to test that theory.

I turned the corner to find him and Marty at their lockers getting changed. Milo was sitting on a bench nearby, lacing his wrestling shoes and not making eye contact with the two bigger boys. He nodded when he saw me. I nodded back, and opened my locker.

"Bill don't know what a gook looks like," Marty said to Stink. "He ain't never been to Vietnam."

"Bill *knows*," Stink said, crossing his arms for dramatic effect. "His cousin sent him snapshots from Saigon, pictures of hookers. So Bill knows, man, and he said she has that gooky-eyed whorehouse look."

His words made Milo flinch, as if he'd been stung by something.

"I heard she's a chink," Marty responded, "but I'm like, if she *is* a chink, why don't she go to the colored school? How's that even legal?"

Milo's brow creased cartoonishly low and his leg began to twitch.

"She ain't colored enough for the coloreds," Stink shrugged, "but she *ain't* white, and she ain't a chink. Once she sets herself on fire to protest meatloaf day in the cafeteria, you'll see how wrong ya were."

"Jesus Christ!" Milo yelled, stomping his foot on the floor.

My back tensed. I tried to play it cool as I changed my clothes, but my nerves were on high alert. I prepped myself for a fight that I wasn't looking to join.

"I'm fuckin' disturbed that you two made it past fifth grade," Milo said. "She's half Japanese, not Vietnamese, and it's *legal* for her to be here because *school segregation ended fourteen years ago!*"

"Not down here," Stink huffed.

Which was true. Every school in the state remained segregated despite *Brown v. Board of Education*, and they'd stay that way for the foreseeable future.

"Watch yourself, spazoid," Marty said. "Just 'cause you're a dork don't mean ya can suss out a chink from a gook from a jap from a goddamn space alien."

"I don't have to suss shit out," he scoffed, "Hana *told me* she's half Japanese, that's a pretty good fuckin' indication. Y'all just quit it with the 'gook' shit."

Then Milo sighed and sat back down. I could tell he was exhausted by the argument. It was understandable. Trying to reason with these guys was like debating with a goldfish.

"You really talked to her?" Marty asked.

"Believe it or not, Marty," Milo sneered, "asking works better than trying to decipher Bill's secondhand jerk-off pictures."

"Talked to who?" I finally asked, before Marty could reply.

"The new girl," Milo said. "Hana. I met her this morning on the way to school. Her family moved into the Criswells' old place, right across the street from us."

"There goes the neighborhood," Stink grumbled.

Milo looked back to Stink and Marty.

"You better be careful," Milo said. "Her pops works for the Browning Corporation, and they just bought stake in the P&P. Hana told me they sent him here to assess the viability of the mill—including the usefulness of the employees."

Marty and Stink looked at each other nervously.

The Cordelia Island Paper & Pulp Mill employed the majority of men in town. Marty's dad, Stink's dad, and pretty much *everyone's* dad worked there—everyone but mine, who was six doors down, and Milo's, who was six feet under.

"Jeez," I said, feigning concern, "if her dad overheard your racist jive, then—"

"*Poof!*" Milo said, spreading his arms like a mushroom cloud. "Your fathers will be begging for change on the street, and they'll sell the mill for scrap."

Stink slammed his locker. Marty was bigger, so he slammed his harder.

"She lied to you," Stink snapped. "She lied about the mill, and she lied about being a jap! I bet she's a V. C. assassin sent here to take me out! High Command knows my boots hit the ground next year, and they're already scared as hell. Every gook in my path is gonna be dead meat!"

"Yeah," Marty yelled, "gook meat!"

The two of them busted up as they walked away. Their laughter came from the gut, bellowing genuine glee. The slaps of their high-five echoed off of the lockers as they headed to practice.

———

Night. Home from school. Done with practice. Done with the day.

I stayed in the shower until the hot water ran out and my fingers turned to prunes. The heat helped the pulsing ache that was building in my neck and shoulders. The first practice back was always the worst, and Dad had pushed us harder than usual. My legs were as stiff as tree trunks as I stepped onto the green bathroom rug.

I toweled off, and then combed my close-cropped hair to the side, like Steve McQueen. I slid on my red pajama pants and a fresh white tank top. Steam drifted into the dark, empty hallway as I opened the bathroom door.

Momma and Dad were in bed. Roy was already asleep. I flipped off the bathroom light and moved blindly toward my bedroom as quietly as I could.

I shut my door, locked it, and then stepped onto my bed. I stood on my tiptoes, arching until my fingers pushed up the ceiling panel above me. I stuck one hand into the opening and felt around until my fingers grazed the handle of my stashbox. I pulled it out carefully and then stepped down off the bed.

In my hand was a yellow Rocky & Bullwinkle lunchbox.

Inside was the arsenal of tools I'd used to get through my brother's death.

I opened it and took stock of my supply—a ziplocked bag

of grass, rolling papers, a half-smoked joint, and three magic mushrooms I was too afraid to eat.

I took the roach from the lunchbox, then put it back in its hiding place.

After the box was secured, I crept down to the kitchen and went through the rarely used side door that led into the garage. I locked it behind me.

I didn't turn on the light in case someone came down for a midnight snack. Instead, I felt my way through the garage, stopping when my hands touched aluminum. Then I squatted and lifted the garage door up as quietly as I could.

Moonlight poured in. I turned toward the car.

God, she was sparkling. Even in the dark.

Bruce's 1962 Chevy Bel Air, baby blue with a 409 mean-machine engine. His car had been the envy of the neighborhood kids. It was the sort of car you waved at when it passed you by. She *was* real fine, his 4-0-9, indeed.

I opened the passenger door and slid into the middle of the bench seat. I pulled the keys from the driver's side visor, where Bruce had left them. I put it in the ignition—I turned it one click, just enough to get the battery going.

The dashboard lit a dull-green color, like a beer sign with a blown bulb. The light blended with the moon and cast the interior in an airy radiance.

I flipped the radio on.

Aretha Franklin sang "Chain of Fools" through the ghostly waves.

I ch-ch-charged the dashboard lighter, and nodded my head with the beat.

Once it heated up, I pulled it from the cradle and lit the joint. It sizzled when it touched. I brought the joint to my lips and inhaled steadily.

I stretched out my neck, and then rested my head on the back of the bench. I closed my eyes and held in the smoke. I listened to the music. I reflected on the day.

I couldn't get Stink and Marty out of my head.

Why'd they have to talk like that? Why'd they have to be such assholes?

As a Southerner, I'd been taught that refusing to participate in bigotry was its own type of rebuke. But as a seventeen-year-old, I was beginning to question that logic. Obviously Milo was too, since he shot back at Stink and Marty even though they could cream him without breaking a sweat.

But he still spoke up . . . and I didn't say shit.

I never fought as hard as I could. Or should.

I exhaled hard enough to push that bummer of a thought from my head.

Smoke filled the cab. The DJ faded up the first bars of the next song.

—*boom, ba-boom, boom, ba-boom*—

—*boom, ba-boom, boom, ba-boom*—

It was then that I heard my brother's voice.

I knew it was my imagination. I knew it was the weed.

But I swear I heard him in the static, drifting out on the back of a song.

"Tell me, loyal listeners, what *does* become of the broken-hearted? Well, it's hard to say, baby, even for me, but when Jimmy Ruffin does the askin,' the question sounds oh so sweet."

God, Bruce loved that song. "What Becomes of the Brokenhearted" had been the crown jewel of his Motown collection.

Jimmy Ruffin sang about the heartbroken world, belting out painful visions in his sad, soulful way. I took another toke and reached for the dial. I cranked the volume up, then exhaled into the green-lit dark. The air suddenly became three-dimensional, a thick, green haze of jungle smoke.

I leaned back in the seat and I thought about my brother and I thought about the war and I thought about hate and rock-n-roll and nothing and nothing and nothing and nothing and nothing at all.

Then I whispered to the radio, a hollow reply.

"I have visions too, man. I have visions, too."

THREE

CRACK THE SKY,
SHAKE THE EARTH

The first few weeks back at school flowed in a forgettable stream of monotony. Class, practice, work, home—there was no big news, no big deals. Even the news from Vietnam was tame; nightly newscasters made it clear the war was on its last leg. Rumors of peace talks loomed, and it really looked like President Johnson might decide to end the war, after all.

So for the first time in a long time, my thoughts drifted to normal teenage things—like the fact that I still hadn't met the new girl. I saw her only in glimpses, usually through the window of Dad's Studebaker as he drove me to school. She walked with Milo in the mornings, but he hadn't offered to introduce me. When I finally asked him what she was like, he just said she was "sorta intense."

I had no interest in adding any intensity to my current state, so I didn't go out of my way to meet her. I let school days stay boring old school days, and weekends be nothing but mindless shifts at the Royal Atlantis, the movie theater where Milo and I worked.

There were only three viewing rooms, so the theater wasn't as majestic as it sounded. But it was the only theater in town, and it had a neon-green sign bright enough to double as a light-house beacon. I was the ticket taker, which was the easiest job in the joint. Milo, however, was the projectionist and pro-bono repairman (he could fix everything from the aperture plate to the popcorn machine.) He did any and every task happily because movies were his passion. He wanted to be a director, or a cameraman, or . . . well, anything, pretty much, as long as it had to do with his obsessive passion for motion pictures.

Me, I didn't have a passion. Not like that, anyway.

Not like Milo and the movies. Not like Bruce and music.

I'd had a *plan*, but that's different.

Now it was gone, too.

But whenever I was taking tickets, I didn't dwell on such things. I was able to work in the blank state of mind I clung to at school. The whole month was like that—blank and familiar. Everything was thoughtless, fantastically so. That entire month was steady, save one day.

January 30th, 1968.

The Lunar New Year.

Tết Nguyên Đán, as the Vietnamese called it.

Tet, for short.

———

Dad and I found out when we got home from wrestling practice.

Momma was sitting in the den, hunched toward the TV screen with a sour look on her face. Roy was on the floor playing with building blocks.

"What is it?" Dad asked. "What happened?"

"An attack," she mumbled. "Some sort of attack."

CBS News was calling it the Tet Offensive. When Dad got caught up on the story, he called it "a goddamn nightmare." Every American embassy, base, and airfield in South Vietnam was hit with simultaneous surprise attacks. As the newscaster droned on, my spirit dwindled—for months, all I'd heard was that we'd been kicking ass and taking names, but now it was clear that peace was out the window. Our troops weren't going anywhere, and neither was the draft.

Now it was all I could think about, *the draft the draft the draft.* I couldn't put it out of my mind anymore, or pretend it wasn't coming. I was no longer able to convince myself that Bruce's death had paid some cosmic debt and left me free from having to worry about being drafted and killed myself.

The fear was in me now, and those numbing efforts were futile. It was just a matter of time before I was smacked out of my grief-induced meditation. I knew it was coming. I felt it. But, in the end, I was still surprised by the force of the hit.

———

The Friday after the Tet Offensive, the Royal Atlantis ran *The Graduate.* Judging by the size of our opening-night crowd, I wasn't the only one who'd heard rumors about how salacious it was. Half of the senior class was there, including all the guys from the wrestling team. They made fun of my work uniform as I tore their tickets to the late show.

My boss, Mr. Dori, always left before the last show. So once the movie started and the lobby cleared out, I abandoned my post and went upstairs to the projection room to bullshit with Milo. Every time I did this, the empty upstairs hallway struck me as creepy; the glow of the fake chandeliers was dull, and the echoes of competing films disorienting. I hurried down the matted red carpet to the small door labeled *Employees Only*. I opened it and went inside.

The small door led to a small room hidden above the crowd. Milo sat in the corner eating a box of M&M's, paying no attention to the machinery or the images they projected.

"Hey," I said.

"Hey, man."

I peered out the opening that the camera lens stuck through. I didn't see any sex stuff happening on screen, just Dustin Hoffman freaking out on a mechanic.

"How's the movie?" I asked.

"Fantastic. The cinematography's amazing. Real Euro-style, I dig it."

"Cool," I said. He passed me the box of M&Ms.

"Wanna hear something messed up?" he asked.

"Always."

"The *New York Times* published the signal the Viet Cong sent their troops before the Tet attacks. Know what it said?"

I shook my head.

"*Crack the sky, shake the earth.*"

The words sent a visible chill down my spine.

"Yeah," he said, "I know."

He leaned on the opposite side of the projector and peered into the theater.

"What are we gonna do, man?" I asked.

"Hope our numbers don't come up until we figure something out."

I finished the box of chocolates and threw it at his head. "You're supposed to be the smart one!"

"Hey," he said, turning, "what can I say? It's a low fuckin' bar."

As if on cue, the audience below us busted up in laughter about something on screen. Milo did his Groucho eyes. I rolled mine in response.

"You better get back downstairs," he said. "It's getting near the end."

"Yeah. See you after?"

"Yep."

I opened the small door to leave, but then turned back.

"Since when do you read the *New York Times*?"

He shrugged and turned back to the theater. I left him there as he watched a third ending flicker like a déjà vu dream.

By the time I got back downstairs, moviegoers were shuffling into the night. I waited until the crowd cleared out, then got the broom and rolling trashcan out of the janitor's closet. I turned on the house lights of Viewing Room 2 and started cleaning. I pushed the broom across the back row in one long motion, shoveling all the garbage into a gross pile.

I dumped that pile, then moved on to the next row.

Then the next row.

Then the next row.

Then the next.

I was nearly finished sweeping when I came upon three pieces of gum stuck to the armrest of an aisle seat. Annoyed, I put the broom down and started peeling. The first two pieces were stale, so they came off easily. But the third piece was fresh. I cursed the perpetrator as I pulled it from the armrest in a gross, unmanageable string. That was when I heard a voice echo from the foyer of the stage-left emergency exit.

"What's the matter, bitch? I thought you like sneak attacks."

It was too ugly to come from the mouth of anyone but Stink Wilson.

I wiped the gum on the corner of the trashcan, and then headed toward the exit to see what was going on. My stomach clenched at the thought of conflict, but my job was also too cushy to lose on account of a jackass like Stink.

The hallway leading to the exit doors was dark and cramped. The light behind me was just bright enough to make out five Cordelia High lettermen jackets.

"Just admit it," another voice said, "and we'll let you go."

"I swear to fuckin' God," a third voice yelled, "get your mudderfuckin' hands off me right now, or I *admit* I'm gonna kick the shit outta every one of you!"

The voice was powerful and feminine. The word "mother"

rang out in that Midwestern sneer I only heard when I watched the Bears lose on TV.

I took a deep breath and approached.

"Hey guys," I said, straining for both calm and volume, "what's the hubbub?"

My teammates stiffened and slowly turned to face me.

That's when I saw the new girl. They had formed a circle around her. Two of them held her arms behind her back. None of them could meet my gaze.

But she did, with eyes darker than the shadows around us. They were windows into a soul that wasn't the least bit scared, which was a hell of a lot more than I could say for myself.

Stink took a step toward me.

"Beat it," he said. Now his voice was steady, eerily flat.

I looked at the new girl. She glared at me silently.

"This is my job," I said, inching forward. "Y'all really need to leave."

"Soon," Stink said, in that same odd tone. "I'm getting information."

"What the hell are you talkin' about, man?" I asked, moving closer.

"You don't think she knew about Tet, Ronnie? You don't think they all knew? Oh, they knew, every one of 'em. They knew, and they laughed. They *loved* it." He turned back to her. "Didn't you?"

Stink reached into his back pocket for . . . I didn't wait to find out.

I was too scared. The fear of playing the odds outweighed

the fear of action. So I rushed him, and swung my left arm under his armpit, grabbing his elbow. I hooked my other arm over his wrist, forming a sloppily executed arm bar.

Then, I pulled.

Stink screamed bloody murder. He sounded like a wild animal. The others loosened their grip on the girl, probably from shock more than anything.

"Sheep," she said, spitting at their feet as she pushed them off.

I shoved Stink farther down the hallway and the others backed away. Their eyes leapt from Stink to me, as they tried to decide what to do.

"Get outta here before you get me fired," I yelled back at them, as I barreled Stink through the doors. He went stumbling onto the sidewalk, but he didn't fall. His friends' eyes, however, dropped to the ground as they followed him out.

"I hope this bitch is worth the trouble you just put on yourself," Stink sneered, then added, "goddamn traitor."

His threats were a relief—I was glad to hear the harshness return to his voice. The way he'd been talking all calm and cold really freaked me out.

The exit doors swung shut, and I was alone with the new girl.

"Are you OK?" I asked.

I took a step toward her, and—*WHAM*—she punched me in the face.

"Jesus!" I yelled, backing off.

"Jesus," she mumbled, looking down at her hand as if she didn't recognize it.

She rushed through the exit doors like a shot. I posted my hand on the wall and shook my head until the stars in my vision cleared. I couldn't believe how hard she hit. If I wasn't bleeding, I was lucky.

She's obviously psycho, I told myself as I rubbed my face. *You did what you could, but she's not your problem, Ronnie. This is not your problem—*

I scoffed at myself for being a chump as I followed her into the night.

I found her lighting a cigarette under the awning of the bakery next door. Her zippo sparked, but wouldn't catch. Her hand was shaking badly.

"Hey," I called to her.

She jumped, startled. I raised my hands in surrender.

"I come in peace. Relax."

I took the matchbook from my pocket. She eyed it skeptically for a moment, and then yanked it from my hand.

"Sorry for decking you," she said. The cigarette swayed between her lips.

"Forget it," I shrugged. "That's what I get for tryin' to help."

"Yeah," she nodded, "it usually is."

She struck a match, and it lit up her face like an amber spotlight. Her eyes were gleaming arches that curved and then sharpened, like an infinity symbol. They weren't slanted, like all those John Wayne movies said they would be—they were full and all encompassing. Her eyebrows and jawline and cheekbones arched in strong, serious angles. But her lips were soft, and her nose was round as a pebble at the bottom of a lake. I'd describe that nose as adorable if I hadn't just been sucker-punched by its owner.

But cheap shot or not, I took the cigarette she offered.

"You're Milo's buddy," she said. She spoke in statements, not questions.

"Ronnie Bingham. I live across the street from you."

"Hana Hitchens," she said, offering her hand.

We shook. I smoked and tried not to cough.

"Your brother died last year in Ong Thanh," she said, exhaling.

"Yeah."

"You guys were disc jockeys or something."

"We were gonna be," I said.

"Trippy," she mused. "Your voice isn't exactly made for radio."

"Whadda ya mean," I asked, forcibly making my voice even raspier than usual.

She smiled, but didn't laugh.

"He was the real DJ," I corrected, *"Bad Bruce.* I was just his sidekick. He wanted me to do the weather report, traffic, stuff like that."

"Bad Bruce, and . . ."

"Raspy Ronnie," I smiled. "What else?"

She finally laughed. It was a soft laugh, gentler than the rest of her.

"I know," I said, laughing too. "I was just a tagalong. But he could have been the next Wolfman Jack if—yeah, whatever. He didn't live long enough to be much more than a record collector."

"But hey," she said, "I bet he had some cool fuckin' records."

"The coolest."

She smiled at that, and exhaled.

"So," I said, changing the subject, "what was goin' on back there?"

"Stupid shit," she scoffed. "Your pals were sitting behind me and talking through the whole movie. I finally told them to shut up, then the ugly one called me a gook and started kicking my seat. So when the movie ended, I turned around and poured my soda into his lap."

I coughed up sour smoke. I tried to imagine the scene.

"Are all you rednecks delusional?" she went on. "They acted like throwing a soda on that limp dick was part of the Tet Offensive!"

"Jesus," I sighed, "that really is crazy. For the record, though, I'm just on the wrestling team with those idiots. But we're not friends."

"If you were, you're sure not now. You've aided and abetted the enemy."

"How exactly are *you* the enemy?" I asked. "Milo told me you're Japanese, not Vietnamese. Come to think of it, he told those guys the same thing. I heard him."

"They don't care if I'm Vietnamese or Japanese or a fuckin' Mongol," she scoffed. "I'm different from them. That's all it takes to be considered an enemy."

She tossed her cigarette out into the street.

I dropped mine onto the sidewalk.

"It was nice to finally meet you," I said, "enemy or not."

"See ya later, Raspy Ronnie from across the street."

With that, she started down the sidewalk, back toward our neighborhood.

"Hey," I hollered after her.

She turned around.

"Come by sometime, if you dig music. I'll show you my brother's records."

"If I dig music?" she snorted, and laughed as she walked away.

I stood in that same spot until her laughter evaporated into the night. I tried to place the feeling washing over me, but it had become so unfamiliar I labeled it an utterly new sensation.

Peace.

Brief and unexpected.

The sweetest sucker-punch of all.

FOUR

MUSIC GEEKS ANONYMOUS

I found Milo in the locker room before practice. I sat beside him on the bench without any acknowledgment, the way only best friends can do.

"Prince Valiant emerges," he grinned.

"Yeah, yeah," I mumbled.

"*Yeah, yeah* my ass! I thought you said what happened last Friday was no big thing."

"It *wasn't* a big thing," I said, embarrassed.

"That's not what Hana told me. And she's as cool as they come, so if *she* says it was a big deal, it was a big deal."

I changed into my shorts and began lacing up my wrestling shoes.

"Stink give you any trouble today?"

"Nah," I said, "I'm sure it's fine. He's all show and no go."

"I hope," Milo said. "Hana said he was acting batshit."

"Yet I'm the one she socked in the face."

Milo started laughing. I chuckled too, and shut my locker.

"You must be one of those pain pervs," he said. "I can't

imagine inviting a girl over to listen to records right after she punched me."

Until then, I hadn't considered the possibility that Milo had the hots for Hana. I couldn't believe it didn't cross my mind earlier, and I felt an awkward sort of guilt creep slowly up my throat. Had I overstepped by asking her to hang out?

"I meant, like, the three of us," I stammered, "not just me and her. I was thinking we should start a record club, since we all live on the same block."

"A record club?"

"Yeah," I said, "a club that meets up once a week to listen to music. Everyone brings an LP and a single, and then gets to swap 'em afterwards. A bunch of kids are doing it, I read about 'em in *Rave* magazine."

"I dig it. Just say where and when."

"Ask Hana if she feels like joining, and we'll figure it out from there."

"I'll ask her after school."

He shut his locker. I stopped him before he walked out.

"Hey man," I said, "can I lay some Best Friend Shit on you?"

"Always."

"Do you like this chick? Like, *like her* like her, or are y'all just friends? Because I don't wanna get in the middle of—"

His laughter cut me off. "If you knew her better, you wouldn't ask," he said. "I already get called 'shrimp' and 'dweeb' enough at wrestling practice. I ain't interested in dating a girl who can kick my ass six ways to Sunday."

"Right on," I nodded. "I just felt like I should ask."

"Why," he asked, "do *you* like her?"

"Nah, like you just said, I don't even know her. But she's a badass chick that'll actually talk to us. So, I mean, what's not to like?"

It was an eternally inarguable point.

———

Hana was into the idea—and just like that, our record club was born. I figured we'd meet at my house, but she insisted on her own. (She was allowed to play music as loud as she wanted. Otherwise, what was the point?)

Our maiden audio voyage was set to depart at 7 p.m. on Thursday.

Be there, or be squarer than square.

So I hurried home after wresting practice to shower, and then spent an hour in Bruce's bedroom, agonizing over what to bring. I chose a full-length I was confident about—*Psychedelic Lollipop* by Blues Magoos—but picking a single was impossible. It was ridiculous, the way I labored over the decision. I was so damn determined to choose something left of the dial, a song that a girl from a big city like Chicago wouldn't roll her eyes at.

After flipping through the shelves for an eternity, I surprised myself by looking in my special stack of vinyls—the singles that had Bruce's letters tucked safely inside. A few singles deep, I landed on one that struck me. It was an old song, a real heart-buster. As I touched the thin paper dust sleeve, a memory shot through me like a jolt of electricity.

Bad Bruce, his shades on for full effect, slowly lowers the 45 onto the turntable.

"For all the four-eyed forlorn lovers out there," he croons, *"here's one with a slow beat for the back seat. And speaking of going parking tonight, how's the weather, Raspy Ronnie?"*

"Too cool for school," I said softly, pulling the single from the shelf, "with a hundred-percent chance of young love."

I held it out to Wolfman, who lay curled at the edge of Bruce's bed.

"What do ya think, Wolfie? "

He farted. Loud. His tail began to wag.

"I'll take that as a yes."

I grabbed the 45 in one hand and held my nose with the other.

He farted again. I couldn't help but laugh.

"Agent Orange ain't got nothin' on you, boy."

His tail flapped back and forth lazily, like a paper flag in the breeze.

Milo was waiting outside. He stood between our front yards, beyond the glow of the porch lights. He wore a black T-shirt, and he'd brushed his hair down instead of back, letting the bangs hover over his glasses in uneven edges.

My side-parted hair and untucked button-down felt stifling all of a sudden.

"What'd ya bring?" I asked as I approached.

"A James Carr single and a full-length by my man Donovan."

"Of course," I nodded.

Butterflies or wasps flew around in my gut as I followed

him across the street. I'd never noticed the peculiar amount of windows Hana's house had. As we crossed through her yard, I could see into the kitchen—*empty*—and the dining room—*empty*—and I could even make out a TV flickering in one of the back rooms. I stepped over a pile of cigarette butts strewn loosely across the grass.

"Oh," Milo said as we climbed the porch, "take off your shoes when we get inside. It's a Japanese thing."

"OK. Should we, like, bow?" I asked seriously.

"Jesus, Ronnie," he scoffed, "just act normal."

He knocked on the door. Through the window, we saw a woman emerge from the back. I assumed she was Hana's mother, though she could've passed for an older sister—a *pretty* older sister. She wore white slacks and a tight, gray sweater. Her hair was dark, like Hana's, but cut in a much more fashionable bob.

Milo and I shared a sideways glance.

"Yoko O-*YES*," he said, bouncing his eyebrows up and down.

The front door opened, and I swallowed my chuckles.

"May I help you?" she asked. I heard zero tinge of Midwest or Far East in her voice. Her eyes were Hana's eyes, dark symbols of infinity.

"I'm Milo, from across the street."

"Ah yes," she smiled, "and you must be Ronnie. Please, please, come in."

We walked into the foyer. Milo and I slid off our shoes. Hana's mother didn't comment.

"Hana-chan," she sang up the stairs, "your callers are here."

A door upstairs opened and slammed. Hana appeared at the top of the staircase, wearing patched jeans and an oversized green flannel.

"Come on up."

I followed Milo up the stairs, and Hana led us to the room at the end of the hall. There was a poster on the door of Uncle Sam wrapped in bloody bandages. Instead of the standard *I WANT YOU*, this Uncle Sam implored *I WANT OUT*.

"Welcome to Basecamp Zero," Hana said sarcastically. Then she opened the door, and I walked into a room unlike any other.

The first thing that struck me was her record collection; she had almost as many as Bruce! *Otis Blue* played low on her high-end turntable. He sang about respect. Two lamps were draped in red silk kerchiefs to mellow the mood. All four walls were covered in posters and concert flyers that read like pure fantasy.

FEB. 15—THE DOORS, CHICAGO AUDITORIUM THEATER, $7.50

CHICAGO TRIBUNE—134 SEIZED IN DRAFT PROTEST

NOVEMBER 26—BOB DYLAN, ARIE CROWN THEATER, CHICAGO, IL

BLACK PANTHERS—MOVE ON OVER OR WE'LL MOVE ON OVER YOU!

But out of all those posters, the one that struck me the most was pinned on the wall behind her unmade bed. It featured a young guy burning his draft card, and read simply—**FUCK THE DRAFT!**

"Cool room," I gulped. "Subtle décor."

She laughed her gentle laugh.

"Can ya imagine what your dad would say if you hung that poster on your wall?" Milo asked.

"He'd put me *through* the wall," I said.

"Mine doesn't give a fuck," Hana shrugged, "but controversy doesn't faze him. If you marry a Japanese girl on the heels of World War II, you sorta have to be comfortable with other people's discomfort."

"I guess controversial parents have controversial kids," I smiled.

She smiled back.

"Did they meet in the war?" Milo asked.

"Nah, my father fought in Europe, not the Pacific. They met when he was in Nagoya, evaluating a company that makes toilet plungers."

"No shit?" Milo said.

All three of us laughed.

"Let's spin some records," she said. "Who wants to kick this show-n-tell off?"

"First things first," Milo said ceremoniously. "All members of the record club are present, so let's vote on a club name. A club's gotta have a name!"

"Any ideas?" I asked.

"Music Geeks Anonymous?" he joked.

"Uh, or, like, maybe The Rock-n-Roll . . . uh, Rebels?" I said, trailing off and scoffing at my own dumb suggestion.

"The Vinyl Underground," Hana said. She grinned.

"Eh," Milo shrugged, "that sounds more like a gang name."

"No shit, man. It's *the* name," she insisted. "The Vinyl Underground."

"Yeah," I said, "I can get behind that."

"Then a gang it is," Milo nodded. He picked up his LP. "Let's spin this one first. It's one of my favorites, 'Fairytale' by Donovan. This is the Hickory Records pressing, so it has a completely different track list than the mass-produced version."

"Trippy!" Hana said.

"Yeah," he nodded, "this first song isn't even on the original pressing."

Hana took the record from him and looked over the packaging. Then she slid the vinyl out of the dust sleeve and sat Donovan on the turntable.

She put the needle on the record and let it spin.

The speakers gave a warm crackle as the needle found the groove. She handed me *Otis Blue* just as Donovan's soft warble eased over an acoustic guitar.

"Put this up for me, would ya?"

I nodded, and went to her shelf. Donovan sang "Universal Soldier," and his exhausted disgust came through clearly. Milo nodded to the music.

I slid Otis back with the *Rs*. I glanced down at the table

beside her bed—it was stacked with newspapers, and a paperback copy of *Been Down So Long, It Looks Like Up to Me.*

When I turned back, Hana and Milo were sitting on the floor. She was hunched forward, examining the liner notes. Her black hair hung in her face, and the lamplight cascaded across it like a stoplight on wet blacktop.

I sat down across from them.

"Were you really at this?" Milo asked Hana.

He pointed to a newspaper clipping on the wall.

THOUSANDS JOIN SPRING MOBE
PROTESTS IN NYC AND SF
HUNDREDS OF DRAFT CARDS BURNED
AS YOUTH TAKE TO THE STREETS

"Oh yeah," she said proudly, "last April. We marched all the way to the United Nations. *Everyone* was there, Martin Luther King even gave a speech!"

"Woah," I gasped, "what was that like?"

"Transcendent, man."

"What does MOBE mean?" Milo asked.

"Mobilization to End the War in Vietnam."

"Were people really burning their draft cards?"

"Hundreds," she said. "My guy, Phillip, burned his before the march started."

"Your *guy*?" Milo cooed. "Aw, Hana's got a boyfriend—"

"Boyfriends and girlfriends are for boys and girls," she snapped. "All that's nothing but a distraction. *Boyfriends, girlfriends, glee club, the debate team*, they're traps the Man uses to monopolize the minds and time of the youth."

"And I thought *I* was cynical!" I laughed. "You win."

"You'd be cynical too, if you weren't tucked away from the real world."

"The real world found me easy enough," I said, harsher than I'd intended.

Instead of responding, she got up and grabbed a 45rpm from her shelf.

"Have you heard of 'em?" she asked. "They're from Detroit." She handed it to me.

AMG RECORDS
MC5
I CAN ONLY GIVE YOU EVERYTHING
(T. SCOTT—P. COULTER)
TIME: 2:36

"I don't see a band listed," I said.

"It's right there—"

"MC5?"

She nodded.

"Is this a Van Morrison cover? From when he was in THEM?"

"Yeah, but it doesn't sound like him or like THEM, or like *anything*."

She pulled the single from my hands and stood up. She

took Donovan off the turntable, changed the speed, and put the single on.

"What's it sound like?" Milo asked.

"Like a revolution," she said, and cranked up the volume.

Suddenly, the song's riff *blared* from the speakers, thick and distorted and nearly unrecognizable. Two bars in, the singer screamed over the music like a maniac. The volume of the recording pushed it beyond any chance of coherence.

"This is wild!" I yelled above the music.

"I know!" she said excitedly. "They're the most epic protest band ever! Word is they're gonna play outside the Democratic National Convention in Chicago!"

"You goin'?" Milo asked.

"Oh yeah, I'll be front and fuckin' center!"

The song ended as quickly as it began. My ears rang slightly. She stood back up, and chose one of her many full-length records. It was the new Bob Dylan album, *John Wesley Harding*.

"Have you guys heard this?"

"Not yet," Milo said.

She smiled, and put the record on. Bobby came right outta the gate with the title track. His voice meandered as the song unwound itself at a soothing tempo.

"So, Ronnie," Hana said, settling back down on the floor, "was your brother drafted, or did he enlist?"

"He was drafted. All he *wanted* to do was play records. Right before his number came up he'd been offered a job at a radio station in Sacramento. I was gonna meet him out there after I graduated and work as his sidekick."

"You guys must've been crushed," she said.

The song changed to a harder tune with a backbeat.

"I was. But honestly, it didn't faze Bruce. He figured he'd be back home by the time I graduated, and the two of us could go out west together. He acted like it was all a gas, one last adventure before his real life started."

Bob Dylan said life was a joke, and I shivered.

"What's wrong?" Milo asked.

"Just listen," she whispered.

We sat in silence until "All Along the Watchtower" ended.

Hana pointed to the records I'd brought. "Are those your brother's records?"

I nodded.

"Would you play me one?"

I'd been planning to play the Blues Magoos LP first—I wanted to tell her that it was the first album to ever use the word "psychedelic" in the title. But when I got up and went to the bed, the vinyl I grabbed was the 45.

The cover featured a photo of Roy Orbison wearing glasses, not shades. He looked almost like Milo, except Roy's hair was still quaffed back.

Below the photo read the title—"Blue Bayou."

"Man," Hana smiled, "I haven't heard that in forever."

"It was one of Bruce's favorites," I told her, handing it over.

She took the Dylan LP off the turntable, and set the speed back. But as she pulled the Orbison single from the sleeve, the envelope with Bruce's letter fell out.

I dove for the letter dumbly, sprawling across the floor before anyone else could pick it up.

"What's that?" Hana asked, as I grabbed it.

"Nothing," I mumbled, shoving the letter into my back pocket.

"Don't be a freakazoid," Milo scoffed. "What was that?"

"*Nothing*," I said, more forcefully. "Look, I gotta go."

I stood, and went to collect my other record.

"Fine," Hana said, "then you're outta the gang."

I hesitated. I looked back at her.

"Gangs keep secrets from the world," she said, "not from each other."

"Yeah, man," Milo said, "what gives?"

I sighed.

Part of me wanted to run out the door and shut down the conversation. Grief is a selfish thing, and it screamed inside my head, demanded solitude and secrecy. But another voice—a soft, lonesome voice—urged me to trust my friends.

I cleared my throat.

"It's a letter," I finally mumbled. "An old letter from Bruce."

I was surprised at how easily the words rolled out.

"He wrote me a lot at first," I went on, "and he always paired his letters with music. It was his way to keep DJing, I guess. So whenever I got a letter, I'd store it with whatever song he chose."

"Damn," Hana said, "that's beautiful, man."

I shrugged.

"Would you read us the letter?" she asked.

I squirmed uncomfortably.

"I'd like to hear it," Milo said. "I miss Bruce, too, ya know?"

"Yeah," I muttered, "I know."

I went to the stereo. Hana sat down beside Milo. They stared at me eagerly, like I was some bonked-out Mother Goose about to read them a bedtime war story. I unfolded the letter, and looked it over. Was I really gonna read it out loud?

Apparently fucking so.

"Bruce sent this to me from California when he was there training. If I remember right, this was the last I heard from him before he went to Vietnam."

I eased the needle onto the wax. Roy Orbison sang about his faraway home.

Softly, I began to read—

Listen to: "Blue Bayou," by Roy Orbison

How's the weather, Raspy Ronnie?

It's great here . . . because I'm writing you from California!

I wish you could hear the stations we pick up from the barracks! KRLA in Hollywood, the Boss Jocks on KHJ-AM— they're incredible! Me and you have got some serious competition out here on the coast!

But otherwise, California isn't exactly how I imagined it. Scratch that! It's exactly how I imagined it! This just isn't how I imagined ending up here.

I thought we'd be cruising Sunset with Wolfman Jack by now, ya know? Having fun in the California sun, going on safari to stay, all that good shit.

But all I've done is run, run, run, climb, climb, climb,

shoot, shoot, shoot, shoot, shoot, shoot, shoot. Seems like they're pushing my battalion harder than the others.

But hey! Last week I went to San Diego on leave, and let me tell you . . . the chicks out there, Ronnie! Good Sweet Baby Jesus, they were out of sight! Wouldn't give me the time of day, though, because of this stupid buzz cut. I have S-O-L-D-I-E-R written all over me. Do girls back home still like a man in uniform? Because out here, not so much.

Crazy, isn't it? I finally made it to California, and all I seem to do is miss Florida. Especially at night, when the scent of gunpowder dies down enough for me to smell the ocean.

But word has it we're shipping off to Da Nang in two weeks. I'm so ready to get this over with. I'll try to scrounge up some medals so you can watch people kiss my ass when I get home, ha ha. I'm counting down the days until then. I count them like I'm in prison. Not that I need to tell you that. You're in high school, after all.

Send my love to everyone, Wolfman included. I miss you, Little Brother.

I miss all y'all. Tell Momma to keep putting those candles in the window.

I'll be home soon,

-Bruce

The song was over before I finished reading. No one seemed to notice.

I folded the note and looked up.

Milo had removed his glasses. He was wiping his eyes with his shirt.

"Sorry," he mumbled, "shit, I'm sorry. That was just . . . that was so sad."

Hana was looking right at me.

Her dark eyes took it all in, and didn't give back an inch.

Finally, her lips curled into a soft smile.

"The sad ones are the truth, man. Go on, play it again."

HOW TO OUTRUN A BULLET

The first meeting of The Vinyl Underground was over by 10 p.m.

Milo called dibs on borrowing the MC5 single. I left the Blues Magoos record with Hana, and she loaned me her new Bob Dylan. I kept it at my side as she walked us out. They laughed as I struggled to get my shoes on, but I didn't mind. Milo held me steady until I got situated.

"This was cool," he said as we crossed the porch.

"Yeah. Solid idea, Ronnie."

"Same time, next week?" I asked.

"Definitely," they both said.

Hana pointed to the Roy Orbison single. "How many of those do you have? The ones with the letters."

"Fifteen, I think," I said, knowing damn well.

"Could you bring more next time?"

I clammed up for a moment. I was surprised she asked.

"Sorry if that's weird," she continued, "I just never got to meet him. But when you read that letter, I felt like I almost did."

"Yeah," Milo said, "I wanna know what happens next."

You know what happens next, I thought.

"Sure," I smiled, "I'll bring more next time."

"Groovy," Hana said, grinning.

I blushed and looked at my shoes.

"Well, I should get going," Milo said.

"Me too," I said.

"Bye, guys."

I followed Milo down the front steps, and we crossed the street in silence. The two of us shared a smile in the dark, and then went our separate ways.

I looked at the vinyl again as I climbed the stairs of my porch. It was the first time I'd been able to listen to Bruce's records without plummeting into the void—and I knew it was the others who'd held me in place. My family considered grief a private thing, but finally sharing a little had proven shockingly cathartic. If my friends could understand it, maybe they could help me bear it.

I was still smiling as I fumbled my key in the front door and walked inside.

"Hey, Ronnie," Ramrod called from the dining room.

He was sitting next to my dad, looking over a chart of wrestling matches that were graphed together like the branches of a family tree. He'd turned nineteen last week and been forced into an unofficial retirement from wrestling.

Now Lewis had the prestigious title of Unpaid Assistant Coach. The job came with only one benefit—free beer at scheduling meetings. A half-dozen empty bottles of Jax surrounded the poster board.

"Hey," I said, "what are y'all doin' up so late?"

"Tryin' to see if we can squeeze a scrimmage in before finals," Dad said.

"County's coming up that soon?"

"Barely a month away," Lewis said.

"And what happens the week *after* county finals?" Dad asked me, grinning.

"Uh, I dunno . . . what?"

"Your birthday!"

"Oh. Yeah."

"I talked to Adams the other day," he continued, "and he said—"

"Talked to who?"

"Sergeant Adams? The recruiter? I'm sure you've seen him in the halls. We were talkin' the other morning, and he said now that the D. E. P.'s in effect, boys under eighteen get a signing bonus if they enlist early."

"D. E. P.?" Lewis asked. "What's that?"

"Delayed Entry Program," Dad said, and then looked back at me. "That's why I thought ya should know. We can talk to him together sometime, if you'd like."

"That's OK, Dad."

"Suit yourself. But I don't see the point of waiting 'til you're eighteen, when you can enlist now and get yourself some spending money."

I don't know why I didn't walk away. Normally I would've. But instead I held Bruce's letter tighter and said, "I'm not enlisting, either way."

Dad calmly put down his pencil. He crossed his thick arms, and a curious look spread over his face. Lewis pretended to keep working on the schedule.

"Since when?"

"Since, I don't know, since always? You've never *asked* me if I was enlisting, Dad. You just assumed, I guess."

"Well, *gee-whiz*," he said sarcastically, "I guess I did just assume. I guess I just *assumed* that if *my* older brother died defending *my* country . . . well, I guess I just assumed a *man* might feel obligated to honor him and his sacrifice."

I sighed.

"You got somethin' else to say?" he snapped.

"I just . . . I dunno what to tell ya, Dad. If you wanted to send a boy over there to get revenge, you and Momma shoulda had Roy sooner."

Dad marched around the table toward me. I swear, the ground shook. I wanted to back away, but I didn't.

"It's not about revenge," he barked, "it's about *duty*. It's about *service*. If you're too arrogant to understand that, the draft board will set you straight quick."

A picture of Hana's poster flashed in my mind.

"Fuck the draft," I muttered, barely audible beneath my breath.

Dad shoved me against the wall by the throat.

I heard the drywall crack behind me before I realized what happened.

"What'd you just say to me?"

His face was inches from mine. I smelled the stale Jax on his breath.

"Nothing," I whispered.

"Oh, no, you said *somethin'*. Now I want you to repeat it."

"No. I–"

"You sure?"

I stayed silent.

"You *sure* you don't have nothin' else to say, smartass?"

" . . . "

He gritted his teeth and let me go.

I took a few harsh breaths. My vision blurred in and out.

"If I knew you'd be giving a communist lecture," he spat, "I woulda told the doctors to finish your voice off for good."

Then he walked back to the table to work on the wrestling schedule with Lewis, who was staring down at the schedule, probably pretending he couldn't hear me or Dad.

I hurried upstairs to my bedroom. I slammed the door behind me. I undressed as fast as I could and got into bed, too angry to sleep.

I flipped off the lamp. I stared into the dark with my hands behind my head.

"Fuck the draft," I mumbled again.

Then I drifted off into a peaceful sleep, chock-full of American dreams.

———

Mr. Donahue wrote in fast, dramatic swipes. He scrawled the words across the blackboard as soon as the morning announcements ended. Then he jabbed at the board with the nub of chalk.

WHAT IS COURAGE?

"What say you, ladies and gentlemen?" he asked.

My ride to school with Dad had been brutally silent, so I was happy that first period started with a discussion. I hoped it would allow me to refocus my mind, because turning it off was getting harder to manage.

A girl in the front of the room raised her hand.

"Bravery?"

"Bravery," Mr. Donahue nodded. "Good. Anyone else?"

"It means having balls," Benji Curtis grinned. "I mean, having guts."

I chuckled and shook my head.

"*Very* good, Benji. That was *such* a good answer, I'd like you to stay after class to discuss it."

Benji groaned.

"Moving on," Mr. Donahue said. "When you picture someone courageous, someone brave, someone with *guts*, who comes to mind?"

"Batman."

"Marshall Dillon from *Gunsmoke*."

"Johnny Unitis."

"Ramrod!" a boy in the corner yelled, which prompted a chant.

Mr. Donahue smiled, but held up his hands, "Those are

all great examples. Now, who can name a courageous person in *politics*?"

Silence.

"Come on, this is Government Two, after all! How about . . . you?"

He pointed to Jamie, beside me.

"Um, George Washington?"

"Very good!" Mr. Donahue nodded. "And why was he courageous?"

"Um, because he was, uh, a general?"

"Yes, but what *political* courage did he show?"

"I don't know," she blushed.

"That's OK," he smiled encouragingly. "You will."

He grabbed a book from his desk and held it before us, moving it from right to left like it was a prize on a game show. The book was *Profiles in Courage* by John F. Kennedy.

"*Profiles in Courage* was written by our late President Kennedy. It is filled with short biographies of senators he believed exemplified courage in politics. Some you will have heard of, others maybe not. But soon, you will know them all well, because this is your final grade."

Huffy hands rose. Blackhead-splattered brows creased.

Mr. Donahue ignored them all.

"There will be no final exam in my class. What there *will* be are profiles in courage. You'll read President Kennedy's book, and then seek out your own politician to write a profile in courage about. This short, ten-page biography can be on any politician, living or dead. I know research papers take time, which is why I'm giving you the assignment now. It will be a lot of work, but this will also be a truly inspiring experience, and I think that—"

Benji raised his hand.

Mr. Donahue sighed, and pointed at him.

"Can I write my paper on the courage it took Kennedy to juggle Jackie and Marilyn Monroe?"

The classroom erupted in a giggle explosion.

Benji's mouth dropped open in genuine shock when Mr. Donahue said no.

———

Second period was my free period, so I figured I'd go ahead and grab a copy of *Profiles in Courage* from the library. As I headed in that direction, I saw Milo at his locker, which was covered in magazine cutouts from *Film Review* and *Picturegoer.*

"Hey," I called as I approached.

He didn't turn around.

"Hey."

He still didn't hear me. He shut his locker.

I put a hand on the back of his shoulder.

He jumped, startled, and spun around.

"Oh, Ronnie! You scared me."

"I was yelling for ya."

"You were?"

"Yeah, as much as I can."

"Damn," he said, "it's my ears. They've been ringin' since last night."

"How come?"

"That MC5 single Hana lent me. I was listenin' to it with headphones, so I wouldn't wake up my mom. I guess I had the volume up too loud."

The bell rang. He didn't notice. Students hustled in both directions.

"Class is starting," I said loudly.

"Oh man, thanks! See ya!"

He started off in the opposite direction.

"How many times did you listen to that song?!" I hollered at him.

But he didn't hear me, which was answer enough.

I continued down the hall, which was deserted by the time the next bell rang. When I reached the library, I found it nearly empty, too.

I took a deep, gratifying whiff of books, that earthy musk of wisdom. I loved libraries, in general—they were the one place so many conflicting ideas could stand being next to each other. I, too, was a mixed bag of interests, not married to any single theme or style. But I was also a senior in high school, which meant I was expected to have my entire future laid out in an orderly, easy-to-read fashion. To lack a plan was to lack definition, lack ambition, and lack a sense of self.

At least when Bruce was alive I'd had a plan. It was *his* plan, but it had been good enough for me. Now, I had no outline to work off of. Now, I was just drifting.

But as long as I was in the library, drifting was OK. Drifting was allowed.

So I strolled the aisles leisurely, browsing acclaimed classics and paperback pulps until I happened to stumble upon JFK's book. There was only one copy.

Tough titty for the rest of the class, I thought.

I took the book to the reading area at the other end of the library. When I walked in, I was surprised to see Lewis sitting alone at a table in the back. He was hunched over a textbook that looked comically small between his shoulders.

I sat down across from him.

"Lewis," I whispered, "hey."

"Oh, hey," he said, looking up. "What ya workin' on?"

I held up the book. "How about you?"

"Biology. Tryin' to get through it."

"What a drag. Biology's the worst."

"The worst of the worst," he said, dropping his pencil in frustration.

"Hey," I said awkwardly, "sorry you had to see that last night."

He shrugged. "No big thing."

"Nah, I was bein' stupid. I was—"

"Stupid to say it to your dad, yeah. But you were right. Fuck the draft."

I gawked, surprised at his reaction. His hazel eyes gave nothing away.

"So if you weren't held back last year, you wouldn't have enlisted?"

"Hell no," he scoffed. "I don't wanna die somewhere I can't pronounce or kill people for reasons even the newsmen can't explain."

"I don't either," I sighed, "but I take the draft exam in six weeks. The closer it gets, the more it seems like a death sentence."

"I know the feeling," he nodded. "Every time I think of goin' over there, I think about your brother. He was the best of us, smartest dude I ever met, the fastest man in the land. So if he didn't know how to outrun a bullet, what chance do we have?"

I wasn't sure what to say to that.

Lewis sighed and picked up his pencil. He looked down at his textbook.

"Hey, Lewis," I mumbled a moment later.

"Yeah?"

"Do you dig music?"

SIDE B

"*Did any one of them ever come back and say by God I'm glad I'm dead because death is always better than dishonor . . . I'm happy, see how I sing even though my mouth is choked with worms?*"

—Dalton Trumbo

SIX

THE CIRCLE TIGHTENS

Thursday Night. Record Club.
Be there, or be squarer than square.

When the four of us sat on the floor together, we took the
shape of a circle. Milo sat beside Hana, who sipped a beer that
Lewis snuck over, then passed it around like communion wine.
At first, she wasn't eager to let another jock join our ranks; but
I vouched that Lewis was nothing like Stink Wilson. Now I sat
between him and the turntable, reading one of Bruce's letters
out loud while its companion piece "Turn! Turn! Turn!" turned
and turned and turned.

Three weeks in this country, and I'm still not used to the
smells. They're harder to deal with than the heat. The rice water
and rot and powder and sweat. BLOOD has a smell, too. I never
want you to learn it. I swear, some days I wish Momma never
humored those rock-n-roll dreams of mine. Maybe I'd cope
with this shit better.

But hell, of course she let me dream. That's what mommas
are supposed to do.

I don't know why I'm bitching instead of telling you I miss you. The world keeps turning out there and that's the way it should be. Don't you forget that, Ronnie.

One last thing: I dunno how you got your hands on those Playboys, but I appreciate the amount of effort it must have taken you to part with them! The Corps can keep Vietnam, man! Give me Miss June, or give me death! Ha ha!

-Bruce

The Byrds' cryptic harmonics ended in time with my recitation. I folded the letter, and switched the vinyl to the B side, "She Don't Care About Time."

"When'd he send you that?" Milo asked.

"Late September."

"I hate that he started regretting his dreams," Hana sighed.

"He didn't," Lewis said. "He wasn't thinkin' straight when he wrote that shit."

I nodded and took a drink.

"What do you guys wanna be when you quote-unquote grow up?" Hana asked.

"A movie director," Milo said.

"Like Sergio Leone?" she asked.

"More like Kubrick, hopefully. I've been savin' for a Super 8 since Christmas."

"Does Mr. Dori know you're finally getting one?" I asked. Mr. Dori relied on Milo to keep the Royal Atlantis running. I always assumed he wanted him to take it over one day.

"Yeah, man. He lets me practice splicing reels at work."

"How about you, Ramrod?"

"I dunno," he said bashfully.

"Come on," she goaded him, "how do you do it? Ramrod! Ramrod! Ramrod!"

We laughed. Lewis blushed.

"I figured I'd play college ball for *someone*," he said, "or get a wrestling scholarship, but no dice so far. I knew flunking last year would screw my GPA, but I never imagined it'd be this bad. So I really dunno what I'm gonna do."

"Offers will come in," I said. "You're Ramrod, man. You're a legend."

"Some church in St. Augustine just started a scholarship fund for, uh, underprivileged kids," Milo said. "I don't think it's a full ride, but it might be worth lookin' into."

Milo was noticeably uncomfortable bringing up Lewis's financial situation. His dad split before Lewis ever met him, and it was common knowledge that his mom had a harder time making ends meet than most.

"For real?" Lewis asked. He didn't seem flustered at all.

"Yeah. I think it was Fifth Ave. Baptist, or—"

"Bethill Baptist," Hana interrupted, "in Jacksonville, not St. Augustine."

"How do you know?" Milo asked.

"Because I read the paper, man. It's my *job* to know, or, it will be."

"I'm not sure know-it-all's a job," I grinned.

"Yeah asshole, but journalist is. I'm gonna have my own

column one day, and I'm gonna write about street-level shit, the way Martha Gellhorn does."

"I didn't know you were a writer," I said, passing her the nearly empty beer.

"I write every day."

"You should write for the school paper," Milo said.

"I've submitted fourteen articles," she scoffed. "They told me my work is too controversial. They want stories about football games and the Salisbury steak in the cafeteria, not about civil rights and the war. I don't know why I bother submitting. Sometimes, I forget high school's a place for conditioning, not learning."

"Could I read them?" I asked. "I love books."

"No fuckin' way. *No* civilians read my work until it's published."

She got up and slid Lewis's Booker T. record from its dog-eared sleeve. She put it on the turntable. Lewis killed the last drop of beer.

"How about you, Ronnie?" she asked as she rejoined the circle.

"Well, I'd planned on going to California with my brother, doin' the radio thing. But now . . . yeah. I dunno."

"You could still go," she said.

"Sure, but that's a tough gig without his coattails to ride."

"What about writing?" she went on. "You just said you love books."

"Enough to be a reader," I said, "but not a writer. I'm like that about a lot of stuff. I just . . . I feel like I've never quite figured out what my thing is."

"Then go to college," Hana said, "and take a bunch of different courses. Tons of electives and shit like that. You'll figure it out, guaranteed."

"Even if I apply for scholarships now, I won't hear back before I turn eighteen. Half of me thinks enlisting's the safest move . . . at least I'd have a say in what I do for Uncle Sam. If I get drafted, I'll be put in the infantry. Sometimes I go, shit, maybe my dad's right, maybe the D. E. P.'s my best bet."

"What's that?" Hana asked.

"It's the Delayed Entry Program," I said. "It's a new way for recruiters to scam high schoolers into enlisting. They offer a cash bonus if ya join *before* you're eighteen, then after graduation they stick ya with a contract the shape of a target."

"*What!*" Hana yelled, stunned. "How is that legal?"

Lewis shrugged. "It's legal 'cause the Man says it's legal."

She took a deep breath and shuddered. Booker T. pounded the hell out of the keys. The M.G.'s backed him up with a stellar groove.

"Bring any more of Bruce's letters?" Milo asked me.

Hana looked at me with her big, dark eyes.

I nodded and wobbled to my feet. I got the 45rpm from the bed and pulled out the letter. Then I took the M.G.'s record off the turntable and put my single in its place. I turned to the three of them before dropping the needle.

I cleared my throat.

"Bruce didn't pair this with a song," I said, unfolding the

letter, "but it seems like he wrote it when things were pretty crazy, so he musta forgot. I paired it with this myself, 'cause, well, it just sounded right."

I set the needle onto the outer groove of the Stones' "Paint It Black."

Ronnie,

Sorry I haven't written. I got the letters you and Momma sent, but I haven't read them. It gets too hard, reading them. But I wanted to let y'all know Bad Bruce is still alive and kicking!

If you've been watching the news, I'm sure you've heard about what's going down. The V. C. are as sneaky as they say, but worse. I mean way worse. We plow them down, and then these fuckers come back up for more. Some of the boys think they're not even real, think that we're out here in the jungle hunting ghosts.

Oh yeah, how's the weather, Raspy Ronnie? It's monsooned all week. These ain't like the tropical storms in FL. This rain is heavy enough to crush a guy. The rain makes it impossible to see and easy to screw up—the best buddy I've made here caught a Bouncing Betty yesterday while walking point. We aren't sure who tripped it, but it blew him right out of his poncho. His name was Jonathan Marconi. We called him Meatball. Kinda fitting now, right?

I went to talk to my sergeant about it earlier. He left me waiting in his quarters, which is where I'm writing to you from now. I'm taking advantage of having a desk and not scribbling on my muddy knee for a change. A second ago, I thought there was someone else in here, but it was just my reflection in the mirror. That's a trip, ain't it? I haven't seen a mirror since I been over here. I didn't even recognize myself—I have that fucking look in my eyes now, man.

But you'd still recognize me, Ronnie. Because I still have the same smile. I just double-checked to be sure. It's the one that's just like yours, Little Brother.

So shout it from the rooftops.

Bad Bruce lives!

—*Bruce*

"That was four days before he died," I muttered. "The letter took longer than usual to come in. By then *we knew* . . . I mean, shit, they'd told us, but still. When Momma found it in the mail she thought maybe there had been a mistake, maybe he wasn't really dead. You remember that, Milo?"

"I remember," he whispered.

I folded the letter. I wiped my eyes.

For the first and only time, our record club was a cone of silence. No one made eye contact. No one took a drink. No one lit a smoke. The stillness seemed thick enough to muffle my words, to cut them off mid-air before anyone heard. Maybe that's why I said what I said out loud.

"I can't let it happen to me."

Instantly, I felt their eyes.

"Not dying," I stammered, "I don't mean that. I mean how they *changed* him. They twisted him up. Jesus, it doesn't even sound like he wrote this! It sounds . . . it sounds broken. It just sounds like he's broken. I can't let 'em do that to me. Bruce would hate me if I let 'em. So fuck that. Fuck them! Fuck Vietnam, man!"

"Fuck Vietnam." Hana nodded.

Milo squeezed my shoulder. It was an act of camaraderie as much as relief. "I just needed you to say it first," he admitted. "If you're out, I'm out. Fuck this war. Fuck the fucking draft!"

I put my hand on top of his and peered into all four of his eyes.

"We'll figure a way out of it," I swore, trying to sound confident.

"But we're prime, man, and no colleges have accepted us . . . so. Shit," Milo said.

Hana put a finger to her lips and stood up.

She took the 45 off the turntable and grabbed the first record she saw—Milo's *Songs of Leonard Cohen*. She put it on and turned the volume low.

She sat back down. She motioned us in.

The circle tightened.

"Listen," she whispered, "I can get you guys out of it."

"How?" Milo asked.

"First, we go to Chicago. I have friends in the underground that can get you papers, fake IDs, that sorta stuff. Once we get those, we take a Greyhound to Detroit. I've got people there that can get us outside of the city, where you can cross the St. Clair River. From there, I should be able to score you a ride to Toronto, where you can get set—"

"Wait, wait, wait," Milo said, holding up his hands. His eyes were blinking manically, and it looked like he might overheat. "You're saying we should go to *Canada*?"

She nodded.

"Hana," I said calmly, "we can't do that."

"Why?"

"Draft dodging is one thing. But deserting to *Canada* . . . that's somethin' else entirely. My family would disown me, if Dad didn't find me and kill me first. We'd be pariahs even after the war was over. We'd have no home here anymore, ever."

"Well I don't give a shit what your parents think," she groaned, "when I give a shit about saving your stupid life!"

"There's another way," Lewis said.

We all looked at him.

"Deferment."

"We can't get one if we're not in college," Milo said.

"Sure you can," he said, matter-of-factly, "I did."

"How?" I asked.

"By bustin' my ass to fail," he said, "and to fail convincingly. It took effort to flunk . . . last year's the first time I ever got so much as a D in school. But I did it. So the draft board had to give me a deferment."

A sheepish grin spread across his face.

"You're a genius!" I said.

Milo bowed toward him, and clapped reverently.

"Pretty slick," Hana said, "but what are you gonna do now? You just told us you screwed yourself out of an athletic scholarship by failing. No college means no deferment for you this time around."

"You're right," he admitted.

"A deferment won't be enough, anyway," she said, "not if the war keeps going this way. LBJ is sending more troops to Vietnam *right now*. You might buy yourself a year with a deferment, maybe two, but unless one of you has an uncle in the senate or something, you'll go eventually."

"What if we become priests?" I spat out. "We could get ordained by one of those backwoods revivals in the Everglades, and then—"

"That's a 4-D classification," Hana said. "Right now, they'd still make you go."

"What about . . . what's it called? Being a conscientious objector?" I asked.

"1-O, man," she said, shaking her head. "You'd go, just without a weapon."

"Jesus Christ," Milo sighed. "Tell me there's something behind door number three."

Hana leaned in closer. We leaned in, too.

"Door number three is getting you guys classified 4-F, *permanently* disqualified for military service. That's the only guarantee that you'll be safe."

"How?" I asked. "You mean like shootin' ourselves in the foot?"

"A few years ago, maybe. That shit won't fly now. Too many kids have done it, and the Man catches on quick. I've read a dozen articles about boys getting charged with dereliction of duty. Poor suckers avoided four years in the jungle, just to spend twenty in jail."

"But something *like* that, right?"

"Yeah," she nodded, "something like that."

"OK," I said, "OK . . . OK . . . OK . . . there must be other ways . . . there must be *tons* of random ways to get disqualified for military service."

"Yeah," Lewis nodded, "there must be."

"Sure," Milo squeaked, "we're OK, we're cool. We've got time to figure it out."

"But how much?" Hana asked.

She looked from Lewis, to Milo, to me, and back to Lewis.

"I don't report back until this summer," he said.

"What about you? Do either of you take the draft exam before graduation?"

Milo nodded in my direction.

The beer in my stomach turned sour. I felt like I might puke.

"When?" Hana asked.

"The day after my birthday," I mumbled. "March 16th. A Saturday."

She patted my hand. The touch was reassuring-ish.

"Then we have a month to figure it out," Lewis said. "We can do that."

"Yeah," Milo said, grabbing my other hand. "That's an eternity!"

I smiled the unconvincing smile I'd perfected over the last few months.

She held my hand then—I mean *really* held it. I looked into her dark eyes.

"Don't worry, Ronnie," she said, "I won't let those fuckers take you. I swear to God I'll kill you myself before I let you die over there."

"Oh Hana," I rasped, "you say the sweetest things."

She laughed and Milo laughed and Ramrod laughed.

But I didn't.

SEVEN

RIDING THE UNIVERSAL
HIGH OF DEFIANCE

Two weeks flew by, but not a single one of our ideas survived incubation—walking into the draft exam and drooling like I was a zombie, pretending to have gone blind, sticking peanut butter up my butt to fake some horrible gut rot—in the end, none of the ideas would play.

Those scams might trick the examiners at first, but as soon as they checked my medical records they'd know it was pure fiction. The paper trail of pediatric checkups haunted us worse than our permanent records.

I was starting to panic. One restless night, I seriously considered lobbing off my trigger finger with a steak knife, consequences be damned. I began to wonder how long it would take me to learn to speak Canadian, or whatever the language of pacifism was. But I kept my defeatist thoughts to myself.

When I was with The Vinyl Underground, I displayed as much confidence as possible. They needed to believe that *I* believed we'd find a way to beat the draft. So every Thursday night, I put on the best face I could—but behind that mask of sanity, I was a blubbering, nervous wreck.

The county wrestling finals were a week away, which only added to my stress. Dad was determined to push our team to victory by any means necessary. He stretched our practices an hour longer and made half the guys wear trash bags over their clothes to drop down in weight. The only reason he started speaking to me again was so he could yell at me when I was on the mat.

The one wrestler who seemed to *enjoy* Dad's end-of-season suicide sets was Stink Wilson. He began showing up to practice early and staying late. I often saw him doing push-ups in the hall between classes. While Dad's intense workouts felt like a punishment to me, Stink took it as a gospel in brutality—and he was a true believer if there ever was one.

I put in more effort than usual at practice as an olive branch to Dad, but upping my game put a physical strain on my already-tense mental state. Two weeks of that torture was all it took for my body to give out. I had to call off work after Friday's practice—my back and legs hurt too bad to stand at the ticket counter. I spent most of the weekend in Bruce's bedroom, listening to records while I straightened out my spine on the hardwood floor.

Sunday afternoon I lay there on the floor with Wolfman curled beside me, and I twisted my torso while Sam Cooke sang "Cupid" on the stereo.

"I always liked this song," Momma said from the hall-way. She'd just put Roy down for his nap, which she did every afternoon at the exact same time. When he was born, my un-expected little brother had put a noticeable strain on Momma. But after Bruce died, tending to Roy seemed like the only thing that gave her peace. I don't mean to say that he was a replace-ment; it was more like his presence offered her a bird's-eye view of motherhood, both the terrible and the beautiful, and this vantage point required a small dose of acceptance to truly grasp the scope.

I saw that peace rise into dimples at the edges of her mouth as she smiled and walked into the room. Wolfman wagged his tail while she ran her finger down the shelf of Bruce's records.

"Your brother had quite the record collection."

"Best in the state, I'd bet."

She picked up a 45, but put it down. Picked up another. Put it down. Then she sat on the edge of his bed, and Wolfman jumped up beside her. She petted him idly.

"Do you collect things, Ronnie?" she asked.

"Nah, not really."

"What about your little book display?"

She meant the handful of books above the desk in my bedroom. I mostly got books from the library, because I only read them once. Unlike records, they never seemed as good the second time. I purchased only a handful, and for no other reason than appreciation of their pure righteousness—*One Flew Over the Cuckoo's Nest, We Have Always Lived in the Castle, Heart of Darkness, Tropic of Capricorn, On the Road, To Kill a Mockingbird,* and *Day of the Guns.*

"Yeah," I said. "I guess the books count. What about you, Momma?"

"Heavens, no." She laughed. "I can't stand the clutter in this house as it is! But your father, he was quite the stamp collector when we first met. Had books full of 'em."

I sat up. When I looked at her, she peered out the window. "Dad collected *postage stamps*? I can't imagine."

"Well," she mused, "it was a *long* time ago, before he went to Korea . . ."

Her voice trailed off. I thought about my brother's last letter, about how different he sounded. Momma scratched Wolfie's neck until his leg began to twitch.

"Was Dad different after the war?"

"You know better than to ask," she snapped.

"But it's just us. Come on, tell me."

"Honey," she sighed, "who wouldn't change after something like that?"

"Yeah," I said, "but what was different about him?"

"He had lots of nightmares—screamed himself awake a few nights. He'd wake up sometimes, those first years back, and not know where he was, and . . . his laugh. His laugh was different, too."

"How?"

"I don't know how to put it," she said. "It was hollow. Like an echo."

"You think he wishes he didn't enlist?"

She thought about it for a good long moment.

"Today," she said, "no, I don't imagine he regrets it. But if you were to ask him when he was over there fighting? Well, it's not my place to speak on it."

"Momma," I asked softly, "why does he want me to go? After everything he's been put through, that *we've* been put through—"

KnockKnockKnock!

KnockKnockKnockKnockKnock! KnockKnock!

The banging on the front door pounded an end to our conversation.

I forced myself to my feet.

"I'll get it, Momma."

The knocking continued as my sore legs descended the stairs. I opened the door to find Milo in his work uniform, breathless with excitement.

"Ronnie!" he panted, "Tonight . . . emergency record club . . . meeting."

I stepped onto the porch and shut the door behind me.

"What's going on?"

He took a deep breath, and tried to explain again. "I'm calling an emergency meeting . . . I told Hana. Can you give Lewis a ring?"

"Sure," I nodded, "but what's up?"

"What do you *think*?" he said, shaking my forearms enthusiastically.

"You . . . wait, you figured it out? You figured out how to beat the draft?"

A proud smile spread across his face.

"Let's just say your birthday present will be one for the books, 'cause when—"

He gasped mid-sentence as I knocked the air out of him.

It was an accident. I'd just never hugged anyone that hard before.

——

I couldn't tell you what record was spinning. It was just something to muffle our voices from any perked parental ears. There were no beers to drink that night, no stashboxes or cigarettes needed. The four of us were already riding the universal high of defiance.

The circle was tighter than ever. Hana, Lewis, and I sat close enough for our knees to touch. The three of us leaned toward Milo like petals reaching for the sun.

"So," he started, "this morning, Mr. Dori and I recalibrated the speakers in all three viewing rooms of the theater. We do it every two weeks. The speakers in Viewing Room 1, the biggest room, are supposed to be set at 85 dB."

"What's dB mean?" Hana asked.

"Decibel," he said. "It's a way to measure sound. But it's complicated, 'cause it measures in multiples of ten. So if silence is 0 dB, a sound ten times louder would be 10 dB, but a sound *a thousand times louder* is only 30 dB, and—"

"Come on, man," I said anxiously, "get to it."

"My point is"—he nodded—"movies in Viewing Room 1 are shown at 85 dB, which is loud, but not *crazy* loud. You get it?"

"Sure," Hana said.

"So I calibrated the system to 85 dB, but when I looked at the volume dial I realized I could crank it *twice as loud* if I wanted to."

"Which means?" Lewis asked.

"Dig this," he said. "It's from a speaker manual in the supply room. Just look."

He pulled a piece of paper from his pocket and flattened it between us. The three of us leaned down toward it, trying to grasp the chart.

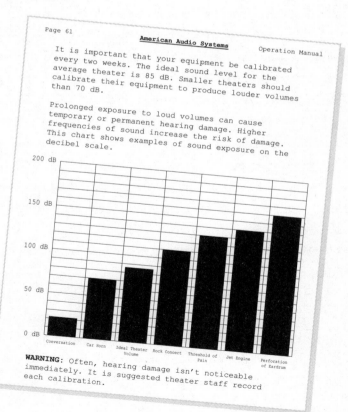

Page 61

American Audio Systems   Operation Manual

It is important that your equipment be calibrated every two weeks. The ideal sound level for the average theater is 85 dB. Smaller theaters should calibrate their equipment to produce louder volumes than 70 dB.

Prolonged exposure to loud volumes can cause temporary or permanent hearing damage. Higher frequencies of sound increase the risk of damage. This chart shows examples of sound exposure on the decibel scale.

WARNING: Often, hearing damage isn't noticeable immediately. It is suggested theater staff record each calibration.

I strained my eyes harder, but I didn't understand.

All I saw were numbers and figures.

I was looking for salvation.

"Milo!" I finally snapped. "Just tell us what it means!"

Milo nodded again, and stood up. He took a deep breath, which made me nervous, because I could see he expected whatever this plan was to be a hard sell.

"What the chart means," he said, "is that if we turn the speakers all the way up they'll be *louder* than the 'threshold of pain,' which would be loud enough to—"

"To what," I snapped, "make me go deaf?"

"Not deaf," he said, "not exactly. But if we can cause *temporary* hearing loss, that's our ticket outta the draft! There's no way a draft examiner will be able to tell the difference between permanent and temporary hearing problems."

"Temporary," Hana said, "like when you go to a concert, then your ears ring for days?"

"*Exactly*! A controlled version of that."

I ran my hand through my hair, disheveling the Steve McQueen perfection. My hand shook slightly. I looked back at the chart, but my eyes were out of focus.

"Your draft exam's the day after your birthday, right?" Milo asked.

"Right. Saturday morning."

"OK," he said, "that's perfect. We'll work our normal night shift on your birthday, and then offer to stay late for cleanup. Once the theater's empty, we'll sneak these two in. All you'll have to do is sit in Viewing Room 1, and I'll do the rest."

"Which is what?" I asked.

"Well, I'll hook up my turntable and put a record on, then calibrate the volume and max it all the way up. I just need to figure out how long you'll need to be exposed to the sound for it to work."

"Jesus Christ," I sighed. "Won't that, like, hurt?"

"Don't be a bitch about it," Hana goaded. "Don't you think it hurts to shoot yourself in the foot? Don't you think it hurts to cut off your trigger finger?"

"Yeah, man," Ramrod nodded, "freedom hurts either way."

I sat in silence, breathing heavily, staring at the chart.

"Unlike cutting off a finger," Milo added, "this damage will be temporary. Your hearing will go back to normal a few days later—a few weeks, tops. I mean, this is the *perfect* plan! Have any of y'all had a hearing exam before?"

We all shook our heads no.

"Exactly," he continued, "so there are no medical records to compare these test results to. All you're gonna have to do is show up and fail."

"You might be a fuckin' genius," Hana said.

"Yeah," Lewis smiled hopefully, "and if it works, can you do it for me?"

"If it works, I'll do it for every guy that lets me."

Lewis stood up, and wrapped his massive arm around Milo's shoulders.

"You *are* a fucking genius," he proclaimed, "no might-be's about it!"

"If it doesn't work, I'll get drafted," I mumbled, "and if it works too well, I'll go deaf."

"That's about the gist of it," Milo shrugged. "But it *will* work, Ronnie. It has to. You've just gotta be brave."

"Yeah," I scoffed, "or a goddamn psycho."

"Be brave or be crazy," Hana said. "Be whatever you have to be to get to the edge of the cliff. It doesn't matter how you get there, what matters is you jump."

EIGHT

SWIMMING WITH SHARKS

"**S**harks pride! Sharks pride! You can't run! You can't hide!"

"Sharks pride! Sharks pride! You can't run! You can't hide!"

The cheer went on and on, conjuring school spirit like a bubbly séance. The majorettes had already warmed up the pep rally, and now the cheerleaders were out there keeping everyone on their feet. I stood in the hallway with the other wrestlers and waited to be announced. The whole shebang was in our honor, so we were expected to make a hell of an entrance.

They ended their cheer with a flourish, and I could hear muffled claps from the crowd. There was a squeal of feedback, and then Principal Yonker's voice flooded the hallway in an amplified echo. "Now, let's give a big Sharks welcome to your very own soon-to-be county champions . . . the Cordelia High Wrestling Team!"

The doors to the gymnasium opened as the marching band started a wobbly rendition of "Louie Louie" inside.

"Let's go!" Ramrod yelled, running into the gym.

He waved at the bleachers like a pro, and the crowd went

wild. We followed his lead, jogging and waving blindly. The cheerleading squad hopped up and down, flapping their pom-poms like epileptics. I wondered how they could jump in those long wool skirts. The majorettes twirled their batons and smiled. Lena, my New Year's kiss, blew me another and I tried not to blush.

The bleachers were made up of any student who didn't use the assembly as an excuse to ditch. I was surprised to see Hana among them, sitting in the third row, clapping for us. Principal Yonker stood center court, at a rollaway podium that faced the bleachers. Behind him were rows of folding chairs meant for us. I took a seat beside Milo.

My eyes drifted back to Hana. She was laughing, mimicking the cheerleaders and waving wildly at Milo and me. She blew me an exaggerated smackaroo. I blushed double-time and looked down. The bleachers erupted in applause again.

"Check it out," Milo said, "your old man's as famous as Cary Grant!"

I looked up as Dad strutted into the gym. His back was straight and his jaw was high. He moved as if we'd already won. He wore a suit, which he rarely did. My teammates gave him a standing ovation. Milo and I did the same. When Dad smiled at us, he didn't look like Cary Grant. He looked like Bruce.

He shook hands with Principal Yonker, and took a seat with the rest of the faculty on the front row of the bleachers. He nodded at us, and we sat down. The marching band finished playing, and then loitered against the wall.

"Now," Principal Yonker said into the microphone, "what

can I say about our wrestlers here that you don't already know? They're the pride of Cordelia Island, one of the greatest groups of athletes in the history of this school!"

The crowd cheered.

"I know it, you know it, and by the end of the week *the entire county will know better than to go swimming with Sharks!*"

The crowd kept cheering. They loved it.

"Before we give them a proper send-off, I'd like to introduce you to one of Cordelia High's former champions, Marine Sergeant Jeffrey Adams!"

"You've gotta be shitting me," I mumbled.

Sergeant Adams, our school recruiter, stood up from the bleachers and waved to the crowd. He looked like a movie star in his dress blues. The kids clapped dutifully—everyone but Hana, who glared at him with white-hot disgust.

Sergeant Adams marched to the center of the gym. His shoes were as blinding as the glare in a rearview mirror. He shook hands with Principal Yonker, who then handed him the microphone.

"*Go Sharks!*" Sergeant Adams yelled.

The cheerleaders went Beatlemania on him.

"I'm Sergeant Jeffery Adams, a proud marine, and a proud graduate of Cordelia High. I wrestled back in my day, too, but I was nowhere as talented as these boys. They truly *are* the pride of this town!"

Cue the applause button.

"Principal Yonker was gracious enough to invite me here to offer you a very special opportunity, the opportunity to become the pride of the entire nation! I'm talking about joining a team that's *never* lost a match, *never* lost a war, *never* known defeat . . . the United States Military!"

Sergeant Adams took a dramatic pause as some faculty members cheered.

"Now," he went on, "when I was your age, I had to be eighteen to prove I had the guts to be a marine. But you boys are different—I can feel it—and your Uncle Sam feels it, too! That's why I've been instructed to offer you a chance to join the military *today*! Every single one of you boys can join right here, right now!"

My eyes cut to Hana. She was squirming in her seat.

"Even you freshmen can enlist!"

Hana was bobbing up and down. She was about to blow her top.

"Trust me," Sergeant Adams grinned, "there's no surer way to make your parents, your country, and, most importantly, your *God* proud—"

"DON'T LISTEN TO HIM!"

A hush went over the gym.

Sergeant Adams stopped talking. Heads and eyes moved frantically, trying to figure out where the cry of protest came from.

I, of course, already knew.

"Don't listen to him!" Hana yelled again. She bolted up from her seat and turned to face the other students. "They'll ship you to Vietnam as soon as you graduate! You'll be in the jungle while this fraud creeps on innocent high schoolers!"

Students and teachers alike gasped. Milo let out a shocked chuckle.

Sergeant Adams looked unflustered.

"Young lady," he said into the mic, "I'll have you know I proudly served in—"

"Don't run your lines on me," she screamed, turning back to him. "There's nothing proud about you, you're a used car salesman of death! You're a-a-a predator! You're a shark! You're the only fuckin' shark here, man!"

That was it. The cussword did it.

The teachers started to move on her, pushing aggressively past the second row of students. But Hana maneuvered away from their grasp, making her way to the very top row of the bleachers. She pumped her clenched fist into the sky.

Then she started to chant.

"We're not eight-teen! Stop the fucking war machine!"

The pure thrill of hearing the word "fuck" sent a jolt through the kids in the bleachers. Tomorrow our classmates would shun her, of course. They'd call her a hippie, a communist, and worse. But the entire student body was mesmerized at her ability to curse in the face of authority; in that moment she was every teenager's hero, politics be damned.

A few of the bolder kids even joined in for fun.

"We're not eight-teen! Stop the fucking war machine!"

"We're not eight-teen! Stop the fucking war machine!"

"We're not eight-teen! Stop the fucking war machine!"

"Shut her up!" Principal Yonker yelled.

But Hana was too fast. She weaved up and down the bleachers, in and out of students, chanting louder and louder.

"We're not eight-teen! Stop the fucking war machine!"

"We're not eight-teen! Stop the fucking war machine!"

Then, from the corner of my eye, I saw Stink Wilson stand up.

I felt my stomach drop.

"Shut up, gook!" Stink screamed. "You're fucking dead!"

Then the gymnasium turned into a riot scene. The cheerleaders and majorettes screamed back at the chanting kids. Lena threw her baton at Hana, but overshot and hit Benji in the side of the head, turning his laughter into a shrill howl.

Stink sprinted toward the bleachers, shrieking death threats that were convincing enough to scare every adult in the gym, Sergeant Adams included. Marty, Bill, and a few of his cronies followed suit. Principal Yonker held his hands out at the charging wrestlers in a lame attempt to reassert his authority.

Stink pushed him out of the way like he was a foursquare ball, but when Principal Yonker hit the court it was with a hollow thud. Dad reluctantly jumped into action, tackling Stink just as his foot reached the bottom bleacher.

Dad held him there in a bear hug, and even Stink Wilson knew better than to fight back. His friends, however, were still determined. They scaled the bleachers after Hana, who'd made it to the far end of the gym.

Lewis stood up and marched toward them.

"Stop!" he yelled. "Don't make me go up there after you!"

The assailants paused, looked at Lewis, thought it over, and gave up the chase. I was thankful their self-preservation still outweighed the sum of their hate. Lewis helped Principal Yonker up, and for a moment I thought things were mellowing out.

Then, suddenly, Milo stood up on his chair.

"Milo," I hissed, "what are you doing? *Sit down, man!*"

He ignored me completely. He was focused on Hana.

"We're not eight-teen!" he screamed. "Stop the fuckin' war machine!"

I put my head in my hands as cheers erupted from the back of the gym.

I groaned. I looked up to see that Mrs. Holstein, the school's sturdiest, meanest matron, had wrestled Hana into a violent embrace. Hana struggled to keep her chant going until Mrs. Holstein's meaty palm finally covered Hana's mouth. But Hana didn't need her mouth to tell me how she felt about the chaos. All I had to do was look into her eyes.

They were smiling.

nine

WAR AGAINST WAR

The Shark Bus, we called it, with a carsick sort of affection; our nickname for the '59 F-5 the school chauffeured athletes in. The only thing up-to-date about that four-wheeled deathtrap was the paintjob—blue against white, with a shark capping the hood like a World War II bomber. There were holes in the seats, and a crack down the windshield. Worst of all was the suspension, which was totally blown.

That drive to county finals was an even rougher ride than usual.

Six of our wrestlers were suspended after the pep rally, which barred them from competing in the tournament. Milo, bless his heart, was the worst wrestler on the team, so no one exactly mourned his loss. But Stink, Bill, Franklin, and Marty were the best of the bunch, and their absence was *definitely* felt. The last-minute shakeup elicited plenty of emotions, but confidence wasn't one of them.

Dad was especially crestfallen. He sat by himself on the front bench, staring at the manicured lawns that lined the road. I sat with Ramrod near the back. He'd helped Dad and Principal

Yonker corral those involved in Hana's protest to the front office, and managed to hang around like a fly on the wall for the aftermath.

"Principal Yonker wanted to expel her outright," he was saying, filling me in, "but Stink's dad asked him to go easy on her."

"No way," I scoffed.

"They're all scared of Hana's dad. They don't wanna ruffle his feathers until things at the mill go back to normal."

"So, what'd he do?"

"Gave her two weeks suspension, same as the others."

"Whew," I shook my head, "I'm sure Stink took *that* well."

"Oh, he was real cool about it . . . all he did was cuss out the principal *and* his daddy, throw a chair across the room, and storm out in a tantrum."

"Stink's tantrums are makin' me nervous."

"Everything about him is making me nervous," Lewis sighed. "I always knew he was a hateful son of a bitch; you can talk to him once and know it. But talk is just talk . . . or, like, I thought it was. But when I saw him get up from that seat, when I saw the others *follow him* . . . I couldn't believe it. I mean damn, Ronnie, I've known Bill and Marty since we were little."

"Not as well as ya thought, maybe."

"Guess not," Lewis muttered, and then peered out the window.

"Ronnie!" Dad hollered over the noise of the road.

Everyone turned to gawk at me as if I was in some sort of trouble. I rolled my eyes, and wobbled my way to the empty seat beside him. When Dad looked at me, his face was stained with the sallow expectation of defeat.

"I'm gonna ask Lewis to wrestle today," Dad said.

"But won't the other teams get mad?"

"Most likely. But I'd moved Marty up to heavyweight, and now that he's benched I need Lewis to take his place."

"Well"—I shrugged—"then let Ramrod wipe the floor with all of 'em."

"That's the plan," he nodded, "not that it'll do much good."

"Well just so ya know, I'm gonna kick some butt for you."

Dad smiled a painfully forced smile. He patted my leg.

"I mean it," I said, and I did. Dad was angry so much I'd grown used to it. Disappointed. Frustrated. Harsh. Cold. But this defeatist shit was too much for me to handle. I was determined to do my best, or some version of it, at the tournament.

"I'm proud of you, Ronnie," he said. "I know you'll leave it all on the mat, and that's all that matters to me. Win, lose, or draw, I'm proud of you."

"Jeeze," I mumbled, "thanks, Dad."

He smiled and patted my leg again.

"But, son," he added.

"Yeah?"

"I'll be prouder if ya win."

———

I lost.

But not, like, right away. I won my first three matches, then lost the fourth by a stupid point. That put me in third place, which didn't help our overall points too much. But I was getting a medal! I'd never won a medal in anything, so bronze was as good as gold to me.

The team did better than expected, too. Ramrod's triumphant return supplied us with a much-needed boost of confidence; we had teammates place in the 126, 138, 160, and 195 weight classes.

Lewis won first place in the heavyweight division, after an *epic* final match against a hulking, two-hundred-thirty-pound Adonis from Fernandina's colored school. Finals were the only chance for segregated teams to compete with each other, and the entire auditorium crowded that mat for the clash of teen titans. It was the first time I'd seen Lewis go head-to-head with an equally talented opponent, and when Ramrod finally pinned him in the third period the cheers and jeers were loud enough to rival Madison Square Garden.

But now that the matches were over, the municipal auditorium was uncomfortably quiet. Sore, stinky gladiators sat waiting for the trophy ceremony to start. I was loafing in the bleachers with Lewis, as he wrapped his knee in medical tape. He winced every time he put pressure on it.

"How bad does it hurt?" I asked.

"It feels like the bone's all twisted. I'm just lucky it didn't snap off. I thought he had me for a minute."

"Me too, man. He was really somethin' else."

I looked at the court below us. The coaches from Yulee and Glenmore were arranging the podiums for the awards ceremony.

The third place podium only looked about half-an-inch high, but I couldn't wait for Dad to see me on it.

Then I spotted the kid who beat me for silver, a bony redhead I shoulda been able to whip easily. He looked up at me and grinned. It was enough to take the wind from my sails.

"I can't believe I lost to that carrot-head," I grumbled, "Bruce woulda *creamed* that kid, easy."

"So you're not as good as Bruce on the mat," Lewis said. "So what? You're stronger than him in a lot of ways, ways that count way more than this."

"Right," I sneered.

Lewis groaned in pain as he stood up. He looked down at me.

"Let's go outside for a minute," he said.

"You think we have time?"

"What are they gonna do, start without us? Who would they give them medals to?"

"Glad you've stayed humble in your old age," I laughed.

Then I stood from the bleachers and followed him out.

Lewis and I loitered outside the auditorium. *COPALL COUNTY WRESTLING CHAMPIONSHIP* was written on the marquee in crooked plastic letters. The sky was dark orange, rimmed in thin hues of pink. A few others stood near us, puffing cigarettes and admiring the horizon.

"What's up?" I asked.

"Just wanna make sure you're still goin' through with it on Friday."

"Of course, man. What better way to spend a birthday than blowing up my ears?"

"Good," he said, without the hint of a smile.

"Why?"

He squinted into the sunset. He didn't say a thing.

"Lewis, what's goin' on?"

"I feel like I should tell you somethin' that I don't wanna tell ya."

"Well you've gotta tell me now, man."

"Yeah," he sighed, "all right. Bruce and I worried about the draft all the time, just like you and Milo. We even cooked up schemes to get out of it. We weren't smart enough to think up a permanent solution like Milo did, but still."

I nodded. He cleared his throat.

"Anyway," he went on, "that's how I got the idea to flunk for a deferment. But when I told Bruce the plan . . . man, he wouldn't do it."

I stood silent for a moment, considering his words.

"Did he, uh, just not wanna retake twelfth grade? He must've thought you'd find another way—"

"He had *plenty* of ways," Lewis snapped, "that's what was so messed up. He had scholarship offers from every goddamn school in the state."

My stomach dropped. Any pride I'd felt from the tournament now burned in the acrid bile that bubbled into my throat. I grabbed Ramrod's arm, and yanked at it until he faced me. His expression rested in the shadowland between heartbreak, anger, and love.

"Scholarship offers? Bruce never told me that."

"He told Coach—"

"*But why didn't he tell me?!*" I cried.

The cigarette smokers and sunset watchers turned, startled. They scurried to the other side of the awning, leaving the two of us alone. I forced a few labored breaths, and tried not to puke.

"I just don't understand," I panted. "I don't understand why he'd do that."

"He thought deferment would ruin his legacy. I tried talkin' him out of it, I swear. But he had it in his head that a warrior on the field should be a warrior off it, too." He put his heavy hand on my shoulder. "That's what I was tryin' to say in there, Ronnie. You're stronger than him in a lot of ways. To buck what society expects of you, it takes a special sorta strength to do that. It takes a brave motherfucker to go to war against war."

I felt tears on my cheeks. The sensation startled me.

"Goddammit," I said, as they fell harder, "I can't believe him."

"Being a hero your whole life can sure make a mess of things," he said. "He thought it'd be easier to walk through the fire than it would be to turn around."

I let go of his arm. I bowed away and wiped my eyes.

Lewis stood beside me, close enough for our shadows to merge.

Together, we stood with that knowledge and watched the sun burn out.

ten

IN THE WORLD OF THE YOUNG

Ramrod's revelation ramrodded through my mind, and all I could think of was Bruce, the war and Bruce, and the war, and the war, and the war. Questions I ached to ask my brother circled in my head uselessly. *Why would you go to war if you didn't have to go? If you didn't need to go? If you didn't want to go?*

I wished I had someone—*anyone*—to talk to about it. But all of our record club meetings were canceled until Hana's suspension was over, and Milo was so fucking grounded he wasn't even allowed to talk on the phone.

I didn't dare ask my parents, either, and not just because my questions could bring more scrutiny to my upcoming draft failure. Now that wrestling season was over, Dad seemed to like me again—bronze was enough to buy some affection, but wouldn't be enough to keep it if I started up with that grief-fueled inquisition.

So day by day, those nagging questions bled over into self-reflection. Was there something I wasn't seeing? Was Bruce's reasoning simply something a coward like me could never grasp? Was I using politics to excuse a lack of courage?

WHAT IS COURAGE?

Three mornings in a row, I spent first period hypnotized by the words on the chalkboard. All of my questions and troubles led back to that deadly word—which is why I decided to take a chance and lay my hang-ups on Mr. Donahue. If he was such an expert, maybe he could help me get my head on straight.

So I lingered after class one day, as the other kids rushed into the hall. Mr. Donahue was sitting at his desk, stacking our worksheets in an orderly fashion.

"Mr. Donahue, do ya have a minute? I've got a few questions about *Profiles in Courage*."

He leaned back in his desk chair casually. "Of course, Ronnie. Shoot."

"Well," I said timidly, "I've been working on the term paper, but I'm not sure how to *define* courage. Is it courageous to follow the rules? Or is it courageous to *break* the rules? Or, like, in some cases, is it more courageous to do nothing at all?"

Mr. Donahue pondered the jumble of questions I'd puked up. Then he cracked his knuckles, straightened his back, and looked up at me.

"Have you ever heard the phrase *courage of one's convictions*?"

I shook my head.

"It means acting in accordance with what one feels is right," he said. "It means jumping into action if the cause is worthy. It also means refusing to act in a way you feel is unjust. Staying true to one's *principles* is what takes courage, Ronnie. The need for action or inaction is situational."

"But what if it isn't that simple?"

His eyebrows arched with curiosity. "Could you give me an example?"

"Yeah," I said, "for instance, uh, my friend and his older brother were both against the war, and the draft. But when the older brother turned eighteen, he got scared he'd disappoint people if he took a deferment. So he let himself get drafted, and was killed in Vietnam."

"Go on," he urged.

"Then, my friend turned eighteen. There was no way he'd make the same mistake as his older brother. So he split for Canada. He knew he'd be called a coward, but he didn't care. He thought the war was wrong, and the draft was wrong, and he refused to take part in any of it."

Mr. Donahue nodded thoughtfully.

"So I guess what I'm asking is, which one of them was actually courageous?"

"Hmm," he mused, "this certainly is an interesting question. By refusing to participate, your friend definitely acted with the courage of his convictions."

"Ok," I nodded, "that's kinda what—"

"Wait," he said, "there's still the matter of his older brother to discuss."

Mr. Donahue removed a nub of chalk from his desk.

He got up, and went to the blackboard. I followed.

"Now," he said, scribbling as he spoke, "*courage of conviction* consists of two principal components: bravery of *thought*, and bravery of *action*. By coming to the unpopular opinion that the war is unjust, both brothers exhibited bravery of thought. But only one of them acted on that belief."

"Right," I said.

"But this is where it gets interesting. You see, there's a variable you failed to account for at play here, Ronnie. A difference between the two of them."

"What is it?" I asked.

"The difference is, your friend knew he could actually be killed in Vietnam. His older brother, on the other hand, likely didn't consider it a real possibility."

Mr. Donahue put down the chalk. He turned to me, and sighed. "Boys are urged to heed the drums of war. In cultures all over the world, to do otherwise means ostracization. So young men are compelled to go to battle, because the risk of combat doesn't outweigh the loss of social norms at home. The possibility they may not make it back to their homes is nothing but a theoretical concept. In the world of the young, death doesn't really exist. Until, of course, it does."

"Oh."

"Your friend *and* his brother acted with the courage of their convictions. His older brother simply didn't have the same knowledge to base his convictions on. But his death, while tragic, allowed your friend to clarify his own beliefs, and act on them accordingly. It's a brutal lesson, Ronnie, but the vital ones often are. The difference between an opinion and an *educated* opinion can be life and death."

ELEVEN

THE DEAFENING
HOUR BEFORE US

I opened my eyes to the morning. It seemed like any other. I groaned and winced as I got out of bed, still sore from the wrestling tournament. I pulled on my Levi's and threw on a button-up, then zombie-walked into the bathroom to brush my teeth and hair. I looked at myself in the mirror.

Eighteen. Old enough to buy booze in Florida. Old enough to die anywhere.

I went back into my bedroom to get my things. I knew Momma was fixing me a birthday cake for breakfast—a tradition in our house—but still, I was in no rush to go downstairs. I leaned my head on the cold windowpane and looked over at Hana's house. I wished I could see her, see all of them, and hash through the plan one more time.

As far as I knew, nothing had changed—I was to bring a 45rpm single with me to work that was at least three minutes long, Hana and Lewis were to meet us at midnight, Milo was to do the rest—but the idea seemed to make more sense when we were all together. In the circle, it seemed genius. Alone, it seemed fucking crazy.

"Ronnie," Momma called from downstairs, "breakfast, birthday boy!"

"Whatever," I mumbled to myself. "Crazy times call for crazy shit."

Then I went downstairs to eat cake.

————

Dad's Studebaker rumbled as the neighborhood blurred by in a pastel rainbow. I rested my hands on my stomach to keep the seatbelt from cutting too tight—after four pieces of Momma's peach yogurt cake, one pothole could make me pop like a zit. But the sugar high seemed to put Dad in an unusually good mood, and he whistled some unknown tune as he steered us toward the school.

"Feel any different now that you're eighteen?"

"Not yet," I said, "just stuffed."

He smiled and nodded. He turned the corner.

"Ronnie," he muttered, "we should talk about the draft exam tomorrow. I'd like to drive you up to Jacksonville myself, if that's all right."

"Sure, Dad. Thanks."

"What time is the exam?"

"Nine," I said, "at Military Entrance Processing Command, wherever that is."

"I know where it is. I drove your brother when his car was in the shop."

"Oh."

We turned onto Racine Street. The sidewalk was filled with kids. The safety monitor stopped us and flagged them across the intersection. A boy and girl near the back of the group held hands. Their arms swayed together—*back, forth, back, forth*—keeping their own special time like a pendulum of innocence.

"Look," Dad said, "getting a 1-A classification tomorrow doesn't mean you'll get drafted. Not for sure. So don't fret about it today. It's your birthday, you should try to enjoy it."

"Yeah," I said carefully, "you're right, who knows how it'll go tomorrow. I probably stress too much. Whatever will be will be."

"It will at that, son."

He pulled to the curb where he usually dropped me off. But as I reached into the back seat for my books, he took hold of my arm. "You have any tests today?"

"No," I said.

"Any work that needs turnin' in?"

"Just some calculus homework. Why?"

"Give it to me," he said. "You've already gotta work tonight. I ain't gonna make you spend your whole birthday bustin' ass. Just pick me up in the employee lot as soon as school lets out. And *don't* tell your mother that I let ya take the car."

"Wait," I asked, skeptically, "I can borrow the car to ditch?"

"Take a joyride," he said. "Have some beers. Enjoy the day."

Stunned, I gave him my calculus homework. He got out of the car.

The engine was still running. I crawled into the driver's seat.

I thought of the coming night.

I thought of Milo. Lewis. Hana.

I thought about the deafening hour before us.

I buckled my seatbelt and switched on the radio. My shoulders eased back in the unfamiliar seat as I got a firm grip on the steering wheel. The car idled in place, perfectly still, but the world outside was spinning.

———

I drove across town, toward Freedom Beach. I passed a mailman and a dog walker, but otherwise the streets were deserted. The hourly WQRX news bulletin said Bobby Kennedy finally announced a presidential run.

I pulled over a block down from the pier. The public parking lot was empty, besides an old fishing truck. I parked beside it and killed the engine. I opened the door and swung my feet out. I removed my Converse and socks, and then rolled up my jeans. I saw that Dad accidently left his newspaper folded in the back seat. I grabbed it, and then stepped onto the toasty pavement.

Up ahead was a plank footpath that led through the dunes. I followed the wooden beams, already sweating beneath my shirt. The sun was harsh in the sky, but I was still happy to see it.

I stepped off the footpath and into the sand. The tide was low and revealed the vastness of the empty beach. I sat up near the dunes, where the sand was fluffy enough to be boxed on a playground. I dug my feet in deep. I opened the paper and held it at an angle that would shield my eyes as I read.

I don't know why I expected anything but bad news.

The first article I came to—short and incredibly brief— was an update on the aftermath of the recent Orangeburg Massacre, which went down just a few hours north of us. The South Carolina Highway Patrol had fired into a crowd of young people protesting segregation at a bowling alley. Thirty people were shot, most in the back. Three of 'em were killed. One was a high schooler, a black kid even younger than me. The paper gave word that none of the officers would be charged or penalized at all.

"Goddamn," I said out loud.

I folded the paper shut. I couldn't stomach any more current events. I stood, put the news in my back pocket, and walked toward the surf. I dipped my foot in—*Jesus!* The water was freezing. Still, I forced myself to go a little deeper, cringing as the water rolled over my ankles. I squinted past the breaking waves to where the ocean simply rose and fell like the breath of a sleeping god.

A few yards out, a pelican swooped down and grabbed a fish. I watched it fly away from everything. I decided it was time to do the same.

I walked back to the parking lot and threw the newspaper away.

———

Last Chance Liquors had been open for exactly three minutes when I arrived, but a short line had already formed at the register. Sad boozers jittered as they waited on the clerk, a young guy with chin-length hair nearly as blond as my baby brother's. I nodded at him as I passed the line, then moved into the first row.

In the sun, the bottles sparkled like brown and green stained-glass windows. I knew booze would help me get through the night ahead, but I had no clue what to buy. So I checked my wallet, and then made my selections on price alone (based on quantity over quality, of course). I loaded my arms with a bottle of Old Crow, a pint of Smirnoff, and a six-pack of Black Label.

I carried it all to the register, relieved that the line had vanished.

"How's it hangin', partner?" the clerk asked.

"Not too bad. How 'bout yourself?"

"Low and easy. ID?"

I took out my wallet and handed him my driver's license.

"It's your birthday?" he asked, perusing it.

"Yep."

"You 1-A?"

"No," I stammered, surprised by his offhandedness. Then added, "I mean, I won't know until tomorrow, when I take the exam."

"Jacksonville?" he asked, glancing up from my license.

I nodded.

"Ya know what, partner? Hooch is on the house today."

"Really?"

"Consider it a birthday present—or a parting gift, dependin' on what Uncle Sam has in store for ya."

He handed back my license. When I took it from him, I flinched.

The tip of his trigger finger was missing.

twelve

THE DEAFENING HOUR AT HAND

I slid my books beneath the passenger seat of the car and hid the booze in my backpack before picking Dad up from school. I held it to my chest like a desperate mother so the bottles wouldn't rattle, and stored them in my bedroom back at home.

My parents gave me my birthday present—a beautiful Seiko Bell-Matic wristwatch with a steel face, brown leather strap, calendar, and alarm. It was the nicest gift they'd ever given me, and it made me feel guilty for the first time since we'd concocted our draft-dodging scheme.

After thanking them for nearly an hour, I spent just as long in Bruce's bedroom choosing a song for the night's ritual. Milo had called from the theater to tell me everything was still a go, and to remind me I needed to be exposed to the sound for *at least* three minutes straight. The timing narrowed my options a little, but not enough to make it easy. Bruce had so many great 45s, it was impossible to choose. Finally, I closed my eyes and touched one of the records in the special stack.

I opened my eyes, and looked at the label—3:17.

Perfect.

I slid the vinyl between the booze, and then crammed Bruce's bomber jacket into the backpack for cushioning. Momma passed down the hall as I did this, and threw me a curious smile. "A little hot for that jacket, isn't it?"

"You'd think," I said, "but Mr. Dori likes to crank the AC as cold as it'll go."

"Men," she scoffed. "Y'all are too hot-blooded for your own good."

"History would certainly agree with you there."

Both of us laughed. I zipped the backpack shut.

"You want another piece of cake before ya run off to work?"

"Momma," I smiled, "nothin' in this world sounds sweeter'n that."

———

I got to the Royal Atlantis twenty minutes before my shift. There was no line at the ticket window. When I looked up at the marquee, I wasn't surprised.

STAY AWAY JOE   DAY OF THE EVIL GUN
PRODUCERS   BLACKBEARD'S GHOST

I strolled into the lobby, where a few folks waited for the five o'clock show. I walked over to the refreshment stand and waved to Susanne, the counter girl.

"Milo's upstairs," she said without me asking.

"Thanks," I said, and headed up to the projection room.

Milo was sitting on the floor, splicing a torn reel of film together. He was too focused on his work to notice me enter.

"You re-editing *Blackbeard's Ghost* until it's watchable?"

He looked up, beaming with surprise. "Argh! Happy birthday, ye asshole!"

He adjusted his glasses and stood. I sat the backpack down and unzipped it.

"What'd ya bring?"

"Liquid courage for before," I said, removing the six-pack, "and some pain relievers for after." I removed the whiskey and vodka.

"Alcohol," he marveled, "the world's remedy for the world."

I unscrewed the bottle of Old Crow and took a pull. The booze blew through my throat like a spoonful of napalm. I shivered, grimaced, and passed it to him.

"You bring a record?" he asked.

I nodded. He took a drink and cringed.

"Jesus!" he coughed. "I dunno how people like this stuff."

"Me either," I said. I took the bottle back and suffered another drink.

"You talk to Lewis at school?" he asked.

"I ditched," I told him, "but I'm sure he'll be here."

"I hope," he said. "I couldn't get ahold of Hana. Her mom wouldn't let her use the phone. But as long as you brought the music, we'll be able to make it work. Just gotta wait 'til the late show clears out."

"What should we do until then?"

"Just act normal," he said, as if we knew what that meant anymore.

———

The theater was slow for a Friday. Only one showing sold out—the 7:10 of the Mel Brooks flick—but even *The Producers'* crowd dwindled by the time the late shows began seating.

I stayed at the ticket podium, though Mr. Dori was gone and there were no more tickets to tear. I didn't go hang out with Milo or flirt with Susanne or do any of the things I normally did but knew I shouldn't do—I was determined to play by the tiny rules until it was time to break the big ones.

So I hung at my post for the long haul until my fancy new watch told me what I wanted to see—it was 10:55 p.m.. All the movies were just about to let out.

So I finally left the ticket stand and began the post-show routine. I pushed through the heavy wooden entrance doors and propped them open with plastic doorstoppers. As I was about to go back inside, Hana called out to me. "The birthday boy under the bright lights."

I was grinning before I even turned around. She stood beneath the awning next door, just like she had the first night we met. She took a drag off a cigarette and exhaled as I walked over.

"Hey!" I said. "You're early."

"Yeah," she said. "Wanted to give you time to apologize."

I stopped walking. She regarded me coolly.

"Apologize for what?" I asked. "I didn't do anything."

"You're right. You didn't do shit."

She exhaled. She inhaled.

She sighed. Smoke drifted away.

"I'm always the outsider, man," she said. "I don't just mean here. It was like that in Chicago, too. Even in the movement, ya know? I've never found a group that's *mine*, that has a fuckin' clue how it feels to be me. But you don't have to know any of that to be my friend. You don't have to say what I say, or do what I do. There's only one requirement, and that's to watch each other's backs."

"The pep rally?" I asked, beginning to understand.

She nodded, and took another drag.

"You didn't have to get up and chant," she said. "You didn't have to get in trouble. But you could've at least tried to stop those guys. You coulda done *anything* but sit there like a fuckin' houseplant. You stuck your neck out for me the night we met, so I'm sticking mine out for you now. But if we're gonna be real friends, I need to know it wasn't a fluke."

Behind us, the crowd began exiting the theater. Many were still laughing from the Mel Brooks flick. A group of women was singing "Springtime for Hitler." I walked closer to Hana so she could hear me. Close enough for our arms to touch.

"It wasn't a fluke," I said, as loud as I could, "I swear. I just didn't know what to do. My dad was there, and it happened so fast, and I just, I just . . . I'm sorry. We're friends for real, and I ain't ever gonna give ya a reason to doubt it again. I've got your back. Whatever it takes, I gotcha."

"You fuckin' better," she said, punching me in the arm. "I don't wanna have to smack you around again."

"I too would like to avoid that," I said, smiling.

She smiled too, and threw her cigarette into the gutter.

"Cool," she said. Then she motioned to the theater, and we walked through the crowd side by side. "You shoulda got in on that chant, though. You really missed out."

"Yeah," I laughed, "maybe so."

"It feels good to raise your voice, I'm tellin' you. Nothing shakes up the party like a strong opinion. Whoever said 'silence is golden' was a fuckin' square."

———

Susanne and a kid named Byron were the only others working that night, and they were too busy closing up to notice me sneak Hana to the projection room.

"There's booze in the backpack," I told her. "Just wait here 'til me and Milo get done. Lewis should be here soon."

She gave me a thumbs-up. I went back downstairs to finish my shift.

I cleaned Viewing Rooms 2 and 3. Byron swept Viewing Room 1. Susanne vacuumed the lobby. With Mr. Dori gone, Milo was our de facto supervisor, and once an inconspicuous amount of time had passed, he told the others to split.

"You really don't mind if we leave?" Susanne asked. "I haven't emptied the grease trap, or cleaned the ladies' room, and I still need to—"

"Forget it," Milo said, "I'll handle it."

It took no more convincing than that for Byron to dip out. Susanne grabbed her things from behind the counter and quickly followed suit. The wind blew the door shut behind them. Milo and I stood in the lobby, alone.

"Wanna flip for who cleans the girls' bathroom?" I asked.

"Nah," he laughed, "chances are we'll be out of a job tomorrow, anyway. Go lock the doors. I told Lewis to meet me outside of the emergency exit."

I nodded, and locked every door in the lobby. Milo went out to get Lewis and I went up to get Hana. I found her browsing the film canisters, drinking a beer.

"It's time?" she asked.

"The gang's all here. The deafening hour's at hand."

The Vinyl Underground haunted the lobby. I sat the bottles on the concession stand, popped the tabs on three Black Labels, and passed them to Lewis and Milo. Hana still nursed hers as she looked over all the Coming Soon posters.

"Let The Vinyl Underground ceremony commence," Milo said.

He raised his beer. We formed a circle and held ours high in the air.

"To the birthday boy," Milo said, nodding at me.

"Nah, to Milo, the boy genius."

"And Bruce," Lewis added, "to Bruce."

"Bad Bruce lives!" Milo proclaimed.

"Yeah," Ramrod hollered, "Bad Bruce lives!"

I was too hard for me to echo the toast, though I was

touched by the sentiment. All I could do was nod. Then we clinked our beers together and drank cheap in the face of power. I chugged half of my beer in a bloated gulp, but my nerves refused to simmer.

"Now," Milo said, "let's get the show on the road."

We followed him up the stairs, beneath the chandeliers and into the main projection room. It was hard for us all to cram inside, and we had to keep tight against the wall so Milo had room to work.

His portable turntable—a yellow GE Wildcat—was already sitting below the projector. He removed the back casing, and hooked wires up to who-knows-what and into who-knows-where until the turntable was plugged into the speaker system.

"Hey, Milo," Lewis asked, "why don't we just use the sound from a movie?"

"Film audio varies from scene to scene, but records are mastered to stay even. So vinyl's the most accurate way to expose Ronnie to the right dB level."

"Damn"—he smiled—"thought of everything, huh?"

"Everything but a Plan B," Milo said, standing up. He wiped his hands on his pants and straightened his glasses. "The turntable's patched into the speaker system. Three minutes of sound at 155 dB will do the job without puncturing Ronnie's ears. Now come on, let's get back downstairs."

He left before I could respond. Hana shrugged, and we followed him back to the lobby. Milo pulled a gym bag from beneath the concession stand and tossed the bag onto the counter.

He unzipped it and removed two rolls of duct tape, one set of earplugs, one set of headphones, and two armfuls of towels.

"Next thing," Milo said, "let's soundproof this place."

He tossed three towels to Lewis and three towels to Hana.

"I thought the theater *was* soundproofed," I said.

"It is. But a little extra padding won't hurt, especially since the sheriff is right up the street. Tape those over the bathroom windows. I'll use the rest to fill the cracks under the doors."

Hana and Lewis each grabbed a roll of tape and headed into their respective bathrooms. Milo began shoving towels beneath the doors of the lobby. I just leaned against the counter, and watched in awe. I couldn't believe a chump like me found friends like this. I took another sip of Black Label and tried not to get all emotional again. Then Lewis came out of the bathroom, nodding confidently. Hana followed soon after.

"Got it covered," he said.

"Same here," she said.

"Same here," Milo nodded.

They turned to me. Milo pointed to Viewing Room 1.

"Ready?" I asked.

"Ready," he nodded, and motioned for Lewis's roll of tape.

My heartbeat kicked up a notch. I was more nervous than I'd ever been.

"Any of y'all holding? *Please* say somebody's holding—"

"Relax," Hana said. She lifted the left leg of her jeans and pulled a joint out of her shoe.

"Wait until we're inside to light up," Milo said. "If the

seats reek tomorrow, Mr. Dori will assume it was just some shithead kids."

"He won't be too far off," Lewis said.

Milo laughed and marched into the viewing room. Lewis and Hana followed. I downed the rest of my beer, then stumbled after them.

The walls inside were lined with copper bulbs burning behind gaudy covers. Matted red carpet ran all the way down the center aisle, and I followed it toward the lifeless screen, straight to the front row where my friends were sitting.

Hana sat between Lewis and Milo. I sat down in the aisle seat, and stared up at the blank, white horizon. We toked and passed and toked and passed with the efficiency of an assembly line.

"I walked the room during the five o'clock show," Milo said, "and I'm pretty sure the best seat is gonna be the middle one in the eighth row."

Hana passed him the joint. Milo had a long toke.

I didn't respond.

"You should've told us to bring earplugs, too," Hana said.

"You won't need 'em," Milo said. "Y'all will be outside keeping lookout."

"*Lookout*," she grumbled. "Come on, man!"

"Yeah," Lewis said, "lookouts are always the saddest of the bunch."

"Not tonight, Ramrod. *This* requires the baddest of the bad on lookout, since the sheriff station's right up on Rosemont.

No one *should* hear us, but in case anyone does, I'll need y'all to distract 'em until Ronnie and I are finished."

"This is bullshit," Hana groaned.

"Hey," Milo snapped, "*you* wanna run all this sound equipment?"

She rolled her eyes.

"Exactly. We've gotta work together."

"You're right," Lewis said, "nothing I can do to help in here except stand around, anyway. But Ronnie, tell me—what song are you gonna spin?"

"We Gotta Get Out of This Place."

"One of Bruce's favorites." He nodded. "Cool. That's real cool."

Hana stared at the ceiling and inhaled the last of the joint. She pursed her lips, and blew a long puff of smoke all the way up to the rafters. Then she tossed the butt of the joint at the screen.

"OK, rock-n-rollers ," Milo said, "let's rock-n-roll."

He stood and walked up to the eighth row. As he did, he yanked off a strip of duct tape about two feet long. The three of us followed behind him.

"What do we need that for?" I asked.

"For you," he said, like it was obvious. He climbed over the middle seat and into the row behind it. He patted the seatback, and summoned me to it. I walked toward him but I didn't sit down. Not yet.

"I still don't understand," I said.

"Ronnie, what we're—what *you're* doing—is gonna hurt. I don't know how much, but I know that if you run outta here before three minutes, you'll still hear well enough to qualify for the draft. So I'm gonna tape you to the chair to be safe."

"It's like in that Burgess book," Hana said. "A clockwork something."

"*A Clockwork Orange.*" Milo nodded. "That's where I got the idea."

"I haven't read it," I mumbled.

"Looks like you're about to live it," Lewis said.

Milo dropped the roll of tape and gripped both of my shoulders.

"Look man, you've gotta trust me. This is Best Friend Shit, OK? I'm not gonna let what happened to him happen to you, I promise."

"I trust you," I sighed. "I trust you, man."

We hugged from either side of the mercy seat.

"Well this is sweet enough to set my ovaries on fire," Hana teased.

"Shut up," we both said, letting go of each other.

I sat down and placed my forearms across the armrests. Behind me, I heard Milo pull off a second strip of tape.

"Oh shit," I gasped. "Wait!"

I jumped out of the seat and stumbled back into the lobby. I grabbed my backpack off of the counter and pulled out Bruce's bomber jacket. The weight of the leather was a heavy comfort as I slid it over my shoulders.

"Ready for takeoff!" Hana laughed, as I returned.

I smiled. The entire thing was getting too crazy not to smile.

I moved across the row and sat back down in the seat.

"OK, Milo, clockwork orange me."

I shut my eyes so I wouldn't panic as he taped me to the chair. I imagined Bruce there with us, leaning against the screen and laughing his ass off.

"Cool," Milo said. "I'm finished."

I opened my eyes and looked down at my silver restraints. I tried to move, but couldn't. I nodded to Lewis and Hana. They nodded back.

"Go out the side exit," Milo told them. "Hana, hide under the marquee. Ramrod, you stake out Rosemont. If *anyone* comes this way, tell 'em the power grid is on the fritz and that the electric company's en route."

"What if they don't buy it?" Lewis asked.

"Then do whatever you need to do. Just *make sure* no one gets in here before the music stops. Stay at your posts at least ten minutes afterward, just to be safe."

"OK," Lewis nodded. Then he looked down at me and smiled. "You got that special kinda courage. Bruce would be proud."

"Thanks," I whispered.

"Crazy times call for crazy shit," Hana promised.

"I'd argue if I could."

Hana and Lewis started off in the direction of the side exit.

"Remember," Milo hollered, "keep a lookout for *ten minutes* after!"

As they disappeared down the corridor, Lewis gave Milo a thumb's up. But Hana flashed us a separate gesture—the sign of peace and victory. Milo and I stayed silent until we heard the exit door shut.

"I'm goin' up now," he said.

"OK."

"I'll yell at you before we start."

"OK."

"The record's in your backpack?"

"Yeah," I nodded.

"I'll grab it. Keep your eyes on the screen. I've got somethin' special lined up to distract ya from the pain."

"OK."

"This is gonna work."

"This is gonna work," I echoed.

I could hear his feet skitter up the aisle and back into the lobby. I could hear the door shut behind him, sealing me inside. Then I heard nothing.

I was alone.

Suddenly, the lights went out.

I was alone in the dark.

But the screen lit up before I had a chance to freak.

"Ronnie," Milo yelled from the projection window, "can you hear me?"

"Yeah!" I yelled back.

"Ok! Hold on while I load this reel."

I heard some clinks and clanks overhead.

"Reel's in," he yelled, "and your song's on the turntable. I'll start with the volume knob at seven, and then crank it fast. It'll be over before you know it, OK?"

"OK," I said. "You have your earplugs in?"

"Affirmative," he yelled, "and I'll wear headphones over those! Now tell me . . . are you ready, willing, and able to rock-n-roll all night?"

I surprised myself by laughing. I felt like a crazy person. I felt scared, excited, drunk, horrified, stoned, and utterly mad.

Bruce loved Fats, I thought, before I screamed, "'TILL THE BROAD DAYLIGHT!'"

My words echoed off the walls around me.

Milo didn't respond.

I heard a familiar click instead—the hum of a movie projector.

I took a deep breath and looked at the screen.

The words COMING SOON FROM PARAMOUNT appeared, and then cut to Jane Fonda floating in zero gravity, stripping off what I assumed was a space suit.

There was a close up of her thighs.

A close up of her stomach.

A close up of her strawberry hair.

Hell of a distraction, Milo, I thought, as the name *BARBARELLA* emerged beneath her half-parted lips. Then came the sound I'd been waiting for: the pop of a needle being placed on a record.

Every muscle in my body tensed.

The song began.

The bass intro itself was loud enough to make me wince. But the pain didn't start until Eric Burdon began to sing and the speakers cranked up at least *a hundred times louder.* The noise made my skeleton vibrate, then it got even louder than that, and high-pitched ringing started somewhere in my brain. Then it got

LOUDER!

LOUDER!

LOUDER!

LOUDER!

The ringing intensified into a shriek.

The song was louder than Armageddon.

I couldn't think anymore. I couldn't even open my eyes.

I felt a swarm of wasps buzz through my head.

Warm blood trickled onto my neck as the song reached the first chorus.

That was when I screamed.

I couldn't help it. I couldn't *hear* it, either, not over the music and the screeching and buzzing and ringing. I was dizzy as a top, even tethered in place. I thought I would barf, like a kid at a carnival. I forced myself to swallow it down.

Somehow, the music got louder.

LOUDER!

I felt like my ears were being cleaned with grenades.

I barfed all over myself. The shrieking and the ringing got louder still.

IMPOSSIBLY LOUD!

That's when the pain overtook me, and the shock of it knocked me out cold.

———

Someone slapped me in the face.

I groaned. They slapped me again.

I opened my eyes. The three of them leaned over me. Concern was plastered on their faces. I lifted my arm—*When did they untape me?*—and rubbed my temples. I felt like I had a migraine, but worse. *Much worse.*

"Did it work?" I asked.

No one answered.

"Did it work?" I said again, focusing my eyes.

All three of them winced. I wasn't sure why. I asked again.

They winced again.

Then I realized Milo's lips were moving, but no words were coming out.

Oh, I thought calmly, *I must've been shouting.*

Now Hana was saying something—but the static in my brain and the ringing in my ears made it hard to compute what it was.

"It worked?" I asked.

Then Ramrod smiled. The smile said it all.

It worked. It worked!

I was raising my raspy voice the only way I could—by quieting all the others. Now I had a chance and a choice; the realization was liberating! Suddenly, all the strange noises in my head rang out like chimes of freedom—*real freedom*—not some ambiguous ideal we were told we had to die to fully earn and enjoy.

That was when I knew Hana was right.

Silence wasn't golden.

It was red and white and blue.

tHiRteen

PHANTOM SOUNDS

The graveyard is empty. I make my way past familiar markers, but they have no names or dates of birth or death; they're nothing but landmarks to let me know I'm on the right track. But it's not my brother's grave I'm drawn to, it's the one directly beside it—the one with dirt piled off to one side, the grave that sits open and waiting.

I walk to the edge of the grave. I peer into the black hole. My shoes are covered in mud or blood. Strange sounds echo from the darkness. I squint into the void—I try to place the phantom sounds swirling beneath me. Suddenly, something shoves me from behind!

I trip forward and nearly fall over the edge. Then, before I can catch my balance, I'm shoved again. I go toppling into the black. Falling deeper! Falling faster! Falling—

I opened my eyes.

Momma nudged my shoulder again. I groaned and rolled over in bed, clasping my pillow like it was a safety device.

"Ronnie," Momma said, "you need to get up now."

The words came in clear enough to get their meaning.

It was time.

I lurched upright, rubbing my eyes in a cartoonish way so she knew I was really awake. She pulled open the blinds as she left and said something I couldn't quite hear. But the fact that I heard her *at all* made me nervous. I'd known the damage to my hearing would be temporary, but last night I'd experienced nearly *total* deafness. As we cleaned up the scene of our crime and got the theater back in order, I was sure I'd be spending the next few weeks spinning the sounds of silence.

But now here I was, less than five hours later, and certain words were already coming in clear. Well, *clear* wasn't the right term. Nothing was clear. All sound was filtered through the ringing in my ears—a high-pitched, unending shriek. Below the ringing was static, like the sound of an untuned radio. Below that was a steady baritone hum. Yet still, I could hear through all that noise . . . just a little bit.

But how much was too much?

"Well," I mumbled, swinging my feet onto the floor, "there's one extremely shitty way to find out."

———

Dad took Highway A1A all the way to Jacksonville.

I pretended to doze on the drive. I didn't want Dad to notice that I was having trouble hearing, not that it was likely; he was too eager to get back onto military grounds to realize anything was up. He'd said *whatever happens, happens* on my birthday, but now it was clear he expected the oldest living Bingham boy to be fit as a fiddle to fight.

"Look, boy," he said, nudging my eyes open.

We pulled into the parking lot of the MEPS—a large, gray building set away from all others with a flag from each military branch prominently displayed. Those flags circled the stars and stripes, which loomed over them like a proud father.

"Right on time," Dad said, as he snagged a parking space. "You ready?"

I nodded at whatever he said.

"Remember, Ronnie, keep your back straight and you'll do just fine."

I nodded at whatever he said.

"I'll be waiting out front. Good luck, boy. I'm proud of you."

That last part was clear enough.

I smiled and got out of the car. I crossed the parking lot toward a cluster of black boys smoking cigarettes by an entrance door. Dozens more stepped off a bus at the other side of the parking lot.

I barely heard the pickup coming up from behind me. The driver laid on the horn just as it roared past, making me nearly trip over my own feet. The truck parked right in front of the entrance. Six guys jumped out of the bed. They looked like me, except excited. Their heads were pre-buzzed, and they marched up the stairs singing some jovial anthem I was plenty happy not to make out. A few of the cigarette boys laughed, but the rest looked as put-off as me when I finally reached the bottom of the staircase.

I sighed. I tried to collect myself, but it was no use. So I trudged up, up, up, up, up the painfully short staircase into the building with the others. Twelve years of public school made sure we all lined up at the entrance desk. The scuff marks on the lemon-scented floor screamed *Property of the Federal Government.*

I kept my eyes low. I only moved when I had to. Once the kid in front of me reached the desk, I watched everything he did. A moment later, I was waved forward. I mimicked as best I could.

"ID," a young guy in uniform said.

I handed him my license. He didn't look up from the paperwork. He ran his finger down a list of names until he found one matching mine. He looked at me. He looked back to my license. He wrote something on his sheet and had me sign a dotted line.

"Follow signs to the briefing room," he said.

He waved the kid behind me forward, and so I moved into the main hall. From there, I followed the other guys into a room that looked like a gymnasium, where actual soldiers were waiting. They ordered us into brand new lines, each one facing a small platform in the front of the room.

The stifling amount of testosterone reminded me of the first day of football practice; except here, the scent of fear proved danker than pubescent masculinity. Once I was in line, I took stock of the surroundings. Out of the hundred or so young men, less than a dozen of us were white. A kid in my row, sweating more than the others, wore a priest collar around his neck.

Another doubly-nervous boy entered, adjusting an eyepatch on his left eye. Before I could dwell on anything, the line-herder nearest me yelled, "Ten-hut!"

Everyone in the room stiffened. The door near the podium swung open, and a short, thick man marched into the room before us. His cropped hair was noticeably graying, and colorful bars ran across his breast. This wasn't some high school recruiter. He was the kind of tough guy they made movies about.

As he stomped onto the platform, his stony expression made every young heart leap into its respective throat. Then he took a deep breath and yelled, "GENTLEMEN, MY NAME IS MASTER SERGEANT JEFFERSON H. MORANO, AND I WILL BE YOUR LIASON DURING TODAY'S EVALUATION!"

He shouted loud enough to cut through the ringing, the static, and the hum. In that way, I found Master Sergeant Morano's voice calming—at least I knew I'd be able to follow orders without drawing attention to myself too soon.

"NOW, I AM AWARE THAT THE BRAVEST AMONG YOU ARE HERE OF YOUR OWN VOLITION, AND THAT SOME OF YOU ARE HERE BECAUSE OUR NATION HAS CALLED YOU TO SERVE. BUT I WANT EACH AND EVERY ONE OF YOU TO KNOW THAT I DON'T GIVE A RAT'S PUCKERED ANUS WHY YOU ARE HERE TODAY! BECAUSE LIKE IT OR NOT, YOU ARE HERE, AND YOU WILL COMPLETE EACH AND EVERY EXAMINATION TO THE BEST OF YOUR ABILITY! I BETTER HEAR A 'SIR, YES SIR'!"

"Sir, yes sir!" the entire room chanted nervously.

"IF ANY OF YOU GENTLEMEN HAVE DELUSIONS OF SHIRKING YOUR DUTY TO THIS COUNTRY, LET ME BE THE FIRST TO DISSUADE YOU FROM SUCH COWARDLY GODDAMN ACTS! BECAUSE IF I FIND COWARDS IN MY MIDST, I SEND THEM TO THAT DARK CORNER OF HELL RESERVED FOR COMMIES, QUEERS, CHRIST-KILLERS, DOPE FIENDS, AND EUGENE MCCARTHY! ANYONE HERE FIT THAT DESCRIPTION? I BETTER HEAR A 'SIR, NO SIR'!"

"Sir, no sir!" we all screamed.

Master Sergeant Morano grinned—his smile was as hard as a cast iron skillet. "ALL THOSE WITH LAST NAMES A THROUGH F, FOLLOW SERGEANT RANKIN TO PHYSICAL! G THROUGH M, FOLLOW SERGEANT CURTIS HERE TO MEDICAL! N THROUGH Z, FOLLOW SERGEANT MCTEIRAN TO THE APTITUDE EXAMINATION! WE WILL BE COMPARING YOU AGAINST YOUR HIGH SCHOOL TRANSCRIPTS, SO IF YOU FAIL THE APTITUDE TEST I BETTER FIND THE PAPER TRAIL OF A GODDAMN MONGOLOID!"

At that, my line started moving forward.

We were led into a locker room twice as big as the one at Cordelia High. Everyone began undressing, leaving only their briefs and undershirts on. I assumed we'd been ordered to strip, so I did the same thing. I piled my clothes in the nearest locker just before we were hustled back into the hall, then to a smaller gymnasium where military personnel stood waiting.

They wore lab coats and held clipboards, so I had to assume they were doctors.

"Straight line! Straight line!" the Sergeant in charge of us yelled.

One of the doctors stepped forward. He was older than the rest—bald, with a stethoscope around his neck. He ashed his cigarette onto the floor, making it clear that he was in charge of whatever was about to happen.

"Young men," he said, "you will now perform a series of physical exercises. Sergeant Rankin will demonstrate each maneuver as we go along. If y'all get confused, just refer to him."

I strained to hear him. My heart was a hummingbird of fear.

The doc looked us over.

"Arms straight forward," he ordered.

We held out our arms like mummies.

"Move your wrists up and down, side to side."

I mimicked the Sergeant and flapped my wrists.

"Now roll your wrists in a circle."

We did.

"Now touch the tip of each finger to the tip of your thumb, like so."

The drills went on that way for what felt like hours—*walk on your heels, walk like a duck, touch your toes*—the doctors took notes as we fulfilled each simple, strange command.

Once the exercise drills ended, the Sergeant ushered us into a larger room sectioned into dozens of workstations, each one walled-off by white sheets on rollers. The room was bright enough and sterile enough for me to be sure—it was time for the medical exam.

They arranged us into new lines, and then left us there to wait on the group of boys before us. The line moved bureaucratically slow. My mouth and stomach felt sour. My anxiety level was rising. My focus was clouding with steam.

I spent the next thirty minutes trying to shut that panic down.

Then, the kid behind me in line said something I couldn't make out. I looked over my shoulder and up at a boy at least a foot taller than me. I recognized him instantly—he was the heavyweight from Fernandina, the one who nearly beat Lewis at the county wrestling finals.

"Sorry man, what'd ya say?"

"I said aren't you Lewis Gibbon's buddy?"

"Yeah," I nodded, "and you're the badass who nearly pinned him at county."

"Nearly don't mean much," he said, smiling a smile that was nearly identical to Ramrod's championship grin. "Percy Johnson."

"Ronnie Bingham," I said, shaking hands with him.

There was a commotion up ahead. Percy turned toward it, and I followed his gaze. Two of the buzzcut rednecks were hooting and hollering, flexing for the doctors. Their annoying hee-haw laughter was loud enough for me to hear.

"What the hell are you doin' here, anyway?" Percy asked. "I can tell ya ain't like those bloodthirsty clodhoppers up there. You aren't enlisting, are you?"

"No way," I mumbled. "What about you?"

"Hell no," he scoffed. "I'm with Muhammad Ali. I've got no quarrel with those people. No Vietnamese ever called me a nigger. Can Uncle Sam say the same?"

"Did one of these instructors call you that?"

"Take a look around you, man. There's a million ways to call someone a nigger. You're just sufferin' from a lack of imagination—"

"Next!" a doctor called, and both of us did an about-face.

I was motioned behind the first curtain. I took a deep breath and followed.

The station was arranged like a general practitioner's office—a gurney, a scale, the whole bit. The doctor checked my weight, height, and blood pressure. He told me to stick out my tongue and say *ahhhh*. Then he flipped on his otoscope.

He stuck it into my left ear.

OK, I thought, *tell me my ears are shot.*

He removed the otoscope without comment. He put it in my right ear.

That doesn't mean anything, he just wants to be sure.

The doctor removed the otoscope from my right ear.

"Pull down your shorts," he said.

"Sorry?" I asked, confused.

"Pull down your shorts, son."

I had a bad feeling about it, even *before* he grabbed my balls and shoved his hand up my ass. Then he sent me into the next station like a common streetwalker.

I stumbled over in a daze. A female nurse sat me down and

drew my blood. *Did it not work,* I wondered, as she filled vial after vial. *Is the otoscope gonna be the only ear exam?*

She slapped a Band-Aid on my arm and sent me into the eye exam.

Cover an eye, read the chart. Cover an eye, reread the chart.

I recited the letters and numbers absently as I focused on quelling my growing urge to flee the building. Then a small man with curly hair beckoned me to Station Four. I followed him around the white sheet. There were two chairs, and a machine with wires and long metal arms to dictate chart readings.

At first, I thought it was a lie detector. Then I saw them—headphones!

A set of headphones attached to the machine.

"Please take a seat," the examiner said.

He had to repeat himself before I sat down. He sat in a chair on the opposite side of the machine. I focused on his mouth, determined to read his lips as well as I could.

"Have you ever had your hearing tested?" he asked.

"No, sir," I said tentatively.

"Your voice," he asked, "are you sick?"

I told him about my scarred vocal cord. He read through my medical history until he was satisfied, then he handed me the headphones.

"This is called an audiogram. The test is simple. Put on these on, and listen for a series of beeps and tones."

I took the headphones. Then he handed me a trigger button attached to a wire—my own personal doomsday device.

"When you hear a sound, press the button."

"OK."

"Put the headphones on now, please."

I situated the headphones over my ears. They were the expensive kind, with noise cancelation cushioning. The sensation of isolation made me dizzy because the headphones magnified the sounds in my head. It was like having two large seashells attached to my ears.

The examiner pressed some buttons on the machine. The thin arms began running up and down the paper, charting my score in real time.

The examiner nodded at me—*let's begin.*

I nodded back. I listened. A few seconds later, a faint succession of beeps panned across my right headphone. I pressed the button. I heard beeps again, louder. I pressed the button.

Then nothing.

I thought I heard more beeps—lower in tone—in my left ear. I pressed the button. The machine arms scribbled across the paper as I pressed the button again. Then I heard more beeps, and I pressed it again. Then nothing.

Nothing.

More nothing.

Then the machine printed my chart out, and he tore the perforated edge. His eyes moved down the page, and then scaled back up again.

Finally, he motioned for me to remove the headphones.

"You've never had your hearing tested?"

"No, sir."

"Have you ever had trouble hearing?"

"Well, at school sometimes, it's hard to hear my teachers."

"I see," the examiner nodded. "Wait here a moment."

He left me alone in the cubicle. I stole a glance at my test results. I had no idea what the readings meant. I tried not to seem antsy or excited or scared or ecstatic or—the examiner returned with the doctor from Station One and Master Sergeant Morano.

The examiner from the first station went over my chart with the other two.

"No sign of congestion or infection," he said.

The master sergeant nodded at him, and he went back to work.

"Mr. Bingham," Master Sergeant Morano said, "just so we're clear, you aren't currently sick? No head colds?"

"No, sir," I squeaked.

"And that rasp in your voice? You're sure you're not sick?"

"It's been like this since I was eleven, sir."

I hadn't considered my voice could throw the whole thing off. I was sure I was screwed, sure that they'd make me come back next week to retake the test, then the next week, then the next, until they got the result they wanted.

"We need to run the test again, to make sure the results were accurate," the examiner said.

"That OK with you?" Master Sergeant Morano sneered. I liked him better when he was screaming.

"Of course, sir."

I put on the headphones. The machine started up. The examiner pointed at me. I picked up the response buzzer.

Beeps. Hums. Tones.

Loud. Soft. Ghostly.

Once the sounds evaporated, the examiner had me remove the headphones. The machine printed out my new chart, and they held my tests side by side to compare the results. I couldn't make out what they were saying to each other.

Then the examiner handed both documents to Master Sergeant Morano.

"Stand up, son," he ordered. "You need to come with me."

———

Dad sat on a bench in the yard of the MEPS building, drinking coffee from a paper cup and chitchatting with a girl around my age, probably the sweetheart of one of the unlucky boys still inside. His face lit up when he saw me walking down the steps of the building.

He shot off the bench and hustled over to meet me. But as he closed in, I saw the wheels in his head turning. By the time he reached me, his expression had melted into a confused grimace.

"Where's everyone else?" he asked hurriedly.

I handed him a piece of paper. I braced myself as he read it.

And reread it.

And re-reread it.

He glared at the 4-F stamped on the bottom right corner.

"4-F?" he asked.

"I guess I'm . . . I dunno, Dad. The classifications are on the back."

He flipped the paper over. His face grew flushed.

"4-F," he read aloud, "Rejected. Rejected from military service . . . for physical, mental, or moral . . . what is this bullshit, Ronnie? Rejected?"

"They said my hearing isn't good enough to qualify."

"Your hearing?" Dad barked. "That's ridiculous! This can't be right."

Dad threw down his cup, exasperated. Cold coffee splashed onto my shoes. He stormed past me, straight up the stairs. By the time I got moving he was already inside, focusing his frustration on the entrance guard.

"That's right," Dad snapped, "Corporal Buford Bingham, United States Marine Corps, retired. I need to speak to your commanding officer immediately."

The guard disappeared into the hallway.

"Dad," I said softly, "come on, let's get outta here."

"Not until I get this straightened out. There's obviously been some mistake."

"This way, sir," the guard called from the hall, waving Dad forward.

Dad followed the guard into the briefing area. I couldn't believe it—I felt like I'd broken out of prison just to walk right back in. But still, I hurried after them.

I caught up as they turned into the medical exam room. I passed the boys currently being poked and prodded by the hypocrites of the Hippocratic Oath.

As Dad began speaking with Master Sergeant Morano, a chill shot down my spine.

"I understand your frustration," I (sort of) heard the

sergeant saying as I approached. "That's why we did two audiograms, to check the accuracy of the results."

"But Ronnie's never had hearing issues before," Dad said.

"Has he had an audiogram before?"

"I-I'm not sure," Dad mumbled. "I'd have to check with his mother."

"Boys come in all the time with undiagnosed hearing problems. Hearing loss can be subtle in day-to-day civilian life. But as you know, corporal, subtleties don't fare will in a war zone."

"But he can't be unfit," Dad said. "My son's a lot of things, but unfit isn't one of them. He . . . he has to be fit. You understand? He, he—"

Master Sergeant Morano shook his head solemnly, and Dad's voice trailed off. He placed a consoling hand on my father's shoulder.

"I blame rock-n-roll," he said seriously. "Kids play it too loud, and it ruins their ears. Then perfectly fit boys like your son come in who I've got to turn away. I'm sorry I can't be of more help."

Dad nodded. Then he started drifting back to the exit.

Master Sergeant Morano turned to me. "I bet you like rock-n-roll, don't you?"

"Sir, yes sir," I said.

He shoved the rejection slip into my chest hard enough to knock the wind out of me. I reeled, but caught my balance before I gave him the satisfaction of falling.

"Then don't forget to take that with you. After all, you earned it."

FOURTEEN

DEAD FLOWERS

That drive home from Jacksonville was the longest ride of my life. I was relieved, of course, but not in a celebratory mood. Victory didn't feel the way I thought it would feel.

Instead of celebrating, I spent the drive rationalizing my disqualification to Dad, blubbering excuses. But his expression remained as stoic as the totem of a blasphemed god. He kept his eyes locked on the road. He didn't say a word.

Then we pulled off of the A1A and crossed the long bridge that led back to Cordelia Island. Below us were miles of marshland, which granted an incredible view of the sunset; a rainbow of oranges and purples overlaid by the purest of blues.

"Really, I'm as surprised as you are," I swore again. "Maybe I hurt my ears wrestling, like cauliflower ear but, like, an *internal* injury—"

I saw Dad's mouth open slightly, and his strong jaw move, but the glare on the windshield made it impossible to read his lips. I leaned over the gearshift to get a better angle.

"Sorry, Dad, but what'd you—"

"I SAID YOU DIDN'T LOSE YOUR HEARING FROM

WRESTLING," he yelled. "IS THAT CLEAR ENOUGH FOR YOU?! HUH?! ALL THAT LOUD MUSIC RUINED YOUR EARS! THOSE RECORDS . . . you and your brother . . . those goddamn records ruined everything."

His voice became an inaudible jumble as he swerved onto our street. His foot was still hammering the gas as he turned in our driveway. We were less than an inch from the garage door when he finally hit the brakes.

Dad said something else, but it just sounded like a growl.

Momma happened to be outside, drawing chalk pictures on our walkway with Roy. She stood when she saw us arrive, and was wiping pink chalk dust off of her hands as Dad and I approached. Roy didn't even notice us; he was focused only on what looked to be a portrait of Wolfman.

"They didn't want him," Dad told her before she could speak.

He stormed past her, onto the porch and into the house. He didn't bother shutting the front door behind him. Momma turned to me for clarification.

"My hearing," I said, moving slowly. "They said my ears are bad."

I handed her my rejection slip.

"Your hearing?" she asked.

"That's what the 4-F stamp means. The doctor said a lot of guys have bad ears, but don't know it until they go in for a hearing test."

"So, now you won't be drafted anytime soon?"

"Now I won't be drafted *ever*, Momma. Even if they revoke deferments or do another one of them troop surges. I couldn't join the military now if I tried."

She reached out and touched my ears, as if she thought her fingers held some motherly healing property. Then her hands dropped to my shoulders, and I saw the tears swelling in her eyes.

She muttered something like a prayer. She clung to me in a death grip, and in that moment of raw relief I finally felt a sense of victory. I sniffed back my own tears and hugged her.

The victory faded a second later when Dad came back onto the porch.

"Where's my bottle of J&B?" Dad hollered to Momma.

"It's in the cabinet, dear," she said.

"Which cabinet?"

"Go on and get it, Momma. I think I'll lay down for a bit. Long day."

"Yes it was," she sighed. "But it's over now. Lord willin', it's over now."

————

I locked my bedroom door and leaned against the familiar wood. I let out a gratified sigh as the absurdity of the day sank in. I felt like David must have felt as he looked upon the beaten body of Goliath and wondered what the hell just happened.

My room was childishly innocent compared to the MEPS building. There were no death dealers here; all I was faced with was a *Robinson Crusoe on Mars* poster and a closet full of clothes washed and folded by my mother.

I tried to square the contrast, but it was all too overwhelming.

So I gave up thinking about it, went to the closet, and dug through my T-shirts. The Vinyl Underground had agreed to go radio silent all weekend to avoid suspicion. But that didn't mean the gang was patient enough to wait until Monday to know if the stunt had worked.

So we came up with signals. If everything went as planned, I was to hang a green shirt off of my windowsill. If it didn't work, I was supposed to hang a red one. If the military figured out I'd tried to dodge, a black shirt would signal to them that I was royally screwed.

On the bottom shelf of the closet, I found a shamrock-colored T-shirt from the '66 Florida State wrestling finals. I unlatched my window and tied the shirt onto the hook like a makeshift curtain. I drank in the breeze as the wind picked up—the shirt danced in the dark. Then I tilted my desk lamp toward it for maximum visibility. Now my victory flag was flying. My bat signal was lit.

Satisfied, I kicked off my shoes and collapsed onto the bed. I was too tired to ignore the ringing, so I closed my eyes and let the sounds untether me from my consciousness. Then I drifted away, far, far away, for a good sweet while.

———

The horrible smell woke me. It was vinegary but worse; like hydrochloric acid, or something else I'd misspell on a biology exam. The fumes were bad enough to make my nostrils burn.

Annoyed, I crawled out of bed and went to the window— and that's when I saw the spiral of smoke rising from the back of my house. Panic alarms flashed in my temples. Unthinking, I ran from my bedroom and went directly into my parents' room. It was empty. I turned and headed toward the stairs, but then I noticed Bruce's bedroom door had been left open.

The sight gave me pause, and my brain clicked back on.

I *never* left his door open.

I walked into his bedroom and flipped on the light.

His records were gone.

I blinked my eyes clear. I couldn't be seeing what I was seeing.

I stopped blinking.

His records were still gone. Bruce's collection of singles—the shelves of 45s—hadn't been touched. But all of his full-length albums had disappeared.

I dashed out of his bedroom. I took the stairs two at a time. I nearly busted my ass when I reached the foyer, but caught my balance on the wall and propelled myself through the dining room, straight into the kitchen.

There was Momma, sitting at the counter. I could tell she'd been crying.

My confusion mutated into a freak out. "What's wrong?" I panted. "What is it, Momma?"

"Your father. He's just . . . very upset."

"*What's going on*, Momma? Where's Dad?"

She dabbed her eyes with a wadded tissue.

"He's in the backyard," she muttered, "but please stay in here, Ronnie. He's having a hard night, and it's . . . he's . . . Lord, he's already—"

I was out the back door before she finished the sentence. The backyard was dark except for the fire that was raging in our fire pit. Then I saw Dad's silhouette, there before the flames. Memories rose in my head like embers: Dad digging that fire pit a decade ago, the year Bruce and I got the chickenpox. Bruce's scout troop had gone camping at Osceola National Forest, but he'd been stuck at home with me. So Dad gave us a camping trip of our own—*He calls us into the yard, smiling in the firelight. He holds a bag of marshmallows in one hand, two chocolate bars in the other*—the inverse image of the nightmare that stood before me now.

The fire was at least four feet high. The flames were a sickly shade of yellow. Their tips flickered an unnatural green. I'd never seen a fire burning colors like that. A bright trail of smoke curled skyward, polluting the air with its toxic stink. Wolfman ran around the yard in circles, barking at the flames.

I noted the empty bottle of J&B Scotch on the patio table. Then I turned back to the fire, just in time to see Dad lift a crate of records above his head.

I ran at him without thinking. "*Dad! Don't!*"

But he hurled them into the flames.

"DAD!" I bawled in complete shock.

He didn't even acknowledge me. He stepped back to watch the records burn.

I took my first look at the casualties—The Four Tops, The Shangri-Las, The Dave Clark Five, The Beatles, The Zombies, The Who—every LP Bruce ever loved was now nothing but kindling. Their sonic grooves wilted like a field of dead flowers. Dad watched, zombified. Firelight danced in his vacant eyes.

"Dad," I wheezed, "his records! What the hell are you doing?"

"These got my oldest boy killed," he said, "and they've turned you into a deaf-mute. So I'm doing something I shoulda done a long time ago."

"What are you talking about? Help me get 'em out! Hurry!"

"No point, now."

He was right. The records, the music, and the memories they held—they were dead now, gone forever. All I could do about it was cry, and I did. Hard.

I wept there, before the fire. Dad walked back to the house.

I heard our back door open and shut. I forced myself to wipe my eyes and chase after him. Dad stormed through the kitchen without acknowledging Momma. He simply moved around her, straight though the dining room. I caught up with him in the foyer, just as he started up the stairs.

I'd never seen him in such a state. It scared the shit outta me.

But still, I followed behind him. When he made it to the top of the stairs, a new burst of panic hit me—*He's getting more records!* I charged up the last few steps, ducking around him to block the door just as he turned to Bruce's room.

A dizzy look crept over his face.

"You best get out of my way, boy. Now."

"Why?" I snapped. "So you can burn more of his stuff? You, you . . . drunk fuckin' *assho*—"

He drove his hands into my chest, and my voice wheezed away.

At first, I didn't feel pain, or even the sensation of falling. I felt more like a spectator watching a kid who *looked* like me get thrown across a room and go crashing into the shelves of vinyls that lined the wall.

When I hit the floor, the pain was there waiting. But my throbbing chest and back got little more than a brief acknowledgment, because Bruce's entire 45 collection came tumbling down on top of me, scattering across the floor.

I looked at the music around me, then looked back to the doorway, stunned. Dad seemed shocked as well. He stood wide-eyed and shaking, unable to comprehend his actions. I heard a faint wail down the hall—the racket must have woken up Roy.

Dad took a step into the bedroom.

"Son, I—"

I recognized the vinyl beside me, it was one from the special stack. Before Dad could get any closer, I grabbed it and ripped the dust sleeve in half, then I pulled Bruce's envelope out.

"You wanna see what you're burning? Here! Look! You're burning the memory of who he was! You're burning all that's left!"

He winced as if he'd been physically hurt by the sight of the letter.

"Ronnie, please. Enough," he moaned. Tears shimmered in his eyes.

"Enough? Are you kidding me?"

Dad took another wobbly step. Then, suddenly, he dropped to his knees.

My whole world shook from that fall.

He covered his face with trembling hands, and he began to cry. I'd never seen him cry before; it just wasn't done in the Bingham household, not right out in the open. But now his tears came in frantic gasps, as if he was physically smothered by grief. The sight of it was a cataclysmic event.

When he looked at me, it was as if the atmosphere in the room had changed.

"You were the one that had what it takes, you were—"

Then he burst into a coughing fit. I couldn't understand what he was saying.

He cleared his throat. He tried again.

"Bruce was never right for the marines," he said. "Physically, yes, but not in the head, not where it really matters. He didn't have the concentration, the awareness. All he ever thought of was these records. That's what got him killed. I know it is, I know it."

I tried to respond. I couldn't speak. Dad couldn't seem to stop.

"But you coulda made it right, made it mean something. You're strong enough; you were always strong enough, strong in the way a marine *needs* to be strong. But all the loud music he pushed on you, all the *goddamn* rock music—"

"That music kept me safe! That music, *his music*, it saved my life." I could feel my own tears coming as I crawled to where he lay. "Nothing I could've done in Vietnam would square what happened, or make it right. All we can do is celebrate who he was, Dad. Don't you get it? Nothing we can do now will justify how or why he died."

He trembled, and then punched the floor with his heavy fist.

"Oh son," he cried, "I'm sorry. I'm so sorry."

I couldn't tell if he was talking to me or Bruce.

Either way, he deserved a reply. So I opened the envelope clutched in my hand and unfolded the letter inside.

"'August 12th, 1967,'" I read.

"What?" Dad stammered, looking up at me.

"'How's the weather, Raspy Ronnie?'" I recited. "'It's be-ya-utiful here in Paris Island, South Carolina. And by beautiful, ladies and germs, I mean miserably hot and disgusting. I tell ya, Little Brother, I feel like a boiled peanut!

"'One day I'm in high school, the next, I'm out here. Am I a chump or what? All and all, though, it's been a breeze. Fuckin' basic training, man. These drill sergeants have got nothin' on Dad's trash talk.'"

Dad let out a tearful laugh. I smiled. I kept reading.

"'Yesterday, a fella told me that we've got our own radio station in 'Nam called the American Forces Vietnam Network. Rolls off the tongue, right? I'm thinking maybe I can score an audition. It sure would be nice to spend my tour in a DJ booth instead of a foxhole. Oh, and as you probably noticed by the heading, I'm countin' on you to keep my chops sharp! So drop that needle on the record, and let it spin.'"

I trailed off. I cleared my throat.

"Does . . . does it say anything else?" Dad muttered.

I handed him the letter. He sat up, now reeling from the booze. He held the letter up to his nose, and focused. "'Play 'Heat Wave' by Martha and the Vandellas,'" he read. Then he looked back to me. "I never could figure out how to work your brother's turntable."

"Here, I'll show ya."

I picked the record up off the floor.

Then I took my father's hand in mine so together we could stand.

Fifteen

THE NEAREST THING
TO NORMAL

Things would never go back to how they were before Bruce was taken away. But the weeks that followed my draft exam were the nearest thing to normal I'd had all year. Mr. Dori never found out what we did at the theater. Stink and the bullies at school began to heed their fathers' demands to leave Hana alone. Life after Bruce had always seemed impossible, and it still wasn't easy, but the world had finally begun to settle.

The day after the fire, my family gathered in Bruce's room and read through all his letters, participating in his DJ ritual as a singular family unit. I swear I could feel him there with us, laughing as Momma searched for his copy of "Day Tripper."

It was a long and brutally heavy day, but allowed us to finally, openly, share our grief with one another. The pain still remained, but now we could bear it together instead of letting is smother us. Day by day, I began to breathe again.

My hearing improved, too—but slowly. Focusing in class was nearly impossible, so I called in sick a lot and did my work at home. I spent most of those days at the beach, which was the one place I could think clearly—the roaring surf was able to drown the phantom sounds away.

My time in the sand was haunted by that then-popular slogan: *Today is the first day of the rest of your life.* It looked good on buttons and posters, but was scary as shit when you were an eighteen-year-old high school senior.

Now that I'd escaped the war, it was time to grapple with the fact that my life would extend into adulthood. I was running out of excuses, distractions, and time. I needed a plan, or at least a next step.

I'd intended on heading to California with Bruce for so long, it felt almost blasphemous to do otherwise now. I'd come to terms with the fact that I didn't really want to be a DJ anymore, but I felt a duty to carry on his legacy somehow.

Hana said I should think about my own legacy. She wanted me to go to college. But my family wasn't as well off as hers, so going to college wasn't as easy as simply *wanting* to go. I'd need some type of scholarship to swing the tuition.

The head of the wrestling program at University of Florida told Dad that my placement in the county finals gave me a slim shot at a scholarship. Dad started a full-on lobbying campaign, but I didn't get my hopes up. The lack of effort that defined my wrestling career didn't bode well for a last-minute free ride.

Milo agreed that a scholarship was unlikely. He encouraged me to stick with California. But he had his sights set on Hollywood, too, so I think the idea of a running buddy appealed to him. He'd finally saved enough to buy his own movie camera—the Kodak Instamatic Super 8 from Sears—and after it left the box, it never left his hand. The camera was no bigger than a drugstore paperback, and Milo was *obsessed* with it.

He began filming everything—record club meetings, walks to and from school, fire drills, church services, *anything* he could. He was determined to make a film about forward thinking in a backward town.

His focus for the project, of course, was Hana. He documented her struggle to get her articles published—she wouldn't let him read them, but he knew that the topics ranged from college protests to rape at rock concerts to civilian deaths in Vietnam—and he filmed her as she pitched the ideas to the uninterested editors of the school paper, the local paper, and the *Florida Times-Union*. He filmed her through every roadblock and every slammed door.

She wouldn't let me read her work either, but I was in constant admiration of her guts and vision. She was so ahead of me, of all of us. She wouldn't take no for an answer, when I hadn't even figured out what fucking questions I should ask.

While Hana faced down the Man through her writing, Lewis engaged in a last-ditch effort to avoid him. His teachers, faculty, and fans wrote recommendation letters to the Bethill Baptist Scholarship Fund for Underprivileged Youth. I helped him fill out his application, and Dad drove him to Jacksonville so he could meet with Bethill's board of directors.

Our paths bent slightly as the sand shifted beneath us, but the four of us hardly noticed; our sights were still fixed on the same North Star—*music*. The Vinyl Underground regrouped the week Hana's suspension ended. Our first meeting was a victory lap, a celebration of our hard-earned triumph over the Man. We laughed and danced to "We Gotta Get Out of This Place" on repeat, and everything slid back into place. Our meetings steadied us; the ritual reminded us we were in it together, no matter what. In The Vinyl Underground, the norms of society seemed shrug-worthy at best.

In fact, the only change I noticed was the slow improvement of my hearing. I yearned for it to come back; being a spectator at a record club was like being drug-free at the Manson Family ranch. While my friends soaked up the music in its sonic glory, I ached to partake! I cursed my ears, perpetually wondering when they'd finally heal. I created timelines and theorized which day my hearing would fully return—but I never would've predicted that the first sound I'd hear was a shot.

SIDE C

"There's no use being defeatist. Despair is the worst vice for a revolutionary."

—Marge Piercy

Sixteen

LATE REACTION IS INACTION

I noticed while I was watching TV. All of a sudden, there was no more ringing, no more humming, no more static. My ears had finally healed. The sound caught me by surprise. I didn't actually expect to *hear* the lame-o sitcom dialogue! I was only watching *Bewitched* because I liked the way Samantha's nose wiggled.

My parents were watching with me, so I tried not to let my excitement show. As far as they were concerned, my hearing problems were legit. I stayed calmly fixed on the TV, though my nerves were popping like fireworks. I couldn't wait until the clock hit 7 p.m. so I could go to Hana's and listen to records with my friends—to *really listen,* to hear every subtlety, every secret pressed into the wax.

Suddenly, ABC News interrupted the show with a breaking news bulletin. *Bewitched* cut to a gray-haired newsman sitting in front of a black background; he read the breaking news with the emotional sensibility of an alligator.

"Good evening. The Reverend Doctor Martin Luther King, thirty-nine years old, a Nobel Peace Prize winner and the leader of the nonviolent civil rights movement in the United States, was assassinated in Memphis tonight. A sniper's bullet shot down Dr. King as he stood on a hotel balcony in Memphis. Within an hour, Dr. King was dead. With the nation shocked, President Johnson expressed horror and will postpone his trip to Hawaii until tomorrow—"

"Good God!" Momma gasped.

I leaned closer to the screen. I tried to process what I heard.

Assassinated . . . postpone a trip to Hawaii . . . What?

"Goddammit," Dad spat in frustration. "I knew this would happen. I knew it! You can only stick your neck out so far 'til they chop it off."

"Buford!" Momma yelled.

"Tell me I'm wrong!" he yelled back, pointing at the screen.

My parents continued bickering as the end of the world began.

———

A few minutes later, I left for The Vinyl Underground meeting. I was too flustered to remember to bring any records, which would've been funny on any other day.

I found Milo sitting on his front porch. He held his Super 8 in one hand and a Grand Funk album in the other. I could tell he'd been crying.

"There a riot in Jacksonville," he mumbled when he saw me. "The radio just said the governor's initiating a statewide curfew."

"Jesus."

"Can't help us now," Milo said as he stood.

We crossed the empty street and trudged up Hana's front steps. Milo knocked on the door. There was no answer. Milo knocked again.

I leaned over to the window. Through the glass, I saw Hana emerge from the living room, wiping her face with a red bandana. She slid it into her pocket as she opened the door.

"Hey," she said. "Sorry, my parents are at dinner. I didn't hear the door."

"You OK?" Milo asked.

"What the fuck do you think?"

Neither of us answered. Instead of going upstairs, Hana led us through the kitchen and into her living room. Lewis was already there, sitting hunched toward the TV as Dan Rather gave an up-to-date report.

"Any new details?" I asked.

He just nodded at the screen. A newscaster was asking Andrew Young where the civil rights leaders planned on eating dinner . . . then they cut to a Budweiser commercial starring Frank Sinatra as a loveable Civil War soldier.

"Turn it off," Hana said flatly.

Lewis flipped off the tube.

"What do we do now?" Milo asked.

She just turned and walked back through the kitchen. I could hear her climbing the stairs. The three of us shared a knowing look—the meeting had begun.

Hana chose the record—*For What It's Worth* by The Staple Singers—and we formed our circle.

"I can hear again," I told the others.

They just nodded, barely registering what I'd said. I didn't fault them for it; I had a hard time caring, myself. Even though I could hear the music, I couldn't focus on it. I couldn't concentrate on anything except *the* thing.

My mind drifted to Bruce; how he'd feel if he were here, how I felt because he wasn't. I tried to resist the pull of the black hole I had inside me. I knew grief was waiting to catch me off guard and drag me back into that nothingness.

"Do y'all believe in heaven?" Lewis asked, snapping me back to the present.

"I don't believe in people living on clouds and stuff," Milo said, "but I believe there's another . . . something. Some great beyond, I dunno."

"I'm not sure I believe in anything," I admitted.

"Reincarnation," Hana said. "That's what happens when we die."

"Is that a Japanese thing?" Milo asked.

"It's a vision-of-death-I-had-during-an-acid-trip thing," she said seriously.

Milo's chuckle fell flat. The circle grew silent again.

Pops Staples grooved into the next song, "Father, Let Me Ride."

"Man," I sighed, "I still can't wrap my head around it."

"Why?" Hana asked. "Memphis can't be that different from Florida, both are full of racist assholes. You Southern boys shouldn't be surprised by any of this."

"Are you sayin' we're racist assholes?" Milo asked. His glasses magnified the hurt in his eyes.

"Are you saying you're not?"

"Come on," I chimed in. "I know you're upset, but that's not cool. Growin' up Southern doesn't automatically make us racist."

Her scoff was cold and firm. It shut the three of us up quick. We could see Hana needed a punching bag, and no one planned to volunteer.

"There's a quote in *Bartlett's* that reminds me of this place," she said. "'All that's necessary for the triumph of evil is that good men do nothing.'"

She shot me a look.

"Are you still pissed about the pep rally?" I asked. "I told you I was sorry. I should've done more, I should've done *something*, but you caught me off guard."

"How can *any of this* catch you off guard? It's all around you! The segregated school, the Confederate flags. I know you see it, and *I know* you know it's wrong, but you still sit quietly until things come to a head! So I don't want to listen to you whine about Dr. King or the pep rally! You didn't have the balls to speak out before shit boiled over, so no one should have to listen to you bitch about it now. Late reaction is inaction and not a damn thing more."

Tears stung at my eyes—tears of anger, tears of shame, tears of regret.

"That's . . . that's so unfair," I mumbled.

"Is it? If you spoke out against the war while your brother

was alive, would he have gone to Vietnam? If you would've told him how you really felt, if you would've made a stand when it mattered—"

"Fuck you, Hana!" I screamed, scrambling to my feet.

I tripped, but caught myself on the edge of her bed. I felt dizzy, sick. Her words had injected a hot shot of *what-if* into my bloodstream, and I was overdosing on the possibilities. I needed air. Fresh air. Fresh air now.

I moved clumsily from her bedroom and slammed the door behind me. I somehow got down the stairs. I grabbed my shoes without breaking stride. I stumbled off her porch and ran barefoot across the jagged gravel street toward home.

I pushed through the door. Most of the lights in the house were off, but the TV was still playing. I walked slowly into the living room. Dad was still watching the news reports, though the volume was turned low. He acknowledged me with a nod and a grunt, and then took another sip of beer.

I sat down beside him on the couch, still dazed by Hana's words. Moments passed. Commercial break, news, commercial break. The TV looked out of focus, and all the world was a bad dream full of bad answers to bad questions that I couldn't help but ask.

"Hey, Dad?" I said, in my shaky dream voice.

"Yeah?"

"How come you let Bruce join the marines if you didn't think he could hack it? Why didn't you try to talk him out of it, or anything?"

Dad sighed. He took a long chug of beer, killing the bottle.

He sat it on the side table, and the glass rang hollow. Then he reached out and grabbed my shoulder, squeezing it with the pressure of love.

"Nothin' I coulda said to change his mind," he mumbled. "Besides, if he was man enough to go to war and I stopped him, what the hell kinda man would I be?"

———

My watch said it was two o'clock in the morning. I couldn't sleep. Only a sociopath could've slept on a night like that. Our entire national trajectory had just been thrown off, and I was afraid my friendship with Hana had been, too.

I wished I'd kept my cool. I wish I hadn't screamed. Because it wasn't her words that set me off—it was the truth they contained. She'd been annoyingly *right*—about me, about the town, about all of us.

I should've spoken up about the war when I had the chance. Maybe I could've saved my brother. Maybe the grief inside me wasn't grief at all. Maybe it was guilt. Maybe. Maybe. Maybe.

All I knew for sure was that it was two o'clock and I was still awake.

Rolling a joint of mind-erasing proportions seemed my only recourse. If it didn't knock me out, then sleep was hopeless. So I got my stashbox from the ceiling and rolled myself the fattest, most promising doobie I could manage.

Then I crept down to the garage.

I pushed the garage door up gently. I looked at the sky.

No stars. Not that night.

I turned around and slid into the front seat of the Bel Air. I turned the battery on and sat the joint on the dashboard. The news bulletins were finally over, and records were spinning again—"I've Gotta Get a Message to You" by The Bee Gees. As I waited for the lighter to heat up, I wondered if King was the only Nobel Peace Prize winner to be murdered by a stranger in a redneck town. I wondered how much it hurt to be shot, if he was conscious after the fall, re-asking all the questions I'd once asked about my brother's death. All that death, all from the slightest pressure applied to the slightest sliver of metal. It was amazing that something as small as a bullet could leave a hole so goddamn big.

My mind drifted down that dark line of thought, when suddenly . . . a figure.

A dark figure stood in the open garage door.

My breath caught. I couldn't react. The Bee Gees sang on.

The figure moved forward. It was Hana. She wore her jacket over a nightgown, like the first time I saw her. But this nightgown was yellow, not blue. Her hair was tied back in a braid, and she'd washed the makeup off her face.

A dying cigarette idled on her naked lips.

I motioned to the passenger door. She tossed her cigarette. I turned down the radio. I pulled up the passenger lock.

"Don't slam it," I whispered, as she opened the door.

She nodded, and slid into the seat. She eased the door closed. Once I heard the latch click, I turned the radio back up.

"Can't sleep?" she asked.

"Not a wink, you?"

"Too restless. I've gone through half a pack tonight. I was just burning this last one when I heard the music. Figured it was you."

"You aren't afraid of being out after curfew?"

"It seemed like a chance worth taking."

Neither of us looked at each other.

"Listen," she mumbled, "I'm sorry about what I said. I was a total asshole. I'm just upset, and, well, fuck. There's no excuse. I'm just really sorry."

"I'm sorry, too. I should've have yelled . . . Plus, you were right. In my book, the real asshole's the one that doesn't wanna listen."

"I think I'm rubbing off on you, Ronnie."

"Scary, ain't it?"

"Fuckin' horrifying."

We both chuckled. The song ended.

The DJ faded up The Grass Roots' "Let's Live for Today." Hana bobbed her head to the guitar riff and ran her fingers across the dash.

"How come we've never gone cruising in this?"

"I'm not supposed to drive it. It was Bruce's car."

"Oh," she nodded. "Well how about this joint? Is it yours, at least?"

"Yeah," I laughed, "it's mine."

"Then light it up."

"Patience, my dear, patience. This isn't just a simple joint.

It's a peace pipe, and once we share it, our truce is eternally sealed. Now until forever."

"That's all?"

"Now until forever," I smiled, "then again after that."

"Deal," she said.

I slid the joint between my lips. She removed the fiery orange dash lighter. The joint sizzled like a grease trap when she touched the tips together. When I exhaled, I melted into the upholstery.

"Peace," I said, as she took the joint from my hand.

"Peace," she said as she hit it.

Then we sat in silence, enjoying the music. Things felt easy between us, as if our spat never happened. We shared the dark and filled our lungs with peace.

"It feels like the world's ending, doesn't it?"

"Yeah," I coughed, "the fall of Rome, part two. I can't decide if I feel lucky to see it go down, or if I wish I was born in easier times."

"We're lucky to be alive while the doomsday clock's ticking," she assured me. "Because now the Man's got nothing over us. See, conformity's enforced through implied consequences. But consequence is no longer an issue if the world's ending."

"Maybe you're right," I said, "or maybe I'm just stoned."

"Maybe both." She smiled.

"So what will you do in a world without consequences?" I asked.

"Hmm," she mused, "you know what I'd *really* like to do? I'd like to blow the ears out of every eighteen-year-old boy in

America. I'd like to make this entire generation ineligible for the war."

"Damn! If anyone could do it, it's you."

"Even if it was just in one city," she continued, "at one school, the word would still get out. Other kids would copy it, and then kids would copy them."

"Then it would turn into a movement."

"A movement"—she smiled—"that's what I *really* want."

She passed the joint back to me, and our eyes met. "What about you?"

"I dunno," I said bashfully, and took a hit.

"You don't know shit about shit, huh?"

"No, ma'am. I sure don't."

"That's why you've gotta go to college," she said. "Take weird classes, meet weird people, read weird books. You've gotta figure out the world around you if you ever wanna figure out your place in it, man."

"The Hana Hitchens guide to success."

"Take my advice," she grinned, "you'll be as pissed off as me in no time."

We both laughed. We both took another hit.

"You've gotta let go of the DJ thing, that's all I'm sayin'. It was your brother's dream, not yours. And what's a dream without a dreamer?"

"Just another ghost." I coughed. My eyes watered.

"So let it go, man. Or you'll never have a dream of your own. Nothing can grow in a shadow, Ronnie. You dig what I'm trying to say?"

I nodded. I scooted closer as I passed her the dying joint. I smelled the smoke on her leather. She exhaled, moving a little closer as she passed it back. We sat like that for an hour. Not speaking. Just listening. Just sharing the dark.

Shoulder to shoulder, so close that our hands almost touched.

seventeen

DEFINITELY PROBABLY
NOT DEAD

Riots rocked the streets of Jacksonville all night. The extent of the damage, injuries, and arrests was not yet known, but the paper said it was bad enough for the National Guard to be deployed. They didn't specify if their orders were to protect or suppress, but the photos showed a city crushed beneath the heavy boot of authority.

Momma had shown me the article at breakfast. It read more like something that would happen in a foreign land, not right up the highway. Here, it was just another carefree Cordelia Island morning.

No moment of silence was held at school for Dr. King, so Mr. Donahue held one himself. Sixty seconds of quiet reflection. Sixty seconds in which he had to send out three students because they wouldn't stop giggling.

As the day went on, I realized most of my schoolmates were completely unfazed by the assassination. The day-to-day cliques just gabbed about their standard Friday gossip, as if the cold-blooded murder of mankind's bastion of love was less interesting than what Jeannie Shepard wore to the baseball game. The killing was too high profile for anyone to be oblivious. This was *active indifference,* and it disgusted me—mostly because I saw more of myself in them than I wanted to admit. I was thankful for the clarity I'd gained the night before, but now I had so many thoughts rolling through my brain it was getting hard to focus. I needed time to process it all. One more new realization might cause my head to overflow.

In an effort to avoid learning I decided to ditch. Lunchtime came, and I went to my locker to grab my things. I cut down the hall toward one of the least guarded exits. When I turned the corner, I saw a J. V. wrestler standing near the fire alarm wiping tears from his eyes. His name was Ernest, and he was one of those misguided Stink Wilson worshippers. I'd written them all off as racist assholes, but maybe I'd been wrong about him.

"Hey, man," I said, stopping.

"Oh," he whimpered. "Hi, Ronnie."

"You gonna be OK?"

"Yeah, it just . . . God, it seems so *unfair*!"

"I know."

"They should be *hung* for this! They should be tarred and feathered and hung in the street!"

"I understand how ya feel, but that wouldn't fix anything."

He scoffed, then blew his nose on his T-shirt. "I just don't get it," he sniffled. "Why would a Chicago outfit do this?"

"You mean *the* Outfit?" I asked. "Holy shit, I hadn't even thought of that! But it makes sense, I heard the mob was also involved in Kennedy's assassination—"

"What're you talkin' about?"

"Martin Luther King," I said. "Isn't that what *you're* talkin' about?"

"No, the P&P! I'm talking about *the mill,* you idiot! They laid a bunch of guys off! My daddy, my uncle, both my cousins—for all I know, they're gettin' canned right now!"

"Wait," I stammered, "where'd you hear that?"

"Suzie told me."

"Suzie Dean? How would she know? She must be messin' with you—"

Ernest shook his head like a child in need of a nap. "She heard it on the radio when she was in the nurse's office. WQRX. The DJ said the P&P announced they're scaling back production and blah blah blah blah."

The fluttering in my stomach hardened into a solid mass of anxiety.

"Tell me the *blah blah* part, too. Did they say *why* they're scaling back?"

"Ask your friend," he sneered. "Her dad's the one doin' the firing. Stink *knew* the V. C. would try somethin' like this! It's all because of them, because of her!"

"Stink's an idiot. I can't believe you'd listen to—"

"He knew MLK was gonna get iced for startin' a race war! Think Stink's an idiot *now*?"

"Jesus," I sighed, "y'all don't even know why you hate what you hate."

I walked away. A wave of exhaustion washed over me as I pushed through the side exit. My head was killing me. It pounded, pulsing in code. A warning. I was just too tired to read the message.

———

The downside of working weekends was that every once in a while I had to stand in the lobby while something premiered I was dying to see. That Friday, there were two of them (*Planet of the Apes* and *2001: A Space Odyssey*) so I was doubly annoyed to be stuck taking tickets. I wondered if Milo could screen us an after-hours double feature, but the idea fizzled as soon as I hit the lobby to clock in.

"Hey, Ronnie," Susanne called, "have you seen Milo?"

"I saw him at school. Why?"

"He ain't here yet."

She leaned over the glass counter of the concession stand as I approached.

"He's not here yet? He's always here before me."

"Not today," she said, "and Mr. Dori is freakin' out. He's been running the projectors himself all afternoon, sprinting back and forth like a nut job . . ."

She trailed off as Mr. Dori trampled down the stairs, rushing into Viewing Room 1 without breaking his stride. Susanne looked at me and shrugged.

He came back out to the lobby a second later. There were sweat rings under his arms and neck; everything but his bowtie was damp.

"Didn't mean to be rude, Ronnie," he panted. "Had to make sure the projector was centered."

"That's OK, Mr. Dori."

"Did Milo come to work with you?" he asked—not panicked, but close.

I shook my head.

"Was he at school?"

"Yes, sir."

"Shoot," he huffed. "He isn't sick?"

"Not that I know of. Have you tried his house?"

"A few times."

"Well, I wouldn't sweat it," I shrugged, "he's probably just runnin' late."

"Maybe," he glanced at his watch, and groaned theatrically. "Time to switch reels! Do me a favor, give Milo a ring every hour. Use the phone in my office. Keep calling until he gets here. If you reach him *before* he gets here, tell him to get here!"

"Will do, sir," I said with a straight face.

But as soon as he was back upstairs, Susanne and I burst out laughing.

"Riots all through Jacksonville, half our town's laid off, but his biggest worry is still gettin' the *projector centered*," she snorted.

"I know," I said. "I'm just glad the weekend's here."

A customer approaching the counter nodded in agreement.

He smiled at Susanne. She smiled back. Then he ordered some Junior Mints.

It was after nine o'clock and Milo still hadn't shown. It

wasn't like him to miss work, but the opening-night crowd kept me too occupied to dwell on it. The lobby was nonstop packed until the late shows started. Only then did the place begin to thin out.

I took tickets from the stragglers like a seasoned expert. I got handed a ticket, ripped it, and gave back the stub. I got handed two tickets, ripped both, and gave back the stubs.

Then, a guy came to the counter without a ticket and threw off my rhythm. I looked up, annoyed. But it was my dad. I was surprised to see him there; my parents usually gave me a heads up if they were coming to the movies.

"Hey," I said. "Are you here for the Charlton Heston one? There's still a few seats left. The previews have already started, but if ya hurry—"

"No. I actually came to talk to your boss."

"What? Why?"

"It's Milo," he said, but then hurriedly added, "he'll be OK. Don't worry. But there was an, uh, *incident* after school today."

Mr. Dori saw us talking and came over. He looked dead tired. "Ronnie," he panted, "everything OK here?"

"Yeah, Mr. Dori. This is my dad."

"Are you the manager?" Dad asked, extending his hand.

"Owner," he corrected. "Frank Dori."

"Buford Bingham," Dad said.

They shook.

"I'm afraid I come bearin' bad news," Dad said. "Milo's mother asked me to let you know that he was hurt in a scuffle on his way home from school, and that's why he missed his shift.

He suffered some broken bones, so he may not be able to come back to work for a while."

Mr. Dori got lightheaded. He grabbed the counter for balance.

"What the hell—?"

I couldn't finish the sentence. A sudden nausea washed over me, as if I'd been kicked in the gut. I clamped my mouth shut, convinced I'd puke on the ticket counter if I continued speaking.

"We should get to the hospital," he said. "I'll fill you in on the drive."

"Go! Go!" Mr. Dori urged. "Just please make sure he's OK!"

I nodded to Mr. Dori. I left the ticket counter unattended and followed my dad away from those damn dirty apes on the screen, through a door that led toward much more brutal monsters.

———

"What happened?" I asked as Dad pulled out of the back lot.

"Your mother and I were finishin' supper," he said, steering us toward the hospital, "when she noticed a cruiser parked across the street. So we walked next door to see if Gladys knew what the fuss was about, and we found her on the porch, crying. I guess the sheriff talked to her before goin' to speak with the girl's parents—"

"Wait," I snapped, "they went to Hana's house, too?"

He nodded. He kept his eyes on the road. "She was ambushed by some kids after school, probably on account of the mill. Milo just happened to be walking with her, wrong place, wrong time kinda thing. Your mother drove Gladys to the hospital, but first she begged me to tell your boss Milo's not playing hooky. Said he loves that job, doesn't wanna get in trouble."

"Who was it?" I asked. "Who would do that to the two of them?"

"I don't know. But the kind of guy who'll mess with a woman, it don't get much lower than that. Proud of Milo for jumping in, though. Hell, I wish he woulda shown that sort of moxie on the wrestling mat!"

I didn't laugh. Dad clammed up.

Soon, the giant mercy cross atop Liberty General loomed ahead of us—a colossal empty gesture made of sleek, red neon. Dad followed it like a beacon. He pulled up to the front entrance. He slowed. He stopped.

"Room 312," he said. "Visitin' hours are over, but if you take the stairs no one will notice you. I'll wait in the lobby. Take all the time ya need."

Room 312. I knocked, but no one answered.

I opened the door slowly. The overhead light was off, but the blinds had been left open—the light from the rooftop crucifix spread a choppy red glare over everything. I could see that the bed nearest me was vacant. A white cloth divider cut off the other half of the room. It reminded me of the ones from the draft exam.

I stepped inside and eased the door shut behind me.

I crept past the empty bed. I peeked over the room divider—

My knees buckled.

I grabbed ahold of the divider until I felt steady. I took a deep breath. Then I forced myself to look back at my best friend lying in the bed beside the window.

I'd never seen anyone I cared for in such a state. By the time they'd shipped Bruce home, he was a clean, dead husk of himself. Milo, however, was still very much alive, and looked to be in an incredible amount of pain. His entire left arm was in a cast, bent at the elbow, dangling above him in an elevated sling. His lips and nose were swollen. Two of the fingers on his right hand were in splints. An IV pumped who-knows-what into his arm. The drugs must have been top notch; otherwise no one could sleep like that.

His glasses were off. He looked so tiny without them. I saw them sitting on the sink. I picked up his specs, and carried them to the bed.

"Milo," I whispered, leaning over him.

Nothing.

I shook his good arm. He groaned a little.

"Milo," I whispered, louder.

He opened his eyes—just barely. I slid the glasses on.

A moment later, he blinked his eyes into focus.

"R . . . Ronnie?"

"Man," I said, forcing a smile, "I'd hate to see the other guy."

"Shit," he croaked, "you mean the *five* other guys?"

"What happened?"

"Help me sit up," he groaned.

I adjusted the bed into an upright position. As he situated himself, he tried not to move his cast, which was nearly impossible. I grabbed a chair from the corner of the room and moved it next to the bed.

"Ya know," he said, "I'd say those dipshits did me a favor, if it wasn't for Hana. The doc says my arm is royally fucked. I need months of physical therapy. He swears this will get me a 4-F stamp."

I waited for him to tell his story. He readjusted his arm. Then he cleared his throat and began. "We were walkin' home from school. I had my camera out, like usual. When we got to the corner of Magazine Street, I saw a hopscotch game in the alley. I asked Hana to let me film her playin' hopscotch. I thought it'd be funny, you know? They were probably already looking for her, by then."

"*Who?* Who was lookin' for her?"

"Stink," he mumbled. He winced when he said it. "Stink and Marty and Bill and Franklin—and that little prick, Ernest. All five of their dads work at the mill."

"Oh, *Christ*," I whispered. I was beginning to understand.

"Hana and me were sittin' ducks, man. But we didn't know it until Marty's Camaro peeled into the alley. He almost ran me over. Seriously. I thought I was roadkill. Then Marty and Bill jumped out of the car and charged me before I even knew what was what. Marty got me in an arm bar, and I dropped my camera. Then Ernest and Franklin went after Hana, caught her before she could . . ."

Milo stopped talking. The red neon light reflected on his lenses, and thin streams of tears flowed from beneath the glowing frames. I hunched closer.

"Stink got out of the car last. He was drunk. All of 'em were drunk, but he was on another planet. He stumbled over to Hana, and he, he pulled a blade out of his back pocket. A switchblade."

My jaw clenched.

"Marty had me stuck, man. I couldn't do anything when . . . shit. Stink held that blade and said 'If you make a sound, I'll cut your yellow fucking throat.' I'll never get those words outta my head, man. I'll never . . . I . . . *Jesus* . . . I tried . . . I tried to—" His voice broke. The words crumbled into a single incoherent sob.

"Everything's OK," I said, trying to reassure him. "Everything's cool."

He let out a heartbreaking laugh. "Are you dense? What part of *this* is OK?"

That's when I finally hugged him.

"Ronnie, shit!" he cried, wincing.

"Shhhhh, shut up," I whispered, "shut up, shut up, shut up—"

He groaned, but hugged me back as best he could. I held him as tight as I dared to. Then he fell into a coughing fit, so I finally let him go. I got him a cup of water from the sink. I held the paper cup to his lips. He drank without comment.

"Is Hana here, too?" I asked.

"Jacksonville. They've got a poison control unit there."

"*Poison*?" I gasped.

"I'm sorry," he groaned, "I just can't handle thinking about it right now—"

"OK," I said, afraid to push too hard, "you can tell me when you're ready. I'm just glad you're, well, not OK, but not dead."

"Definitely probably not dead. I don't think I'd be in so much pain if I was."

I got him another cup of water. He sipped it feebly and motioned me closer.

"Go to the corner of Twelfth and Magazine," he said. "You'll see a hopscotch course in the alley, in purple chalk. It should be somewhere around there, on the left-hand side."

"What should be?"

"My camera," he said.

"Wait, your—"

"*Camera*," he repeated. "It flew outta my hands when they tackled me, but I think it landed right-side up, and I *know* it was still rolling."

"Holy shit."

"I think I got it on film. All of it. I think we can *nail* those guys."

The prospect jolted me outta the chair like a live wire.

"I'll go right now!"

"Good," he croaked. "Take it to Schwartzman Camera *first thing* tomorrow. Tell them I'm in the hospital. Beg 'em to get the spool developed by Sunday."

"You're stuck here until Sunday?"

"Don't worry about that. Just get that film developed. We'll watch the footage together once I'm sprung from this joint."

"OK," I nodded, "I'll get the film developed in the morning."

"And you'll bring it over Sunday?"

"Yeah, man, I'll be there."

"Or be squarer than square," he said. His lips cracked into a painful grin and he bounced his eyebrows up and down in that annoying way of his. Then he shut his eyes and drifted into unconsciousness.

I removed his glasses. I sat them on the sink.

I looked back at my buddy, snoring through a painful sleep, and I smiled.

In spite of everything, I smiled.

Because in 1968, "definitely probably not dead" was a best-case diagnosis.

eighteen

SUICIDE BY QUAGMIRE

I woke craving a cigarette, even though I wasn't much of a smoker. My nerves were so raw my hands shook when I rubbed the goop from my eyeballs. I tossed the sheets off the bed to stop myself from curling back up in them.

Wolfie barked. I rolled over in time to see him sulk from beneath the avalanche of blankets. He looked as annoyed as I was to be back in the waking world. Both of us groaned and got up. I stretched my neck out, and then put on a clean shirt. The sun caught the lens of Milo's camera, which now sat on the edge of my dresser. The exaggerated handle was toy-like, something you might expect to see on a gag camera that was actually a water gun. But the complicated focus and exposure knobs made it clear this was more than a toy—it was an instrument of creation that required a level of dedication to use.

I'd gotten it in the night, as soon as we left the hospital. The camera was exactly where he said it'd be, just to the left of the hopscotch course. The batteries were dead, but the power switch was flipped ON.

It was hard not to tell Dad what might be on the filmstrip curled inside. But Dad could only discipline them through the school, and suspension wasn't good enough. If the camera caught those creeps on film, we might be able to put them in jail.

The possibility of justice fired me up. I threw on some jeans, brushed down my cowlick, and then went downstairs for a quick breakfast before taking the film to the camera shop.

The smell of biscuits cleared my mind as I walked into the kitchen.

"Momma," I said, "those smell *so* good."

I maneuvered directly to the basket of biscuits cooling on the stove. I reached for one, but she slapped my hand away. Roy giggled from his high chair

"Don't pick at those," she scolded. "They're for the Hitchens across the street. I've been meanin' to send somethin' over, but it kept slippin' my mind."

I nodded and sat down. The gesture was obviously because of yesterday—Momma didn't bake biscuits for any ol' reason. It was a process, those biscuits, and she took it as seriously as any expert craftsman would. She used cake flour instead of all-purpose, and threw in an extra half-glob of lard per batch.

"Would you mind runnin' them across the street for me?"

"Sure, Momma. But can I go ahead and eat?"

"Of course"—she smiled—"when you get back."

I rolled my eyes. She wrapped the biscuits in a blue-checkered napkin and kissed me on the cheek as I stood. Then I headed outside with the wicker basket saddling my hip.

I crossed the street beneath the cloudless sky, but slowed

as I reached the house. I had no idea what really happened to Hana, and no clue what I was walking into. My nerves jittered as I strode onto the porch. I told myself to act normal, no matter what. Then I knocked on the front door.

No answer.

"She's still in Jacksonville," a voice rasped. It was almost as gravelly as mine.

I turned, startled. A thin man lazed in one of the rocking chairs at the end of the porch. He held a coffee cup in one hand and a cigarette in the other. I could tell he was Hana's father by the defiant tilt of his jawline.

"Sorry for jumpin'." I laughed nervously. "You startled me. I'm Ronnie Bingham, from across the way. I just came by to give ya these biscuits my momma baked."

"Finally! A little of that Southern hospitality I'd heard about."

He flicked his cigarette into the yard as he stood up to approach me.

"Oliver Hitchens," he said, extending his hand.

"Really nice to meet you, sir," I said, and shook.

Mr. Hitchens could've been twenty years older than my dad, or maybe five years younger—his smile had retained its youth, though I could tell by the lines around his eyes that this man was no virgin of life. His dark hair was slicked back, and he sported a righteously hip goatee that was entirely white. He wore a black polo shirt tucked into brown chinos. He was barefoot.

He held the basket to his face, and breathed in.

"These smell incredible. Please tell your mother we appreciate it."

"I will."

"Can I get you a cup of coffee?" he asked. "It's been days since I've chatted with someone who isn't cursing or threatening me."

"Uh, yeah, sure. That sounds good."

"Great." He smiled.

He took the biscuits and his coffee cup into the house.

He was back a moment later, holding two fresh mugs.

He handed me a cup. I sat down beside him.

"So," I mumbled, "how, uh, how's she doing?"

"How much do you already know?" he asked, looking over at me.

"Not a lot. I talked to Milo last night. He's the boy that was with her. He was too doped up to say much. But I saw how bad off he was, and I expect she got it even worse."

"Yes," he sighed. "They had to pump her stomach, and do two chemical scrubs. She has some internal bruising, but nothing's broken. Except maybe her spirit. She's a hard girl, but this . . . this was something else. She had to be sedated once she fully grasped what they did to her hair."

"Her hair?"

"Her hair is gone," he said flatly. "Those boys, those *scum*, they told her that they were going to make her look like Ho Chi Minh."

"I don't understand—"

"They *scalped* her. They sawed off her hair with a switchblade."

I spilt coffee onto my jeans. My hand was shaking. I hunched over and put the cup down. He fished a pack of Lucky Strikes from his pocket. He offered me one, but I declined. It felt weird taking smokes from an adult.

He shrugged and slid one between his lips. He lit up and took a contemplative drag.

"Have you lived here long?" he asked, exhaling.

"Yes, sir, all my life."

"Has it always been such a hateful place?"

"I never used to think so. But lately, I've been wonderin' if maybe I just never noticed."

"Ah, the power to *not* notice," he mused. "A luxury those like you and I have. But it's lazy, as all luxuries are, so I'm glad to hear you're avoiding the urge."

"Hana doesn't give me much of a choice."

"No," he grinned, "she's not a fan of staying out of the fray, is she?"

I shook my head, and picked up my cup. The coffee tasted bitter and right.

"Did you know I only took the job here to get her out of Chicago?"

"Really?"

"Oh yes," he nodded. "No one *wants* these hatchet jobs. Restructuring always means layoffs; they're horrible things to be a part of. But Chicago had gotten too dangerous for Hana, and we had to get her out of the city. She was getting into too much trouble—serious trouble. We've always encouraged her to speak her mind, but the groups she was getting mixed up with were dangerous."

He took another drag. He cleared his throat.

"We thought a small town would do her good. Keep her out of trouble. I knew the mill evaluation would take six months, at least. So we figured that would be a nice little cooling-off period for her. Life's a gas, huh, kid?"

"You couldn't have known what would happen," I said.

"No," he scoffed, "I should have. And if I'd done a better evaluation, I would have. Christ, what was I thinking, bringing her to a place like this?"

I felt silly trying to comfort a grown man, but I stammered on.

"I'm gonna try my best to get justice for her, sir."

He let out a deflated chuckled, and my words trailed off.

"Did Hana tell you I served in World War II?" he asked, leaning back.

"Yes, sir, she's mentioned it."

"I was as young as you," he mused, "maybe younger. The war was coming to a head, but I was still eager to fight. I still *believed* in the fight. I'd just made it to the front when the Krauts surrendered. I'd barely fired a shot, but I still went along with the other troops to get liquored-up and celebrate. We walked to a town called Troyes, near Paris, expecting a party.

"We found everyone gathered in the town square. I thought it was a celebration, but as we got closer, I realized it was a mob. They had four local girls strung up, with nooses around their necks. An onlooker said they'd been accused of having relations with Nazi soldiers. The oldest looked fifteen, if that. Do you know what they did to those children?"

I shook my head—no.

"Well, first they stripped them naked. Then, they sheared off their hair to make sure the girls were *properly* humiliated. After that, they threw the ropes over the archway of a church, and lynched them from it. And I just stood there, with the others. I just stood there and watched."

I kept my eyes locked forward. I didn't know what to say.

Mr. Hitchens took a drag. "That was justice to the town of Troyes." He exhaled. "I suspect there's a similarly skewed definition of the word down here."

"Maybe so," I mumbled, "but I have to try."

"Well, I wish you luck." He nodded. "I appreciate what a friend you are to my girl, you and the other boy, Milo. I imagine she's really going to miss you two."

"Miss us?" I asked. "Where's she going?"

"She hasn't told you? She must be waiting until it's official."

"Until what's official, sir?"

"Her writing career," he said. "My college roommate was just promoted to foreign bureau chief at the *Chicago Tribune*. I sent him some of her recent Vietnam articles. Have you read her work?"

I shook my head.

"It's damn good," he continued. "Her focus has shifted to exposé-type articles; there's real depth to them. My buddy at the *Tribune* thought so, too. He threw her name in the hat for an internship with their foreign correspondents."

My head started to hurt. I tried to focus on what this meant.

"Foreign correspondents . . . like, does that mean *war* correspondents?"

"It depends. Do you consider this suicide-by-quagmire in Vietnam a war?"

———

I picked up the film on Sunday. The developer looked troubled when he handed me the reel—I took it as a good sign; maybe it meant we had enough to nail those assholes to the wall for good.

When I got home, I saw Hana's mother struggling with a load of groceries. I jogged across the street to help, eager to hear about Hana. Her mom said she'd just been released from the hospital and was resting in her bedroom. She made it clear no visitors were allowed. It pained me not to see her, but what could I do?

Pace my porch aimlessly.

Back and forth, back and forth, looking from her window to Milo's driveway, then back to her window again. The film felt heavy in my pocket. I was excited to have it. I was nervous to watch it. I waded in that ambivalence until Gladys Novak's Impala cruised down our street.

I stopped pacing and smiled.

I rushed down the steps and crossed into their yard as Milo

labored out of the car. His cast seemed to throw him off balance. I wrapped my arm around him until he got his footing. I shut the car door for him and tousled his increasingly shaggy hair.

"Missed ya, man. How do you feel?"

"Like one of Ramrod's tackle dummies," he said.

I believed it. His face wasn't as swollen, but purple bruises had replaced the puffiness. His cast was almost comical—the damn thing was bigger than him!

"That's enough, Ronnie," his mother said. "Milo needs to rest."

"Mom," he whined, "I've been stuck in bed for two days! I need some human interaction or I swear to God I'm gonna go nutso."

"Spare me," she scoffed, but her eyes softened. "Promise you'll be careful."

"Always," he said, and smiled.

As soon as she was inside, Milo turned to me. "Did you find the camera?"

"I found it."

"Did they develop it?"

"Picked it up this morning," I said.

"OK." He nodded. "Let's watch it in my room."

"OK."

He looked over at Hana's house. "Is she back yet?"

"Yeah," I said, "she got home earlier. I tried to see her, but her mom said she's resting."

"Oh," he said. His eyes looked troubled.

"Hey, has she ever mentioned an internship with the *Chicago Tribune*?"

"I don't think so. Why?"

"Just curious," I lied. I was afraid saying more would upset him.

"Oh . . . well, whatever. Come on, let's go see what's what."

I kept my arm around him as we walked into the house.

Milo's room looked like the production tent of an under-funded movie—the floor and bed were littered with notes, storyboards, and ideas for his documentary. It was a bedroom in name only, and I had to wonder where he actually slept.

His projector was a tiny, shoebox-sized thing called a Kodak Brownie. It faced a white sheet tacked to a bare wall. I handed him the spool of film. He fastened it onto the roller, and then carefully fed the filmstrip into the Brownie.

Then he stopped.

"I hate this," he sighed. "Fuck. My favorite thing about movies is seeing the world through different eyes. It's such a drag that this is what you see when you look through mine." He stayed still another moment, then got up and killed the lights.

We sat next to each other on the floor and faced the blank, white sheet.

"There won't be any audio," he said.

"Can you narrate for me? Just so I know what's happening?"

"I can try. But you've gotta brace yourself, Ronnie. If the camera stayed in focus, this won't be easy to watch."

He switched the Brownie on. The small device was surprisingly loud, and it *taptaptaptaptaptaptap*'ed like one of those cheapo card shufflers, ticking madly as the gears wound the film into place. The Brownie ticked along like that for nearly a minute, projecting nothing but white light.

But then . . .

FADE IN:

EXT. ALLEYWAY—DAY

HANA stands at the end of the hopscotch game. Our P.O.V. is the final chalk block. She pretends to hold a jump rope as she springs from one square to the next, one foot and then the other then four hops then two hops with both feet—on and on, until she reaches the end.

She laughs, and we get the impression the cameraman is laughing, too. But then she looks beyond the camera, and her smile disintegrates. Her eyes glow with rage and fear.

Turn as a blue Camaro BLAZES into the alley. MARTY HOUSTON and BILL MARGARET exit the car. They look identical in their letterman jackets and khaki slacks. They GRAB for the camera. The picture blurs.

"Now we'll see what we got," Milo said, leaning in.

I watched the silent chaos of the camera spinning through the air. Finally, the picture steadied. The focus was a little off, but I could plainly see Franklin Buckley holding Hana in a chokehold.

EXT. ALLEYWAY—DAY (RESUMING)

At first, STINK WILSON is just a smudge. All that's clear is his letterman jacket . . . until he pulls a knife from the back pocket of his jeans. The knife, that vicious metal, is clearly visible through the blur. Stink points the blade at Hana's mouth as he speaks to her in silence.

"He was accusing her of being a spy," Milo mumbled. "He said he, he said . . . he said he was gonna make sure everyone in town knew she was Viet Cong."

EXT. ALLEYWAY—DAY (RESUMING)

Hana spits in Stink's face. Stink grabs her by the hair and snaps her head down. He brings the knife to her scalp, and his arm moves with an unfathomable amount of violence. He doesn't cut her hair, he saws it like a maniacal carpenter.

In the corner of the frame, MILO drops to the ground. Stink continues sawing until there's nothing left of her hair but stringy, uneven patches, like a botched Wild West scalping. Blood drips onto the concrete. Then Stink punches Hana in the gut, and she goes down. She curls into a ball on the dusty concrete as Stink walks out of frame, toward the Camaro.

Hana tries to stand. FRANKLIN BUCKLEY kicks

her in the ribs, and then looks at her with
something close to pity. Stink walks back into
frame carrying A SILVER TIN.

"What is that?" I gasped. "What is that, man?"

"Gasoline," Milo said flatly.

"No, no, no, no!" I screamed, but it was no use. Tears
blurred my vision as I watched Stink douse my friend in gasoline. Her silent cries were like invisible shrapnel that blew
straight through my heart.

I turned to Milo. He was crying, too. But he wouldn't look
away.

I forced myself look back at the screen. Then I felt his broken
hand reach out in the dark for mine. I took it and squeezed. We
held hands like horrified children as the filmstrip flickered on.

EXT. ALLEYWAY—DAY (RESUMING)
Hana lies broken on the pavement, soaked in
gasoline. Her few remaining strands of hair
are stuck to her face. Stink tosses the gas
can aside. He is laughing. He leans over her
and says something undoubtedly cruel. His hand
slides into his pocket.

"What did he say," I whispered, my voice an incorporeal
shudder.

"He said . . . *You wanna make a statement, bitch? Here's
your chance.*"

EXT. ALLEYWAY—DAY (RESUMING)

Stink pulls a matchbook from his pocket. Hana screams a silent scream as he takes a match out. He lights the match . . . but then, after a horrifying moment, he blows the flame out and throws the matchbook at Hana's face. Then Stink drunkenly stumbles away. A beat later, his friends follow. Hana lies still.

FADE TO BLACK

We sat there for I don't know how long. Finally, Milo let go of my hand and flipped off the projector. The room turned gray. A lone sliver of sunlight snuck through the covered window. I was thankful for the shadows—I was shaking badly, crying messy tears. I felt like I had to use the bathroom. I tried to get under control.

Milo looked a little better than me. He'd stopped sobbing, anyway.

"I blacked out," he said. "When I woke up, she was still on the ground. I wasn't in a lot of pain. The doctors said it was shock. But I got to my feet and flagged down this geezer mowin' his lawn across the street. Then I think I passed out again."

When I looked over at him, he turned his eyes away.

"If she swallowed that gas she coulda died," I said. "You saved her life, man."

"All I did was run for help," he mumbled. "And she was still in danger from inhaling the fumes and absorbing the gas through her skin. Lassie coulda done a better job."

I let out a sad, soggy chuckle. Milo stood up and turned on the lights.

"So what do we do now?" I asked.

"Take the film to the sheriff."

"OK. I'll call Lewis and see if he can meet us there."

"Good thinkin'." Milo nodded. "A little star power can't hurt! I'll get this shit together, you can use the phone downstairs."

I nodded and went downstairs. I had to stop in the hallway to take a breath before I could talk to anyone. I was still utterly overwhelmed by what I'd seen.

"Jesus," I whispered to myself. "Come on, man. Come on." I pushed off the wall and cut into the kitchen. I yanked the plastic phone off the cradle and dialed.

"Hello?" Lewis answered.

"Hey, it's Ronnie. You busy? Milo and I could use your help."

"Then say no more. Your one-man cavalry's on the way."

———

Milo and I walked downtown. I had the film in my pocket, and carried his Brownie projector in case the sheriff didn't have one. I'd crammed the *Cordelia High School 1966–1967 Yearbook* under Milo's left armpit so we could identify Stink and his supporting cast.

The sheriff's station was a single-story building on Main Street, catty-corner to the courthouse. Lewis was waiting on us, reclining on a bench in front. I hadn't told him much about the film—there was just no way to accurately describe the horror. He needed to see it for himself to understand.

His biceps stretched the sleeves of his letterman jacket as he waved us over. His smile faltered when we crossed the street, and he took stock of Milo's injuries.

"They did this?" he asked softly. "Our teammates really did this to you?"

Milo replied with a single nod.

Ramrod nodded back. His fists clenched. His eyes hardened.

"Come on guys," I said, "lets stick it to 'em the right way."

Lewis took a calming breath. His shoulders eased slightly. He turned to the station and focused back on the task at hand. He grabbed the yearbook from Milo and the projector from me, and then he set off across the street. I wiped sweat from my brow and followed. Milo tripped walking up the curb, but I caught him.

Lewis held the door. I helped Milo inside.

The interior of the sheriff's station reminded me of the *Andy Griffith Show*—the reception area led into a big, open room filled with desks and a holding cell. A door in the corner opened into a hallway. Three deputies stood around idly, drinking coffee and chatting comfortably with one another.

We approached the receptionist, a gray woman with a gray expression. She seemed to take all her arthritic aggression out on the keys of her typewriter.

"Excuse me, my name's Milo Novak. I have somethin' to show the sheriff pertaining to my case."

"Case number?" she asked without looking up.

"Um, I don't remember the number."

She stopped typing and raised her hands as if to say *Then why are ya wasting my time?* Ramrod stepped in front of Milo.

"Go get the damn sheriff," he snapped.

She scowled at him. Lewis didn't look away.

Finally, she turned to the deputies. "Wilcox!"

The youngest-looking deputy jogged over. He had a sunken leanness about him, and a sun-bleached mustache covering his upper lip.

"Seems these boys have information regardin' the Hitchens case."

The deputy gave an airless chuckle at the mention of Hana's name.

Then he nodded, still grinning, and disappeared into the hall.

"Waitin' area's over there," she said, pointing to a bench.

She went back to typing. The three of us took a seat.

"Young Mr. Novak!" a voice thundered a moment later. A dinosaur of a man came into the room. His skin was blotchy and red. Something about his smile tied my stomach in knots. The star on his chest bounced as he moved toward us.

"Sheriff Milton," Milo said, "I have somethin' you've gotta see."

"Of course," he said, and then he turned to Lewis. "And looky who you brought with ya! Ramrod Gibbons! Hell, boy, it's an honor to meet you."

He extended his hand and Lewis shook it.

"What're you doin' with this bunch? Workin' security?"

"No, sir," Lewis said, "just hangin' out with my friends."

"I didn't catch your name," Sheriff Milton said to me.

"Ronnie Bingham, sir," I mumbled.

Sheriff Milton stuck out his meaty palm. I shook it, too.

"Is there a projection screen here?" Milo asked.

"Yes siree! Just follow me, boys. We'll get y'all set up."

We followed Sheriff Milton into the hallway, which led to a small conference room in the back of the building. Deputy Wilcox joined us. Lewis sat the Brownie on the end of the conference table and the deputy pulled a projection screen down from over the blackboard. He and I sat on one side of the table. The Man sat on the other. Milo stayed standing so he could run the projector. He loaded the film, then switched the Brownie on.

"This is a film of what happened," he said, "and it *proves* the guys who attacked us were Adam Wilson, Franklin Buckley, Ernest Thorogood, Marty Houston, and Bill Margaret—just like I told ya when you came to the hospital."

Milo spoke clearly and evenly, and a sense of pride swelled in my throat.

Lewis flipped the yearbook to Stink's photo and slid it across the table. Sheriff Milton looked it over. Milo turned off the lights.

The reel began to spin.

I couldn't stand to watch it a second time. I turned my gaze to the sheriff as the film flickered in his eyes. Milo narrated, and even paused the film at one point to highlight a crystal-clear image of Stink's face.

Lewis moved his chair up to the screen. I could see his muscles tensing, his jaw tightening, and his eyes narrowing. At one point I thought he might flip the table over, or tear down the screen, or just straight up explode.

Milo's voice broke near the end of the film. I was thankful when it ended.

The deputy turned the lights back on. Milo leaned on the projector, emotionally exhausted. Lewis stayed hunched toward the now-blank screen.

I hated that Milo had to rewatch his own sad movie. I hated that he had to retraumatize himself. But it was gonna be worth it. Because the sad ones were the truth, as Hana liked to say, and now that the sheriff knew this, justice would demand to be served.

Sheriff Milton yawned. He leaned back in his chair.

"That was quite a picture," he finally said.

"It was," Deputy Wilcox agreed. "But I gotta be honest, Sheriff. I ain't so sure them boys in the movie are the same boys in that yearbook, there."

"It did leave a lot to the imagination," Sheriff Milton nodded.

"Come on," I stammered, "that's Adam Wilson! Stink—I mean *Adam*—he's threatened Hana in public a *bunch* of times! The entire school can vouch for that!"

"Half the town has threatened the Hitchens family," Sheriff Milton said. "All that filmstrip showed me are a few boys in varsity jackets. Coulda just as well been Mr. Gibbons, here."

"What?" Lewis yelled. When he stood up, he towered over

the table. "I ain't like them! I ain't one'a them! Goddammit, I ain't like them!"

"Sit down big boy, 'fore I put ya in cage to cool off," Sheriff Milton sneered.

Ramrod shuddered, enraged. Then he stormed out of the room.

"Don't you think I know who did this to me?" Milo asked. But all hope had been drained from his voice. His four eyes were fixed on the floor.

Sheriff Milton stood up slowly to adjust the crotch of his ill-fitting kakis.

"What I think," he said, "is trauma makes an unreliable witness. We need *hard evidence* for charges to stick, and I'm sorry boys, but this film ain't it. It coulda been tampered with, coulda been edited. It's damn near *impossible* to say."

"But Super 8 cameras don't work that way," Milo pleaded. "I'll show you—"

Sheriff Milton interrupted Milo by clearing the phlegm from his throat.

"Tell ya what, son. I'll ship the film and this yearbook here to the FBI office in Jax. They got fancy thing-a-ma-do's that can match these pictures to the boys in that movie. If they are who ya say they are, we'll bring 'em in and put 'em down."

"We aren't leaving that film," I snapped.

"I'm afraid ya have to. It's evidence in an active investigation. But don't fret fellas, this case is our top priority. I've got my best man on it, right Wilcox?"

Deputy Wilcox burped loudly, then walked into the hall.

———

I left the station with my head hung in defeat. When I looked up, I saw Lewis seething near the crosswalk. His T-shirt was damp with perspiration. I could see the cuff of his letterman jacket sticking out from the corner trash can he'd stuffed it in.

Milo noticed it, too. He was nearly in tears again.

When Lewis walked over, neither of us said a word about it.

"I think I need a drink," he groaned.

"I think I'm too nauseous," Milo replied.

I looked down the street, in the direction of the ocean.

"Come on," I said, "I know what'll make us feel better than that."

———

My strawberry cone was melting by the time we got under the boardwalk. It was low tide, and the shadow of the pier stretched a thousand feet. I put the projector on a rock to keep it from getting wet. I was sticky with sweat and sugar, and had to admit to myself that the ice cream didn't help me a bit.

But at least Ramrod had cooled off a little. He chomped down the last of his sugar cone, and then wiped his dirty hands on his pants before placing them on Milo's shoulders.

"I'm sorry I wasn't more help."

"It's OK, man," Milo said. He even forced a smile.

"Nah," Lewis mumbled, "it ain't. I'm supposed to be the

head of the team. I'm supposed to keep those guys in line. I'm supposed to . . . I was supposed to look out for you, man. I shoulda at least been more help in there, but I freaked. I'm sorry."

"It wouldn't have mattered, anyway," I sighed. "I shoulda seen it sooner. The millworkers voted Sheriff Milton into office, so *no way* he'll crusade for the daughter of the guy that laid them off. Even if the evidence is right in front of him."

"But they can't *ignore* it," Lewis said. "They can't pretend it didn't happen!"

"Sure they can," Milo said. "Everyone ignores what's happening in 'Nam, in Memphis, in D. C. This won't be any different. No one cares."

"Piss on that," Lewis growled. "I wanna hear Marty make fun of your glasses after I rip out his eyes. I wanna hear Stink talk his racist shit once I turn his fuckin' skin inside out."

I hate to admit that part of me was excited by his threats. Part of me wanted blood. But the softer, saner, side of my brain knew what I wanted didn't matter.

"No," Milo said, as if reading my mind. "That's not what Hana would want. She'd say revenge is for assholes, or somethin' like that."

Ramrod deflated. He knew Milo was right.

"But we've gotta do *something*," I said.

Milo tossed his cone. He knew I was right.

The three of us stood silent. I leaned against a barnacle-covered post. Milo winced as he sat down beside the projector. Lewis peered into the horizon. The question of what to do drifted between us in the rhythm of the waves. I shut my eyes and let my mind roll with the tide. I thought of the weeks I spent walking that shoreline, waiting for my ears to heal . . .

"We can't get justice," Lewis sighed, "we can't even get revenge."

"Poetic justice!" I said suddenly. "Maybe we can at least get that."

"What do you mean?" Milo asked.

I walked over to him. Ramrod joined me.

"Once," I said, "Hana told me she wanted to blow the ears out of an entire senior class. If she could disqualify a whole school from the war, she was sure other kids would be inspired to do the same thing."

"You're saying *we* do that?" Lewis asked.

"That's *exactly* what I'm saying. It'd be a double-whammy, man! How many times have you heard Stink talk about goin' to Vietnam? We wouldn't just be keeping our classmates safe, we'd be royally screwing those sons-of-bitches!"

"Revolt turned payback by default," Milo smiled. "That sounds like Hana."

I sat down on the rock beside him. I put my arm around his small shoulders.

"It's not revolt," I said, "not activism or payback. This is Best Friend Shit."

Ramrod's shadow covered us. He nodded boldly. "Let's do it."

"For The Vinyl Underground." Milo nodded back.

I squeezed him close to my side.

It was Best Friend Shit, all the way.

SIDE

D

"Today's pig is tomorrow's bacon!"

—Hunter S. Thompson

nineteen

KING MIDAS IN REVERSE

Once we agreed on the idea, we had to actually make a plan. For the first time in our lives, we could say that we really did our homework—it was how we stayed connected to Hana, who'd become something of a ghost. She never returned to school. She never returned our calls. Whenever we went over to her house, we were turned away.

Still, we tried our best to stop the circle from breaking. The three of us darkened her door every Thursday night, records in hand. We didn't expect her to hang out with us, but she needed to know that we tried. Her parents were gracious rejecters—*She isn't up to company yet. Hana needs time to herself. Hana needs to be, wants to be, demands to be left alone*—and once we were denied, we would go to my brother's bedroom and continue working on our plan.

The more we talked about it, the more I liked it—not only would we be saving our classmates from the threat of war, but we'd be throwing a wrench in the lives of Hana's assailants. It was a *big* idea though, and big ideas tend to involve tons of small, but important, details.

For instance—there were 132 kids in our senior class, at least half of whom would be caught up in the draft after graduation. But we couldn't exactly invite them all to the theater, so we had to figure out a way to bring the theater to them. Our school auditorium was the most logical space. There was no seating on the main floor, and there was a balcony we could utilize. So there was plenty of room to fit all the seniors inside, but only one viable opportunity for us to pull it off: senior prom.

THE VINYL UNDERGROUND
OPERATIVE BLUEPRINT

CLASSIFIED: TOP SECRET

LOCATION: Cordelia High School Auditorium, Senior Prom

OBJECTIVE: Blow the ears out of Cordelia High's Graduating Class of 1968, disqualifying them from the draft, saving their lives, and royally fucking over Stink Wilson, Marty Houston, Bill Margaret, Ernest Thorogood, and Franklin Buckley.

ESSENTIAL MISSION MATERIALS:

- Coach Bingham's keys to the school
- The Royal Atlantis speaker system
- Transportation for sound equipment
- A prom committee insider informant
- Three baseball bats
- Two bicycle chains
- One record player
- One totally righteous record

MISSION OUTLINE: EVE OF THE SENIOR PROM

1.) Milo will pretend the speaker system in Viewing Room

3 needs repair. The speakers will then be loaded into Mr. Dori's work van, along with all the speakers in the storage room of the Royal Atlantis. The combined systems emit 170 dB of sound, loud enough to blow the ears out of the students and chaperones.

2.) The day before the prom, Ronnie will steal his father's work keys and replace them with a dummy set of keys. After their shift at the Royal Atlantis, Milo and Ronnie will drive the speaker system to the cafeteria loading dock, located in the alley behind the school.

3.) The Vinyl Underground will enter through the cafeteria, and then place the speaker systems around the auditorium for maximum impact.

4.) A base camp will be set up on the second-floor balcony, overlooking the auditorium. There, they will set up the record player and secure the two largest speakers facing the crowd at an angle by chaining them to the front-row pews.

5.) All speakers will be wired to the record player and camouflaged.

MISSION OUTLINE: NIGHT OF THE SENIOR PROM

1.) Confirm timetable with prom court—currently, prom court crowning ceremonies are expected to take place at 11 p.m.

2.) Ramrod will attend the prom, so not to draw suspicion from the "popular kids." Milo and Ronnie will again sneak through the cafeteria, and then take the elevator to the second-floor balcony, overlooking the dance.

3.) At approximately 10:45 p.m., Ronnie and Lewis will

barricade the exits shut with baseball bats, like they did in *Attack of the Brain Eaters*, trapping everyone in the auditorium. This way, chaperone/teacher keys will be useless. 4.) At approximately 11 p.m., when they announce the king & queen dance, Milo will drop the needle. The Vinyl Underground will escape down the east stairwell as the senior class is blitzed, assaulted, and saved by rock-n-roll .

We had it all figured out—besides, of course, how we could get away with it. If we got caught we'd be expelled, at the very least. Plus, it wouldn't take much detective work to realize that I'd dodged the draft the exact same way. A dereliction of duty charge would put me in jail for who the hell knows how long.

I thought it was scary shit, but Milo seemed unfazed. He assured us he had the perfect cover, but he wouldn't give us any details. The not knowing made me crazy, and the closer we got to the prom the more panic attacks I suffered. If I didn't have marijuana, I swear I woulda ended up in the loony bin.

But I did, so I didn't. I just smoked my anxiety out. My nerves stayed even, in a functional sense, but the depression that had eased up after the fire began creeping back, waiting to corner me when I was alone and vulnerable.

Usually it was when I was smoking in my brother's car, gazing up at Hana's bedroom window. The blinds were never open, but I imagined her inside. It was then the depression would whisper:

How's the weather, Raspy Ronnie? Lonely, with a chance of being alone? Remember whose car this is? He's dead. He's gone.

Remember whose window that is? She's gone, too.

But you're still here. You're just fucking fine. Are you bad luck, or what? Raspy Ronnie, you're King Midas in reverse— everything you touch turns to shit! You're—

I'd turn the radio up until I drowned the voice out. I'd focus on the music and think about the good times we had in that room, the good times I had in that car with Bruce, and I'd tell myself to be brave. I'd tell myself to fight as hard as I could, as hard as I should. I'd turn the music up as loud as I had to and find peace in the fact that soon we'd crank it loud enough to penetrate Hana's fortress of solitude.

We'd crack the sky.

We'd shake the earth.

We'd rattle and roll it, too.

twenty

OUTSIDE THE GATES OF EDEN

Milo took care of almost all the set-up work. My main job was stealing the keys to the school from my dad. I overanalyzed the task, but then again things had finally cooled down with my family, and I wasn't eager to mess it up by fumbling my part in the mission and getting busted snatching my dad's things.

So every day I shadowed him, and every day he dropped his work keys and his house keys in the Marine Corps ashtray on his bedside table. There were six keys on the work ring, and a rubber shark keychain so he knew which set was which. All I needed to do was pull the old switcheroo—get a set of dummy keys to replace his and slide the shark keychain on them so he couldn't tell the difference. I'd have the entire weekend to switch them back before he'd need his keys again.

Still, stealing from him made me nervous. And messing up the plan made me nervous. And everything about the whole thing made me nervous, so I double and triple checked every day—and his keys never left the ashtray.

The Monday before prom, I had crept into my parents'

room to see if Dad's keys were in their place when Momma called to me from the foyer. "Ronnie!"

Her voice made me jump. I rushed out of their room and found her standing at the bottom of the stairs. She was smiling, bobbing eagerly in place.

"What is it, Momma?"

I walked down to meet her. She kept smiling. She handed me a white manila envelope.

I flipped it over. UNIVERSITY OF FLORIDA popped out at me in blue letters. I tore the top of the envelope and pulled out the first thing I touched. It was a letter printed on thick stock paper. A cartoon alligator grinned up at me. I heard Momma's breath catch.

"Dear Mr. Bingham," I read aloud, "congratulations on your athletic scholarship to the University of Florida for the Fall 1968 term."

Then she hugged me, smashing the acceptance letter between us. I felt lightheaded and overwhelmed. Momma let me go. She took the envelope from me and pulled out a school brochure with a class catalog.

"Accounting! Agriculture! Anatomy! Art!" she read aloud, punctuating each one like she was shocked the subject was offered. "Biology! Civics! Civil Engineering!"

While Momma scanned the schedule, depression whispered in my mind: *Disc Jockeying, West Coast Wandering, Dead Sibling Dream Fulfillment—see any of those in your fancy college schedule, Raspy Ronnie?*

Momma let the paperwork fall to her side. She was out of breath.

"There's so many choices!" she said, chest heaving. "It's overwhelming."

"You're tellin' me," I sighed.

———

I was high above the stars, looking down on them all. The prom committee spent Thursday afternoon hammering, cutting, stringing, and toiling away. I saw veins pop out of a boy's forehead when he hoisted the giant moon over the corner of the stage. I watched sweat trickle down a girl's brow as she cut out symmetrical stars.

I was on the balcony of the auditorium with Milo.

I leaned on the railing and watched them decorate for the dance. The theme of the evening was *A Night Beneath the Stars*, and dozens of cardboard constellations had been wrapped in aluminum foil and hung from the ceiling with fishing wire. Silver, blue, and white streamers were taped along the walls and around the doors. The large, silver moon floated above the DJ booth.

Milo paced the center row of the balcony. He rubbed his chin with his free hand, like a beat-to-shit version of *The Thinker*. After nine or ten laps, he stopped—he nodded to himself, seemingly satisfied with whatever he'd just thought up.

"OK," he said, as he came to the railing, "here's what I'm thinking. We'll put the turntable and the receiver here, and we'll set the two main speakers *here*. Our bicycle chains should be strong enough to secure 'em to the back of this bleacher."

He patted the top of the very first bench. I gave him a thumbs-up.

"We'll hide the bass amps *there*," he said, pointing under the stage, "behind the grating, facing this direction. We'll run the other speakers *there, there, there,* and *there,* right down the sides of the room. That'll make a wall of sound loud enough to blow Phil Spector's fuckin' wig off."

Suddenly, the balcony doorknob gave an amplified *click*—both Milo and I jumped. I spun around instinctively, expecting to see a teacher or, even worse, my dad, but it was only Lewis. He eased the door shut behind him.

"Sorry I'm late," he said.

"It's all right," Milo told him. "We're talkin' about speaker positioning."

"I wanna hear all about it, but *first*, I've got news."

"Yeah?" I asked.

"Bethill Baptist offered me one of their scholarships, man! I can't believe it, I really can't—it's enough to cover two semesters at Gulf Coast State in PCB!"

"Lewis," Milo smiled, "that's *amazing*!"

"I know! And I'm so relieved I don't gotta blow out my ears. If I messed up my hearing permanently, I'd be worthless on the field. But now, if I get my grades up, I can walk onto the team, maybe even get a second scholarship to play ball."

I didn't mention my own scholarship offer. If I decided to go to college, Milo would no longer have a West Coast traveling companion. So I needed to make up my mind before I laid any of it on him.

"I'm so happy for you, man," I told Lewis. "You really deserve it."

"Thanks, Ronnie."

"Hold up," Milo said, "if we get busted for this, you might lose your scholarship. Maybe you should sit it out, Lewis."

I gulped cartoonishly. He was right.

Ramrod stood silent for a moment, considering this.

"Well," he finally said, "we're not gonna get busted, are we?"

"No," Milo said confidently.

"Cool." He shrugged. "Then catch me up on the plan."

You can be brave if he's being brave, I assured myself. I almost meant it.

"The plan's the same," Milo said, "unless there was a change on your end."

"Nope," Lewis said. "I asked Beth again the other day, and she told me the crowning ceremony will be at 11 p.m. If the head of the prom committee don't know, then we'll be doin' guesswork either way."

"Let's assume Beth knows," Milo nodded. "Those two doors *there* lead to the hallway, and that door *there* is the emergency exit, which opens onto the veranda. You and Ronnie barricade them during the prom court announcements, and then we meet back up here. If everything goes accordingly, we should be able to start the music and get the hell outta here before anyone grasps what happened."

"But even if we make a clean getaway," I said, "all the equipment will still be here. How are we gonna explain that?"

"I told you not to sweat it," Milo groaned. "I'll worry about all that."

I scoffed.

"*Trust me,*" he urged. "I got it covered like a towel around Brigitte Bardot. It's just better if y'all don't know the details yet, that's all."

He sounded more confident than Lewis and I, so we both went along.

"OK," I sighed. "Then is there anything else we should go over?"

"Just my camera placement. I think I'll hide it near the back exit, where the wrestling mats are stored. That way, everyone will be running *toward* the lens—"

"Wait," Lewis said, "you're not really filming it?"

"Of course I'm filming it. I need it for my movie."

"Woah, woah, man, I—"

"*Don't worry,* I'm not gonna document what *actually* happens. I just wanna show the important part, that a freak rock-n-roll occurrence kept an entire school out of the war."

"Freak rock-n-roll occurrence." Lewis grinned.

"I do like the sound of that," I admitted.

"Good," Milo said. "That reminds me, did either of you choose a song?"

"I figured we'd use the same one as last time," Lewis shrugged.

"I'm still thinking about it," I said, "I'll come up with somethin' righteous."

"Just pick one already," Milo huffed. "The prom's on Saturday!"

"We know," I groaned, "we know, we know."

"If *you know*, then get it figured it out! And make sure the jam's rockin' enough to bring the fuckin' house down."

———

Thursday night. 7 p.m.
Be there, or be squarer than square.

It was 7:17. It was the first Thursday that the three of us hadn't shown up on Hana's porch. Our weekly statement of solidarity felt pointless that night. The prom was forty-eight dwindling hours away—we'd be making our real statement soon enough.

So instead of the record club meeting, I sat in my bedroom and toiled over my *Profiles in Courage* term paper. It wasn't going well. I couldn't concentrate.

I finally gave up on working, and started to look at the brochures that came with my college acceptance letter. They stressed me out instantly, and it was too early to get stoned, so I put them away before my anxiety kicked into gear.

I stood up and stretched. Then I looked out my window—at her window—and wondered if she wondered why I hadn't darkened her door. I wondered if she ever got that internship with the *Chicago Tribune.* I wondered if she would really go to Vietnam as a correspondent.

She hadn't mentioned it to Milo. Lewis didn't know jack, either.

"Like that means anything," I scoffed at myself.

Then I walked across the hall to Bruce's bedroom to look for a song we could use at the prom. I hadn't spent much time in there since the fire. The weight of the room remained, as did the significance of everything in it, but the seal had been broken on that horrible night, and now it wasn't the same.

Oh well, I thought, as I ran my hand over his 45s, *at least there's still magic in the songs.* I flipped through his singles, sticking to the rock-n-roll section. I knew genre didn't matter as long as the volume was dialed in, but it didn't seem right to blow out eardrums to Peter, Paul, and Mary. So I flipped through the vinyls until I narrowed it down to two options—"My Generation" by The Who, or "Wild Thing" by The Troggs. Milo and Lewis could choose between them.

"Wild Thing" didn't scream *revolution* the way "My Generation" did, but it reminded me of Marlon Brando and motorcycle jackets . . . and Hana.

Hana in black leather—a revolution unto herself.

I pulled out the two singles, and then the vinyl in the next row caught my eye. It was the B side of "Like a Rolling Stone," a song called "Gates of Eden."

The sight of it made me weak. I was suddenly desperate to talk to my brother and ask him for advice. I shook the sadness off. I took the prom night 45s into my room and sat them on my dresser so I wouldn't forget 'em.

Then, without forethought, I ripped a piece of paper from my notebook, grabbed a pencil, and walked back across the hall to his bedroom. I took the Bob Dylan single off the shelf. I held it to my chest like a familiar heart.

I flipped his stereo back on. The speakers *popped,* surprised to be revived. I placed the adapter on the center of the turntable, and then set the speed to 45rpm.

I took the single out of the sleeve.

I sat it on the turntable, B side up.

I dropped the needle, and let it spin.

The acoustic guitar came strumming in hard. Bobby sang the way Bobby sings, with a weary rage that only otherworldly omnipotents like him find a way to impart. I flattened the piece of notebook paper on the floor.

I began to write.

Hana,

Usually, this is where Bruce would ask, "How's the weather, Raspy Ronnie?"

I wish I couldn't answer the question. I wish I couldn't walk outside and check. I wish I was too busy doing what I should be doing right now—listening to records with you and Milo and Lewis, geeking out and jiving and vibing and laughing and talking. That's why I chose the song "Gates of Eden," because that's how it felt when we were up there together, safe from the dangers of this terrible bullshit world.

I wish I knew what to say to you. I'm no good at this. I hate what they did to you. I hate it so, so, so, so much. I hate that I wasn't there for you again, and that I can't be there for you now.

But I understand you not wanting to see anyone. I wouldn't either, and don't expect you too. I'm only writing to ask you to open your window on Saturday night at 11 p.m. That's the night of senior prom, if you didn't know.

You see, now that The Vinyl Underground's fearless leader is MIA, all we know to do is fulfill the battle plan she laid out for us: AKA we're gonna blow the ears out of every graduating senior at the fucking school! We're gonna make them all 4-F, and we're gonna do it just like last time, with a killer song. I can't choose between "My Generation" and "Wild Thing," but keep an ear out for one or the other.

If you hear it, it means we brought your protest vision to fruition. If not . . . well, I just hope I don't chicken out. That's one of the reasons I wish I was with you right now; you're the bravest person I know, your courage fucking radiates off you and seeps into the pores of everyone around you. I sure could use some of that spare bravery right now. You're gonna have to bottle it for me, because I'm not sure how I'm gonna decide what to do next year without it.

That's right, I got into FSU. I still can't believe it. I haven't told Milo, or anyone else—I just don't know if it's

what I want . . . See, I'm not even brave enough to make
up my mind without your input! God, respecting your opinion
so much is a pain in the ass.

I miss you a ton. Not just for your brains, or guts. I
miss you 'cause you're Hana, and my world is a drag without
you in it. But anyway, enough cheese. Give Bobby a spin,
smoke a J if you have one. You aren't required to think of
me while you do, but if you happen to I won't mind.

Fuck the draft. Fuck 'em all.

—Ronnie

———

Hana's mother opened the door. She smiled.

"I began to think you wouldn't come tonight, Ronnie.
Though I'm sorry to say that Hana still isn't—"

"She's not up for company, I know. But would you give her
this?" I handed her the 45. The red label was partially covered
by my letter. She looked down at it, confused.

"Of course," she said graciously. "Will there be anything
else?"

"Just tell her the B side's the sad one, and that the sad ones
are the truth."

twenty-one

TOY SOLDIERS

Friday I was nothing but nerves. I wanted that stupid school day *done with* already. I couldn't walk to class without passing the auditorium, the sight of which made my guts do backflips. To make things more annoying, a dozen or so of the popular kids were on a last-ditch campaign for prom court, so the building was plastered with signs and paper banners.

When the final bell finally rang, I was the first one out of my calculus class. But my stride was stunted because the election day rush had the hallway more clogged than usual. I was stuck behind a line of swing voters being pandered to by Margret Jones, the frontrunner for prom queen, who was handing out free cookies.

"Hey! Ronnie!" she called.

I used it as excuse to push through the line. She smiled when I approached.

"Just remindin' you to vote for me," she said, handing me a cookie. "If you've already voted for someone else, there's still time to change your ballot."

"Nah, you've got my vote."

I bit into the cookie—*chocolate chip and raisins*—and tried to keep the combo down. Then, suddenly, Stink Wilson shoved through the crowd and wrapped his arm around Margret's shoulders.

I took a step back. My mind went whiteout clear. I hadn't seen Stink since wrestling season ended. I hadn't seen the bastard since he did what he did.

"You don't need to beg losers like him for votes," he sneered. "You're a shoe in, babe."

Margret blushed. I tossed the cookie onto the ground.

"What's wrong," Stink snickered, "jealous of my date? Don't worry, I'm sure you and your dweebie little boy-toy Milo will make an *adorable* couple."

A ticker tape of words ran across my mind:

. . . IF YOU HIT . . . PUNCH . . . KILL HIM . . . IT WILL BE RUINED . . .

I gritted my teeth and wrung my hands tight enough to draw blood.

But I didn't punch him.

"I want you to remember calling him a dweeb," I said.

"What was that, traitor? I couldn't hear ya."

"Don't worry," I said louder, "you will."

———

"I still can't believe my boy isn't goin' to prom," Dad said again. He steered the car onto our block. My knees twitched—it was almost time to swipe his keys, and I was anxious as hell.

"I just think it's dumb."

"Well, yeah, of course it's dumb. But it's *the prom*. I'll never forget *my* senior prom. I took Bettie Green. Man oh man, was she a looker! She wore a pale blue dress, and we won a dance contest to 'Texarkana Baby.' I still remember the way that dress matched the back seat of my old—"

"Ugh. Gross, Dad."

He laughed as he pulled up to the house. He killed the engine and nodded toward Hana's place. "It's about her, isn't it?"

"Nah," I said, "it's not about her. It's about everyone else."

———

Dad went into his bedroom to take a nap after work. The nap deviated from his normal routine—not much, but enough to get me sweating. I got the dummy keys from my stashbox where I'd stored them. The keys were six random spares from our kitchen junk drawer, but once I slid on Dad's shark keychain, he'd never know the difference.

I pressed my ear to the door and waited to hear his gait on the stairs. Five minutes passed. Sweat beaded along my hairline. Twenty minutes passed. I tried to relax, to remind myself that this wasn't *Mission Impossible* or anything.

Dad's footfalls on the stairs! Go!

No. Not yet.

I forced myself to wait. I counted *5, 4, 3, 2, 1* to be sure he'd made it past the foyer. Then, finally, I opened my door and rushed across the hall. I moved into their bedroom with my sights laser-focused on the keys in the ashtray.

I grabbed them. I slid off the stupid plastic shark and put it on my dummy keychain. I sat the dummy keys in the ashtray. I put Dad's keys in my back pocket.

"Ronnie?" Dad said from behind me.

I jumped like a wet cat on a subway rail. My head and eyes spun out of sync as I whirled around to face him. He was standing in the doorway, totally confused.

"Uh, hey," I stammered, "I was just seein' if Momma left my clean underwear in here. She was supposed to wash 'em, and, uh—"

"Your underwear aren't in here, Ronnie."

"Oh."

"You have a phone call downstairs. It's your boss."

"Ah, OK. Thanks."

If he was wise to what I'd done, he didn't show it. So I followed him downstairs, my core vibrating with cautious optimism. I picked the phone off the kitchen counter.

"Hello?"

"Ronnie," Mr. Dori said, "can you come in early tonight? The sound system in Viewing Room 3 blew again, and the speakers need to go in for repairs. I'd have Milo deal with it, but his arm—"

"Of course, Mr. Dori. Let me throw on my uniform and I'll head down."

"Good man, Ronnie, good man."

I hung up the phone. In my mind, I heard the sound of gears shifting.

Now we're rolling!

"Bang! Bang!" Roy yelled from the living room.

I turned and followed the noise. Roy had six toy soldiers spread across the killing fields of our shag carpet. Four of them lay on their side or back—obviously dead. Roy held the other two, and was impaling one with the extended bayonet of the other.

I got down on the floor beside him.

"Aren't they on the same side?" I asked.

"Bang!" he squealed again, tossing the impaled soldier onto his back.

"Guess not."

"Bye-bye," Roy giggled, as he smashed the surviving soldier onto the fresh corpse of the other. "Bye-bye-bye-bye-bye-bye!"

Then Roy slid the little green soldier around and around in circles. He was trying to say something through his laughter, but it was hard to make out. I thought he was asking me to get him something to drink.

"You want your juicey?" I asked.

"*Boosey!*" he cried, frustrated, "Boosey! Boosey!"

It hit me like a hammer to the throat—*Boosey. Brucie.* Bruce. That was what he used to call Bruce. I hadn't been sure he *remembered* Bruce anymore, let alone the military fatigues he wore in the photos he sent home.

"That's right, buddy!" I said. I touched the top of the army man's helmet. "Bruce was a soldier, just like this guy!"

"Wa Boosey," he said, staring up at me with his big little-kid eyes. I wasn't sure if he was saying *where*, or *want*, or, well, who knows. Both amounted to the same disappointing response.

I cleared my throat. "You know Bruce—*Boosey*—he isn't here anymore, buddy. But he's—"

Suddenly, Roy threw the toy soldier across the room. It slid beneath the television. He began laughing all over again.

"Bye-bye, Boosey!" He giggled. "Bye-bye-bye-bye Boosey! Bye-bye!"

———

Viewing Room 3 had a sign taped on the door—Closed for Repairs. I ducked inside, holding two vinyls in one hand and a bike chain in the other. The overhead lights were on, and every inch of the room looked sticky. Milo was up front, trying to unlatch the compartment beneath the stage. I sat my things down and pulled Dad's keys from my pocket.

I held them behind his left ear and started jingling.

He whirled around fast as a carnival ride.

"You got 'em!"

"Oh yeah," I nodded, "I got 'em."

He patted me on the shoulder proudly, and then stepped aside so I could pull the speaker compartment open. It took me four hard pulls, but the grating finally gave, screeching as a cloud of dust rose around us.

"Jesus," I gagged, "when's the last time this was cleaned?"

"A week before never," he coughed.

Milo crawled beneath the stage and disconnected the wiring. He shimmied out the way he'd gone in, and then brushed his dirty hands on his pants. His glasses looked like they'd been tinted with chimney soot.

"All right," he said, clearing his throat, "pull her out."

"By myself? It's huge!"

"I'd help ya, but I'm supervising." He lifted his cast for effect.

I rolled my eyes, and then worked the speaker out from under the stage.

"God," I wheezed, "this is the biggest speaker I've ever seen."

"Wait until you see the ones behind the screen! Now come on, let's load her up. Mr. Dori has the work van parked behind the fire exit."

I lugged the speaker across the carpet and into the side-stage foyer. Milo held the doors open, and I dragged it onto the sidewalk. The Econoline van sat waiting, white and windowless, covered in dead bugs and bird shit.

"This thing must weigh a ton," I panted, leaning on the speaker.

"Just 120 pounds. But the bigger ones weigh 370 pounds each."

Milo unlocked and opened the back doors of the van. "Now you just gotta lift it in," he said.

I let out an exhausted laugh. He patted me on the back. I felt his finger splints *tip-tap-tip-tap-tip-tap* on my spine.

"Hup-two, soldier. We've got seven more speakers to go."

———

Everything seemed different in the shadows. I crept the halls of Cordelia High, fascinated by the alien vibe the building had in the dark. It felt strange being inside the school at night, but the sense of unease was also thrilling.

It was well past midnight, and we were waiting on Lewis to show. I'd gotten all the speakers into the van by myself, but now I was sore and exhausted. I'd need his help to unload them and get them where they needed to go.

We'd been waiting for over an hour.

When I first pulled the van to the loading bay, part of me wasn't sure Dad's keys would work. But both locks on the aluminum door clicked open, and I coasted the van into the cafeteria stockroom. It was that easy to get inside the school.

Milo and I handled the small jobs that needed doing. I unlocked every door on our route to the auditorium—*out the kitchen, through the cafeteria, into the hallway, and into the auditorium*—and to the balcony—*through the kitchen, up the service elevator, down the second-floor hall, through the concourse, onto the balcony*—while Milo went to get three baseball bats from the gym storage room.

As I headed back to the stockroom to meet him, I stopped at one of the many trophy cases that lined the halls. Here was a photo of my brother and my dad, standing together. Bruce was in his wrestling singlet, holding a trophy. Dad stood beside him, smiling proudly. It was taken just after he won county finals.

"I wish I woulda done this sooner," I whispered. "I'm sorry, man."

But his eyes had no trace of regret or resignation.

His eyes said he made his own fate.

I touched the glass, then went back to the stockroom to wait for Lewis. Milo was already there. I found him digging through a storage fridge. When he came up for air, he was holding two cartons of chocolate milk.

"Hey," he said, tossing me one, "what do ya think Hana's doin' right now?"

"Beats me," I shrugged.

The tab of the milk carton was stuck, and I had to rip it open with my teeth.

"When you were workin' on your movie," I asked, "did she ever say anything about wanting to go to Vietnam herself? Like, to report on the war?"

"Not to me."

I nodded. I drank down the entire carton.

"What gives?" he asked.

I figured I might as well tell him. "When you guys were in the hospital, I talked to Hana's dad. He told me she's up for an internship at the *Chicago Tribune*. She'd be working with the foreign correspondents. When we're at war, 'foreign correspondent' means *war* correspondent. Those reporters go to 'Nam, man."

"Holy shit," Milo muttered.

"Do you *really* think she'd do that? You think she'd go to

Vietnam after everything that's happened? Just for her writing career?"

"I doubt it. She's wild, but she's not crazy . . . well, actually—"

"She can't!" I stammered. "I—*we*—can't let her go there, man."

"I agree," he nodded, "but how do we talk her outta somethin' if she won't speak to us? We've gotta give her space. And when she *does* wanna talk, let her be the one to bring this stuff up. She's been through hell, and she doesn't need us on her case about anything, even Vietnam. You dig what I'm saying?"

"Yeah," I groaned, "I dig."

Suddenly, Milo froze. "Do you hear something?" he whispered.

I concentrated. The hum of the industrial freezer made it almost impossible to hear the pounding on the hallway door that led outside.

"That must be Lewis, right?" I mumbled.

"Has to be," he nodded.

The knock came again, louder.

"Totally definitely must be," Milo said. "Let's go check."

We each picked up a Louisville Slugger before we moved into the hall. A figure loomed beyond the thin pane of glass on the door. I gripped the bat tighter. We crept forward.

Lewis smiled at us through the glass.

Milo and I both sighed. I unlocked the door and let him in.

"Sorry I'm late."

"It's cool," Milo said. "Not like we're doin' a bunch of illegal shit. No rush."

Ramrod chuckled. I locked the door and we headed back to the cafeteria.

"You think this is really illegal?" I asked.

"*Hmm,* let's see," Milo mocked, "if we forget about the breaking and entering part, we've still got dereliction of duty—and robbery, for taking the speakers—and auto theft, attempted assault, probably, since someone's eardrums could bust—"

"Probably kidnapping, too," Ramrod added.

"Jesus. Forget I asked."

Our footfalls echoed the lay of the land, as it changed from stucco flooring to cafeteria tile.

"Look!" Milo said. He pointed to a dolly in the corner of the room.

"Thank God," I said, "I can't carry those speakers another inch."

Milo stepped onto the dolly, and Lewis grabbed the handles. He rolled Milo into the kitchen, through to the storage area, and to the van. When I caught up with them, Lewis had already unloaded one of the speakers. He lifted it onto the dolly like it was nothing. Milo grabbed a bike chain and a cinder block from the back.

"I thought y'all said these were heavy," Ramrod grinned.

I scoffed, then led them to the service elevator. I opened it with Dad's keys. Lewis rolled the speaker inside, and we all squeezed in.

I inserted the key and pressed 2.

As soon as we got to the second floor, Milo moved ahead of us. I helped Lewis balance the speaker as he pushed it toward the balcony. Milo was already there, holding the doors open— inside was only darkness.

"Take it to front row," he said.

"Aren't there lights?" Lewis asked.

"I couldn't find a switch," he shrugged.

"I'll bet it's downstairs," I said. "Hold tight."

I jogged to the stairs and took them two at a time. I reached the auditorium in less than thirty seconds. I went through the door nearest to the stage. The three large bay windows of the auditorium made it surprisingly easy to see. The moonglow was bright enough for me to find the panel of switches along the wall.

I flipped every single switch ON.

The auditorium lit up like an amusement park.

The stage lights—filtered with blue and pink gels—were positioned facing the cardboard constellations dangling over the dance floor. The colors reflected off the tinfoil stars, creating beautiful sparkles of light.

I wished Bruce and Hana were there to see it.

But they weren't. So I went back upstairs.

I reached the balcony as Lewis lifted the speaker onto the front pew. He picked it straight up like a medicine ball and he held it in place while Milo situated the cinder block underneath it.

"OK," Milo said, "that's good."

As soon as Lewis sat the speaker down, Milo threaded the

bicycle chain through the handle and under the gap on the back of the bench. He hooked the chain shut, but he didn't lock it. The speaker leaned forward, forward . . .

But the bike chain held. It stopped the speaker at a perfect slant, nearly eye-to-eye with the front railing.

"I *knew* the chain would work," Milo said.

"How?" Lewis asked. He leaned on the railing to catch his breath.

Milo smacked the speaker. Lewis and I jumped out of the way reflexively.

It didn't budge.

"Because," Milo grinned, "this fucker's American made."

————

It took three hours to get everything in place. Lewis and I did the heavy lifting. Milo hooked up the turntable, the receiver, and all the wiring. I had no clue how he rigged the speakers together, and I didn't bother asking. I just did my best to make sure none of it looked out of the ordinary.

The underside of the stage was hollow, so it was easy to hide the bass amps there. A little redecorating was all it took to hide the smaller speakers against the walls. We turned off the balcony lights, and then covered the switch with a strip of tape marked OUT OF ORDER.

Once we got all the speakers hooked up and camouflaged, Lewis and I climbed onstage to inspect our handiwork. I looked up to the balcony—it was completely blacked out. No one would be able to see us. I looked around the room.

"I don't think I'd be able to tell," I said.

"Me either"—Lewis nodded—"I think it looks good."

Then a familiar crackle filled the room—the sound of speakers powering on.

"Milo!" I yelled up to the balcony. "Don't turn that shit on!"

"Get out on the dance floor," he yelled back, "I gotta test the speakers!"

"Hell no!" Lewis yelled.

Milo leaned over the balcony railing, shadowed and annoyed.

"Calm down," he said. "I'm not even gonna turn the volume knob to *one*. But we've gotta make sure all the speakers are working. You know we do."

"What are you turnin' it up to?" I asked.

"Not even halfway to one."

"Do *half* of that half," Lewis said.

"OK." Milo nodded. "I'll put it at zero-point-two-five percent, cool?"

Lewis and I nodded hesitantly.

"Then get out there, y'all! It's closing time, last chance to dance!"

The two of us hopped off the stage. We nervously walked to the middle of the dance floor, where the stars above were the brightest. The speakers called out to us with the itchy sound of a needle running onto a record.

Then sound came from all directions.

"Shit," Lewis said, and covered his ears.

Milo was spinning The Troggs B side, a love song called "A Girl Like You."

Even with the volume knob at 0.25 percent, the music was loud enough to be *loud*. The drums were their own miniature marching band. The singer's sneer came from every corner, and it was fully enveloping. It made me feel like I was pressed *inside* the wax, like I was a part of the whole thing. The surround sound sensation was overwhelming, but at least it wasn't loud enough to hurt.

Lewis lowered his hands from his ears.

"It's not even cranked to *one*?" he yelled. "It's loud as hell!"

I nodded.

"It's gonna work, Ronnie!"

I nodded again, and then sang in a mock melody, "I wanna blow the ears out of this school, ba ba ba ba-bah, ba ba ba-ba."

Lewis laughed. I laughed. The music rocked. The music rolled.

Milo came down to join us.

"What a lame party," he shouted. "If you squares won't dance, I guess I will!"

A grin spread beneath his glasses, and he began to do the Twist—the slow soul twist—using his plaster arm to guide his hips like a rudder. He sang the "ba-bah" backups as he danced.

"Ba ba ba ba-bah," Lewis bellowed, and started dancing around with Milo. His moves were surprisingly graceful. I laughed and joined in.

I did the Mashed Potato. Lewis twisted, twisted, twisted the night away.

We were really doing it. It was actually going down.

My buddies and I danced freely. The stars above took on a strange, magical luster, as shiny and fake as the innocence they'd been strung up in honor of.

But that didn't matter while the song played.

What mattered was it was working.

What mattered was we were doing it.

What mattered was we were.

twenty-two

THE BIG FUCK YOU

"**R**unnin' late for work?" Momma asked.

As far as she knew, I was on my way to the theater.

"Nah, our schedules are messed up 'cause a viewing room's closed."

"You shoulda just gone to the dance," Dad said, his eyes glued to the TV.

"I'm surprised you're not a chaperone, Dad, if you think so highly of it."

"No need," he said, "I've already got my queen right here."

Momma smiled. Dad didn't turn away from the *Newlywed Game*.

"Can't argue with that," I said. "See y'all after work."

I kissed Momma on top of the head, waved bye-bye to Roy, and petted Wolfie on the floor. On my way out the door I grabbed my backpack, which held a button-up shirt, jacket, and tie—my camouflage for the dance—and my birthday bottle of Old Crow, which had been too gross to finish.

I made sure Dad's keys were in my pocket, then walked

onto the porch. A soft breeze picked up from the east, and I was thankful for it. When I got nervous I tended to sweat, and I was already sweating bullets. I wiped my brow and strolled down the steps, pausing for a moment to gaze up at Hana's window.

The window was closed. The shades were drawn.

So I hustled across my yard and into Milo's. His mom was working the night shift, so we were gonna lay low at his place until it was time to rock-n-roll. Lewis was already at the school— he was the only member of The Vinyl Underground *attending* the dance, because his absence would raise suspicions. He was also working recon, so if something went wrong before we got there he was to wait for us in the alley behind the school. If everything ran smoothly, we were set to meet on the balcony at 9:30.

As I cut into Milo's backyard, I laughed; it had slipped my mind that Lewis took Lena Mills as his date! After trying to hit Hana with her baton at the pep rally, Lewis couldn't resist squiring that bigotous bitch onto ground zero himself. I hopped up Milo's stoop and rapped on the back door.

No answer.

I looked through the dining room window—Milo was in the kitchen, talking on the phone. The sleeve of an unbuttoned dress shirt was pulled up his good arm, but the rest was draped over his cast like a dishtowel. He was pacing anxiously.

I tapped on the window. He stuck up an annoyed finger—*wait*.

So I slid off my backpack and took out the bottle of whiskey.

I had myself a pull, just enough to steady the nerves. Then the door opened.

"Sorry," Milo said, waving me inside.

"You OK? You looked pretty frazzled just now."

"Method acting," he grinned.

"What's that mean?"

"Let's go upstairs," he said, ignoring me. "I wanna show ya some of the footage I've edited together for the short film I'm working on."

I passed him the bottle. He took a nip, and we trampled up the stairs.

"You think that shirt's gonna fit around your cast?"

"No," he groaned, shutting his bedroom door behind us.

"So much for blending in."

"Don't count me out yet," he said, and flipped on his projector.

He turned off the lights and we sat side by side on the floor.

"I want your *honest* opinion, OK?"

I nodded. He nodded back, and loaded the film.

Then the flickering skeleton of the first Milo Novak movie came to life. No dialogue or music had been added yet, but the visuals alone were effective—beautifully, tragically so. Newsreel clips of the King assassination juxtaposed with war zone footage from Vietnam. He spliced shots of cheerleaders and surfboarders together with a local funeral service. He contrasted protest foot-age with us, The Vinyl Underground, hanging out, laughing, smoking, making asses of ourselves for the camera. The very last part was Hana, lots and lots of Hana.

We saw her dancing around in her bedroom, her wild hair flying free, then quick—*a half-second clip of Stink scalping her*—then Hana walking to school, smoking coolly, then quick—*Stink punching Hana*—then back to Hana—brave, beautiful, badass Hana, The Wild One personified.

As I felt the first hint of a tear sting my eyes, the reel flickered to a stop.

"Milo! That was . . . *damn*! That was incredible!"

"You think?" he asked.

When he turned the lights back on, I saw he was blushing.

"Yes! Holy shit, yes."

"Thanks," he smiled, "it's getting there. The footage tonight is what's gonna make or break it."

"It's already too good to screw up," I swore.

"We'll see," he muttered.

"That footage of Hana . . . when did the sheriff give it back?"

"Yesterday."

"Well, what'd the FBI say?"

"He claimed it was inconclusive, which means he never sent it."

I nodded slowly.

"Fuck him," he scoffed, "fuck 'em all! I'll have this film finished by July. Then we can take it out to L. A. and show some movie studios what I can do."

"We?"

"Yeah, *we*. If I'm gonna sneak it onto the desk of Hollywood bigshots, *someone's* gonna have to distract their secretaries for me. Plus, I figured you might wanna talk to radio station producers, stuff like that."

He slid off his dress shirt and tossed it next to me on the floor. I tried to do the math on first semester at FSU. If I went to California for the summer, I could still make it back before school started. Probably. Maybe.

"I'm in," I told him.

"Righteous! We can hitch to Chicago on our way back for the Democratic National Convention. Hana says it'll have the biggest anti-war protest in history."

"I dunno, man. That sounds like a lot."

"Just say you're in," he urged.

I thought about the draft exam, the movies, the fight. I thought about how I'd never deserved a friend like him at all. So I thought up a way to make it work, while avoiding bogging down the mood of our night with the college conversation.

"Roy's birthday's August 30th," I said. "As long as we're back by then, I'm in."

"*Woo-hoo!* We'll make it work! From rednecks to the red carpet, baby!"

I laughed apprehensively.

Milo got a blazer out of his closet and tossed it on the floor beside his shirt.

"Hold the right sleeve of the blazer out straight," he said.

Then he pulled a pair of shears from a pile of discarded film clippings.

"What are ya doin' with those?" I asked.

"Blending in with the crowd. It's just gonna take a little more effort on my part. It ain't easy being the only rose in an asshole parade."

"By any other name, my friend." I laughed, and did just as he asked.

————

We stuck to the alleyways.

We wore slacks, jackets, and ties—not tuxedos, but close enough. We'd altered Milo's outfit by cutting his shirt and blazer from the seam to the armpit so he could shove the cast through, and then rigged it together with electrical tape. At first glance, it was passable, but up close he looked like a broken toy whose replacement part didn't fit.

I held the bottle of whiskey. Milo held the Super 8. We walked cautiously, not in a hurry. Every few blocks, a car would race down the streets parallel to us—drunken classmates trying to get their dates revved-up and taking the phrase literally. We never quit moving forward, although my back would stiffen and my hands would grow clammy until the engines roared onto different avenues.

It wasn't until we reached Racine Street that we finally stopped.

"In through the loading bay," Milo recited.

"And out through the east stairwell, which I unlocked last night," I answered.

He gave a thumbs-up with his functioning thumb, and we got moving again. We crept slow as slugs to the edge of the alley. We were less than a block from the school.

"You gonna tell me the getaway plan now?" I asked. "Do we sneak back later and get the equipment, or—"

"No. Once we get out, don't stick around. The rest of the plan will take care of itself, I promise."

"That's reassuring," I scoffed.

"Tell ya what, Ronnie, if it doesn't work, you can break my other arm."

"Hell no. You'd be callin' me twice a day to come wipe your butt."

"Once a day, tops. The pain meds for my arm really clog my plumbing."

My animated grimace sent us both into a laughing fit. I took a drink to burn away my chuckles, and then passed Milo the bottle so he could do the same.

Then we got moving again. I could see the auditorium ahead of us—"The Beat Goes On" vibrated through the three large bay windows, which reflected blue and pink lights and gave the night a bubblegum sort of radiance. Cigarette tips brightened and dulled like fireflies on the veranda.

We moved closer. The next song the DJ spun was The Mamas and the Papas' version of "Dedicated to the One I Love."

Perfect timing. The smokers on the veranda tossed their cigarettes and hurried inside to slow dance. Anyone still outside
was too busy twisting tongues to notice us.

Milo looked at me. I looked at him.

"You ready?" I asked.

"As I'll ever be."

We walked forward. We kept our heads down and shoulders
high, and tried our best to seem nonchalant as we crossed onto
school grounds. We hugged the shadows as we made our way
toward the back of the building.

No one noticed us turn into the alley.

But then Milo clutched my wrist like a bear trap.

"*Look*," he whispered, nodding forward.

I squinted, then I saw the hunk of metal, low to the ground,
parked right across from the loading bay. A car, a Chevy, a
Camaro—Marty Houston's Camaro.

We hunched down. We kept against the wall. Watching.
Waiting.

Nothing.

"I don't think anyone's in it," I whispered.

Milo crab-walked to the car, and huddled beneath the
bumper.

Slowly, he made his way to the side window. I held my
breath.

He gave me another thumbs-up—*empty*.

I sighed with relief, and then we both hustled to the loading
garage. I pulled out Dad's keys and unlocked the door. I raised
it up just high enough for us to slip through.

Milo crawled under. I followed.

I lowered the door gradually, but it still *clanked* when it hit the floor.

We froze again . . . but there was nothing. No sound but the sweaty thump of my heart. I locked the door. Still nothing.

I got up and helped Milo to his feet. We stood in the dark for another moment, catching our breaths. Then we went through the cafeteria and crept into the deserted hallway. It only took us a few seconds to reach the service elevator.

I put the key in the elevator—the doors groaned open.

I pressed 2. The elevator doors closed.

We were safe.

"Out of all the places that asshole could have parked," I said.

"I know, man."

The elevator doors opened.

We made sure the coast was clear, and then headed toward the balcony. Once we were halfway down the empty hall, I spotted Lewis coming our way. He was walking fast, but he didn't seem nervous. He smiled his shiny championship smile.

"Ramrod, you dreamboat," Milo hollered, "ya look like 007!"

His massive frame was barely contained in the rented tuxedo he wore.

"Guess what we just saw in the alley," I said.

"Guess who I just saw *up here*!"

"Uh, who?" Milo asked.

"Our fearless leader is outta hiding."

"You mean Hana?" I stammered. "She's here?"

"Come on," Lewis said, "see for yourselves."

We walked to the balcony in a straight line like a French battalion.

"No one's noticed anything?" Milo asked.

"So far, so good," Lewis said.

"What about your date," I asked, "where's Lena?"

"With her girlfriends at Stink's table. Him and his buddies offered to share their flasks with 'em, I think. I'm not sure. I told her I wouldn't go over there."

"Forget her," I said.

"Forget who?" he grinned.

When we reached the doors of the balcony, my guts climbed into my throat. I couldn't believe Hana was here. Milo stepped forward and opened the doors. The music got louder. I squinted into the dark.

All I saw was a silhouette lounging in an aisle seat, watching the kids below slow dance to Frankie Valli's "Can't Take My Eyes Off of You." Then the shadowed spectator took a drag off a shadowed cigarette.

Hana. It really was her.

Milo didn't hesitate. He hobbled down the aisle to where she sat. He wrapped his good arm around her shoulders before she noticed we were there. She jerked back, startled, but then I heard her laugh.

When she stood up to hug him, the fake starlight brought her into focus—she wore her motorcycle jacket as always. Her once-illustrious hair now barely reached her ears, but the psychedelic shag gave her an even cooler vibe than before.

I approached slowly, as they held their long-suffered embrace. Their eyes were closed, as if they were having a discussion in which all words were wanting.

Then, suddenly, Hana's eyes shot open. They fixed on mine.

I cleared my throat as she let go of Milo and came toward me.

"Hey," she said, tossing her cigarette absently.

"Hana!" I said, with mock surprise. "For a second, I thought you were Audrey Hepburn."

"Fuck off," she said, and hugged me.

With her hair gone, I could feel the unblemished softness of her cheek. It hinted at vulnerability that I never imagined was there. I breathed that moment in, the leather and the smoke and the secret things buried beneath them.

"I'm kidding," I whispered. "Audrey Hepburn's got nothin' on you."

She laughed into my shoulder. It felt so good to hear that laugh.

So goddamn good.

"What are ya doin' here?" I finally asked.

"What do you think? I read your letter."

I blushed as she broke away.

"I can't let you guys go through with this," she said. "Not on my behalf."

"You can't?"

"Not if you're spinning a predictable song like 'Wild Thing,' I can't."

She unzipped her jacket and pulled out a single in a blank dust sleeve.

She handed the vinyl to me.

"This is the song, Ronnie. It's an advance promo copy, and it's not like *anything* the sheep downstairs have ever heard before. We've gotta play one they're unfamiliar with. *Only* the unfamiliar can shake a sheep up enough to jump outta the herd. If we wanna make a *real* statement, this is the song we do it with."

I slid the vinyl out of the dust sleeve.

Text was stamped on the label in dark-blue ink.

—MC5—
"KICK OUT THE JAMS"
PROMOTIONAL DEMONSTRATION PRESSING
FOR THE BROTHERS AND SISTERS OF MC5

"What's that?" Milo asked, joining us.

"The song Hana wants to use."

"Is it three minutes long?" he asked.

"3:17," she nodded.

"Then tonight is ladies' choice."

Below us, the DJ flipped to his next tune—"Hanky Panky." It was the *furthest thing* from unfamiliar. The crowd looked thankful for a dance they could do by the numbers. A blur of tuxedos and gowns hankied and pankied all around the room.

"Hey," Lewis called, "let's go out to the hall so we can talk."

We followed him up the aisle. Once we were in the hallway, it almost felt like a record club meeting. Now that the doors of the auditorium were closed, the prom was nothing but a program on an unwatched TV in another room.

We leaned on the lockers. I passed around the bottle. We tried to drink ourselves brave.

"Don't ya think Lena noticed you're missing?" I asked Lewis.

"Maybe," he said, removing his bow tie, "but Lena and her friends are more interested in drinkin' than dancin', anyway."

"I'd go dance with you if I could," Hana said.

She locked her arm through his as she took the bottle from his hand.

"Be careful what you wish for, girl," he said with a wink.

She laughed—God, she had the best laugh.

I couldn't stop looking at her. I knew I had been missing her, but Jesus, this was pathetic. I'd steal a glance of Hana—*her neckline is more visible now, delicately pulsing*—and turn away. Then steal another glance—*an apprehension in her eyes, a hesitation that was never there before*—and turn away. I knew I loved her in that inherent way you love a friend that you admire, but for the first time I realized my feelings might not be so stock; no "friend" had ever made me think the kind of cheesy-ass thoughts popping into my brain.

"I'm glad you're here," Milo told her. "None of us fuckers can cuss like you."

Her laugh tapered off, and her face grew flush. She took another drink.

"I'm glad, too," she said. "Sorry I shut you guys out. I've been having a really hard time. I keep getting these . . . *episodes,* I guess you'd call them . . . where I feel like I'm having a nightmare, except I'm awake. It's so freaky. They've made me too nervous to go *anywhere*, to talk to *anyone*. This is the first time I've left my fuckin' house in weeks. I almost turned around, too, until I saw Lewis in the stairwell."

She passed the bottle, but I didn't feel like another drink.

"That's so shitty," Lewis sighed. "Trapped in your head, trapped in your room. Damn. I'm sorry."

"It is what it is," she shrugged. "You find ways to pass the time. Mostly I was writing and packing."

Milo shot me a telepathic look—*Don't get on her case about Vietnam!*

I turned my eyes away from him.

"Aw man, you're moving?" Lewis moaned. "Say it ain't so!"

"Back to Chicago." She nodded. "My father has a few months left at the mill, but I can't stay here anymore. You guys know that I can't."

"I know," he sighed. "I understand." He took the bottle from me.

"But this is good news, believe it or not," she said. "One of my articles finally got traction, and the *Chicago Tribune* offered me an internship!"

"Hana," Milo gasped, feigning surprise, "and after all those rejections!"

She smiled, and I had to look away. It made me think of my brother's smile, locked in the glass trophy case downstairs. Her smile made me worried, but her excitement made me angry.

"I know! I wish you coulda filmed me when they called. I flipped my fuckin' lid! There's no better place for a blowhard writer like me than the Windy City."

"Does this mean we'll finally getta read your work?" he asked.

"We'll see."

"Best answer I could hope for," he said. "Me and Ronnie were talkin' about Chicago earlier, actually."

"Oh yeah?" she asked, looking to me.

"Yeah," I mumbled, suddenly as incapable of looking at her as I'd been to look away. "We were talking about going up for the convention—"

"Do it!" she blurted out. "You come too, Lewis. The Vinyl Underground should be raising our voices together! It'll be so badass!"

"Sign me up," Lewis grinned.

"Yeah," Milo nodded, "let's go."

"How about it, Ronnie?" Hana asked, her smile now beaming double-time.

Just say yes, I screamed to myself, *don't say anything about Vietnam or war correspondents, don't start trouble now or you'll ruin the entire plan.*

"Well, Hana," I said in a measured tone that lasted all of two seconds, "I'd say yes . . . but I know the reason you're goin' to Chicago is to work with goddamn foreign correspondents so you can go to Vietnam! Your dad told me!"

I stormed away before Hana could respond. My angry march picked up speed, and soon it turned into a blind run. I was on the verge of tears, passing classroom after classroom, defective incubators of youth. I didn't stop running until I reached the stairwell. Then, without thinking, I punched a locker.

"Shit!" I yelled, in much-deserved pain.

I leaned against the fist-indent and cradled my throbbing hand. Then I slid down, down, down the locker, until I was on the floor. That's when I finally shut my eyes and let the heavy tears come. I was really crying hard, and it was a struggle to catch my breath. My dad would be ashamed to see me blubbering in public.

"You sure know how to boost morale," Hana said.

I opened my eyes as she sat down beside me.

"Huh?" I muttered.

"Milo and Lewis got into an argument right after you ran off. Milo wanted to set up his camera downstairs, but Lewis said it was too risky."

"Why didn't Lewis just set it up for him?"

"He offered," she said. "Milo didn't wanna risk an amateur mistake."

"Great," I sniffled. I wiped my nose with the sleeve of my blazer.

"Are you crying?"

"No," I spat, turning away. "My eyeballs get sweaty

sometimes, is all. Quit lookin' at me like I'm a chump. I'm not cryin' over you, goddammit."

"I'm glad. You don't have a reason to cry."

I scoffed.

"You don't." She swore, shoving me. "It's just an internship. I'm not going to Vietnam, or Indochina, or anywhere else. I'm not even eighteen yet! Nothing's gonna happen to me."

"You sound like my brother, ya know that?"

She sighed. She took my swollen hand in hers.

"Bruce is who showed me how vital war correspondence is, man."

I looked at her side-eyed.

"I'm serious," she said. "You don't know what I was like before we met. I hated the troops, all of the troops. I *hated them*, draftees or not. I used to go to bus terminals and airports just to yell and throw garbage at 'em. I called them baby killers, murderers. That's how I saw them, until I met you.

"When you shared those letters with me, I realized how wrong I'd been. Most of the boys in Vietnam aren't monsters, they're kids like us. The word *infantry* even fuckin' stands for *infant*, and now I understand why; that's exactly who the Man wants over there . . . not murderers, but kids. Your letters showed me that. I didn't see Bruce as a soldier, but a courageous kid with big, beautiful rock-n-roll dreams! I just want the other boys to have the chance to define themselves. If the American people could get to know the troops on a personal level, they'd never let this war drag on. Not if they really understood the price. I'm sure of it."

I didn't respond. Her hand held mine.

I felt drunk and drugged and painfully sober all at once.

"You know what?" I finally mumbled.

"What?"

I let go of her hand.

"Fuck the rest of the soldiers," I snapped, stumbling to my feet.

"You don't mean that—"

"Fuck you, too!" I spat. "You can wax poetic all ya want, but I know you'll go over there the first chance you get! Somethin' in that jungle hypnotizes hardasses like you, but I always assumed you were too smart to fall for it. I thought you were smarter than Bruce."

"Fuck me? Fuck *you*!" she snapped. "You need to look at—"

"No, *you* need to look! When you're dying in the elephant grass, you need to look back on this moment. Think about how you left me alone, just like my brother did! Think about what you—"

"Hana! Ronnie!"

Ramrod sprinted toward us. His eyes were huge and panicked.

"What the . . .?" I gasped. The worry in his yell drained the rage out of mine.

I stood up. Ramrod ran faster.

"Help me up, jerk," Hana grumbled beneath me.

I reluctantly offered her my hand. She took it. Our palms were still warm when I pulled her to her feet.

"Ronnie," Lewis panted, reaching us, "they're, shit, they're about to start!"

"But it's only ten o'clock," I said, checking my watch.

"They're settin' up right now! We gotta move!"

Lewis set off back in the direction of the balcony.

"Your eyes are sweating again," Hana mumbled.

"Oh, shut up," I whispered, wiping my face. "Let's go."

Hana and I jogged after Lewis. We couldn't catch up with him, so we kept pace with each other instead, staying side by side in an unspoken truce. When we reached the balcony, Lewis was halfway down the center aisle.

I didn't see Milo anywhere.

"He must be on his way," Lewis said, without me asking. "I can see his camera from here. It looks like he's got it all set up."

I peered over the balcony. Sure enough, the dance floor was now meant for spectators only. The entire room was gawking at the stage, where Beth Tulum stood, situating her microphone stand.

"I bet she told me the wrong time on purpose," Lewis scowled.

"Forget it. We're still solid gold."

He nodded, and then grabbed the baseball bats from the center bench. He handed one to me. My hand pulsed around the curve of the handle.

"Give me one," Hana demanded.

"No," I said, "stay here in case Milo's not back in time. Go ahead and put your record on the turntable. All you'll need to do is drop the needle when the king and queen slow dance is announced. Drop it *no matter* what, whether we're back here, or down there, or nowhere. You got it?"

"Yeah," she nodded, "I got it."

"And *run*," Lewis added.

"Oh yeah, as soon you put the needle on the record, run your ass outta here as fast as you can. The east stairwell's unlocked. It's the closest one to the auditorium, right over there—"

"OK," she nodded.

"Give 'em hell," Lewis said.

She grinned. "Give it to 'em right back."

With that, Lewis and I headed into the hall. But when we turned toward the elevator, I stopped.

"What is it?" he asked.

I patted my slacks. I checked the pockets of my blazer. "The keys! I left them on the balcony!"

"I bet Milo has 'em. We'll take the stairs."

We made a U-turn and pushed through the heavy doors of the east stairwell. We were vibrating now—our energy fed off each other, and kept rising, rising, rising, rising, *rising*.

Our shoes hit the first floor.

"I'll block the emergency exit," I said, "you get the doors in the hall."

"Cool." He nodded. "Meet me here. Two minutes."

"Two minutes," I echoed, slapping his massive back.

Then we busted into the hallway without another word.

We ran as fast as we could, slowing only to cut around the thankfully empty corners. When we neared the auditorium, I heard Beth Tulum's voice coming through the walls. I slowed down a little, to try and make out her words. Lewis sprinted past me, baseball bats pumping like extensions of his arms. He jetted to the door next to the stage.

The sight of him snapped me back on task. I rushed into the foyer and barreled through the doors and outside, onto the terrace bordering the auditorium.

The air was thick and hard to swallow. I gave up catching my breath as I plastered myself against the wall. My feet moved forward cautiously, but my heart was a runaway train.

The veranda was deserted—there were no more smokers or face-suckers, it was only me and the bat. The three huge church-like windows bathed the shadows in bright-blue light. Beside the nearest window was the emergency exit.

I jammed the Louisville Slugger into the center of the door handle and forced it all the way through into the second handle. Then I thrust the bat in even farther, until it wouldn't budge. I gave it a test tug—the doors caught as if jerked by an invisible leash. There was no way anyone could break out in three minutes.

I felt confident as I ducked back beneath the portico and reentered the school. I cut left, and took off running toward the stairwell, but as soon as I turned the corner I slammed right into Lewis. I bounced off him like a racquetball. I hit the floor hard.

"Shit," I groaned, "I thought we were meeting at the stairwell—"

He grabbed my hand and pulled me up.

"One of the bats is missing," he whispered, panicked.

"*What?* How's that possible?"

"I dunno, I dunno, but the bat in the side-stage door is *gone*, man. It's fuckin' gone!"

"Uh, we, uh, Milo! He has the *keys*! We need to find him and lock the door!"

Suddenly, a wave of applause swelled from the auditorium. Lewis and I froze. The crowning ceremony had begun.

"There's no time, Ronnie. You go find Milo, and you *play that record!*"

"But what about the door," I yelped, totally unnerved.

"I've got the door," he said.

"What the hell does that mean?"

He slid off his jacket, puffed out his chest, and rolled his shoulders.

"What do ya think it means? I'm the best barricade in six counties. I can hold the doors shut myself. If anyone asks later, I'll say I was trying to push 'em open."

"But your ears," I said, grabbing as much of his bicep as I could. "You already have a deferral! You don't need to risk your sports career, you don't have to—"

"I know I don't have to."

He gripped my trembling arm right back.

"So don't," I persisted. "If we hurry, we can find another way."

"You know," he said, "whenever me and Bruce played against a school we couldn't beat, your brother would call a special play. The coach didn't know about it, the guys on the team didn't either. It was just between us. When a game was hopeless, he'd slap me on the back and say *Bubba, it's time for the Big Fuck You.*

"Then the two of us would walk onto that field and cause as much damage as possible. Maybe we couldn't change the scoreboard, but we could put a wrecking ball through it. It feels like that's what we're doing now, like your brother called this play long before we stood here. This is all him, Ronnie. Bad Bruce *lives.*"

He smiled his championship smile and his eyes lit up like two gold rings.

"Bad Bruce lives," I echoed.

Then I watched in awe as he charged into the auditorium.

He pulled the heavy doors shut behind him. I stood there a moment, totally blanking on what I needed to do . . .

Milo! Shit!

I sprinted to the stairwell in a mad dash. My legs and throat and heart began to burn, but I kept going. I tripped more than once as I lunged up the stairs, but I didn't slow down until I flew through the doors of the second-floor hallway.

I gasped for air, regaining my bearings. *That way,* I remembered, and ran.

I'd never pushed myself like that before, and never would again. So much was happening so fast; I couldn't catch up, no matter how I punished my muscles. But I had to try. I had to try. I had to try.

So I fought forward until my legs began screaming.

My heart pounded, pounded, pounded, pounded, pounded—

Stopped.

The sight of the baseball bat caused my heart to stop.

"You better tell me *right now*, you commie fuck!"

Stink's words coated the walls of my skull, refusing to be fully processed. I couldn't focus on anything but how scared Milo looked trapped against the wall.

It took me a moment to realize I was standing still.

"You know I'll do it," Stink screamed at Milo, "so tell me what you're up to before I break your other arm! Before I bash your fuckin' brains in—"

Stink swung the bat.

I flinched—the shock of the swing slapped me out of my daze.

Stink must have seen Milo setting up his camera. He must have found the bat barricading the door. He must have followed him up the elevator—

Stink swung again. He missed again.

Milo crouched in a wrestling stance, dodging and darting frantically over what little ground he held. He was trying to lure Stink away from the balcony.

My legs began moving forward.

"This is your last chance," Stink howled. "Ya think anyone cares what happens to you? They didn't before—"

He swung again and nearly landed a head shot, but Milo jumped back just in time. That's when Milo saw me coming up from behind. I nodded at him and kept moving.

"Ya think your mamma will mourn a traitor?" Stink yelled. "Ya think—"

"You know what I think?" Milo suddenly said.

His coolness threw Stink off guard. This was my chance.

"I think it's gonna be hilarious when you realize just how fucked you are. Because you're right, I *am* up to something. But what you don't know is—I'm pinning it all on you, you inbred afterbirth-looking Nazi bitch!"

An animalistic scream clawed out of Stink's throat. He hoisted the bat above his head like a sledgehammer.

As he swung down, I lunged. I tackled him with a force that would have made Ramrod proud. The two of us went flying through the balcony doors headfirst. We tumbled to the aisle in what felt like slow motion. I glimpsed Hana standing at the record player, mortified by the sight of us. Then time sped up again, and we collapsed on top of each other.

We grappled violently as we tumbled down the aisle. Punches compounded punches as we gained momentum, rolling, rolling, down and down—until my head smashed into the hard edge of the balcony.

My vision went gray . . . then dark gray . . . then black . . . and then—

Flash!

Starlight. Sparkling starlight. Cardboard silver tinfoil starlight.

I blinked myself back to a blurred plane of consciousness.

I was lying against the edge of the balcony. Below me, the crowd clapped for Rachel Harris, who'd just been crowned prom queen of Cordelia High—but in my confused state, I was positive the cheers were meant for me.

Ronn-ie! Ronn-ie! Ronn-ie! Ronn-ie!

I pushed myself up onto my elbows. I was seeing quadruple.

Ronn-ie! Ronn-ie! Ronn-ie! Ronn-ie!

I reached for the guardrail, determined to give the crowd their money's worth. Then Milo appeared outta nowhere and pulled me to my feet. As I wobbled for some sort of balance, my eyes managed to focus on Stink—he was on the other side of aisle, reaching for the fallen baseball bat.

"Don't let him get the bat!" I gasped.

I spun Milo around by the shoulder.

"Christ!" Milo said.

Milo ran across the aisle fearlessly, and I followed as best as I could. We were locked on Stink like a torpedo, with no plan of attack beyond *charge.* But he reached the bat before we reached striking distance, and he came at us swinging.

Milo and I backpedaled, bobbing and weaving defensively as Stink swung for a kill shot. He was desperate to draw blood, to win whatever private war he was waging. The tip of the bat got closer with every mad swing and clumsy step.

Right before we reached the center aisle, he connected.

The Louisville Slugger crashed against the top of Milo's cast. Milo cried out and fell backwards, knocking me down with him. I tried to get to my feet, but he was dead weight on top of me. We were stuck on the floor, between the bleacher and the balcony.

Stink looked down at us. He caressed the bat. His lips curled into a poison smirk. The veins in his neck bulged. He tightened his grip.

He raised the bat into the sky, paused for a moment, and then swung it straight for Milo's skull at a thousand miles per hour.

"No, mudderfucker!"

All of a sudden, the loudspeaker slid off of the bleacher and crashed down, knocking him over like a bowling pin. The bat flew from his hand as the enormous speaker pinned him against the balcony railing.

My mouth dropped open at its hinges.

I looked up at Stink—he wore the same expression.

I twisted and turned, trying to make sense of what happened.

Then I saw Hana in the second row, holding an unhooked bicycle chain.

Milo crawled off of me, and we somehow stumbled to our feet. When I reached the center aisle, I looked back at Stink—he was foaming at the mouth like a rabid weasel, struggling to get free.

"Come on, you chickenshits," he spat through bloodstained lips. "Get this thing, get this thing off me. Fucking hippies . . . Gook-chink whore. You can't do this you, you, you can't do this, goddammit!"

"You're in The Vinyl Underground," I said, "we do what we want here, man."

An abrupt round of applause rose from the crowd.

"Ladies and gentlemen," the DJ announced, "please circle the floor as your king and queen have their first slow dance of the evening."

Milo ran to the turntable. But I stayed there, looking at Stink. His face was inches from the speaker grating. I glanced out at the crowd—I saw all of Stink's friends loitering near the back. I even saw Sergeant Adams, standing with the other chaperones. As the spotlight centered on the freshly minted royalty, Hana came to my side.

She pointed at the exit nearest the stage—Lewis stood there like a landmark, waiting to push against a flood of boys who'd no longer have to navigate the government implemented rite of passage commonly known as death.

Lewis looked up at us.

He shot his fist into the air like a totem of defiance.

Then he turned back to the doors.

"Here we go," Milo said.

I closed my eyes and smiled.

Milo dropped the needle onto the record. The crackle of the speaker was loud enough to make Stink scream. Hana turned and knelt beside him.

"You know," she whispered, "you made me so afraid—afraid of you, afraid that everyone's like you—God, what a joke. Now I see how fuckin' wrong I was to be afraid. You were already trapped, weren't you? You've always been trapped. You're just another sheep chained up in a prison of your own hate."

The needle found the groove.

"I hope, in a way, that this breaks your cage."

Then a voice boomed through the atmosphere like a thunderstorm. Screams of shock rose from the audience as the noise blasted from the hidden wall of speakers, distorted and insane and impossibly loud. Everyone in the crowd must have thought it was God himself.

Commanding them.

Demanding them.

To:

KICK THE MOTHER

OUT JAMS FUCKERS!

Hana grabbed my hand and dragged me up the balcony.

Milo ran ahead of us. He pushed into the hall just as the drums began beating. Then a buzz saw guitar blew right through existence itself—

YEEE

I... I...

WANNA

'EM

EEAH! I... I KICK OUT!

We made it into the hallway just as the song began.

I don't know if I was laughing or crying as we ran toward the stairwell at the other end of the school. All I know is that it felt like a victory lap, not an escape. All I know is that Hana's hand held mine, pulling me forward as she always did.

I felt zero trepidation, only a hyperawareness of my own existence. We pushed into the stairwell, and descended the stairs like a pack of hyenas, laughing madly as we sprang toward the waiting world. The music shook the outer doors of the building as we pushed them open. We ran into the schoolyard panting desperately, cackling gloriously.

"*Holy shit*," Milo wheezed, "we did it! Oh, man! We really—"

Then the three huge windows of the auditorium exploded. Our jaws dropped open in disbelief as shards of glass and rock-n-roll cut through the fragile night.

twenty-three

LAST CHANCE TO DANCE

(From the *Cordelia Island Register*, Sunday May 25th, 1968)

FOURTEEN HOSPITALIZED AFTER
SENIOR PROM PRANK DISASTER

Fourteen people were transported to Liberty General Hospital on Saturday night after being exposed to dangerous levels of noise during the Cordelia High School senior prom.

The event took place in the Cordelia High School auditorium around 10:30 p.m. on Saturday night, said Fire Chief David Tweel. It is suspected to be the result of a prank gone horribly wrong.

As Cordelia High seniors Benji Curtis, 18, and Rachel Harris, 17, were being crowned king and queen of the prom court, a prankster allegedly barred the doors of the auditorium shut.

Once auditorium exits were blocked, a profane transmission was broadcast into the dancehall at a deafening volume, Tweel said.

"I've never heard anything like it," Shannon Chaney,

17, said. "The noise was loud, like a bomb. I saw a couple kids' ears start bleeding. No one could get out of the room, and everybody started to panic."

The sound was broadcast at a volume well past the threshold of danger. The frequency of the sound waves then shattered the three large windows of the auditorium, Tweel said.

"It was just crazy," Teacher David Corona, 46, said. "There was a lot of confusion. I and the other chaperones were trying to get the children to cover their ears, when bam! The windows exploded. I've never seen anything like it."

The adult chaperones led the students to safety through the broken windows. At that time, the occurrence was thought to be the result of an audio system malfunction. It wasn't until authorities arrived that it became clear it was intentional.

"Once we got on scene, it became apparent there was more to it," said Sheriff Francis J. Milton. A carjacking had been reported earlier in the evening, and the vehicle had been transporting a large amount of audio speaker equipment.

Upon an initial sweep of the scene, the stolen speaker equipment was found arranged around the auditorium in a pattern designed to create the dangerous sound that damaged the ears of everyone in the room, Sheriff Milton said.

The suspect, who is a student at Cordelia High, was found unconscious on the second-floor balcony. Police transported him to Liberty General Hospital for emergency medical treatment.

"It looks like a senior prank that got out of hand," Sheriff Milton said. "You know, play music real loud, scare the be-jabbers out of everyone? The irony is, our suspect ended up the butt of his own joke. My men found him trapped beneath one of the speakers. Lord, he may as well have stuck his head inside of that thing."

Thirteen others were transported to Liberty General Hospital for injuries related to the incident, including hearing loss and dizziness. Seven were treated for wounds suffered from shattered glass. Dozens of other students were treated for injuries on-scene.

"We've had some pretty out-there senior pranks in the past," said Cordelia High School Principal Emmett Yonker, "like when the girls' volleyball squad snuck a pig into the boys' locker room in '66. But I've never seen anything on this scale. What conspired tonight is troubling, extremely troubling."

"The damage to the ears of our students and faculty, as well as the building itself, will take time to properly assess," said Principal Yonker.

Classes at Cordelia High resume Monday morning, per usual. The auditorium will be closed for the foreseeable future.

The investigation is still underway. The suspect's condition has been described as serious but stable. Charges are pending.

"People are saying that noise we heard was music, but I don't believe it," said Tracy Sullivan, 17. "It sounded like, I don't know, craziness. It sounded, for a second, like we were in hell."

I kept my eyes on the newspaper. Dad sipped his coffee and stared at me across the breakfast table. Momma was on her knees, knotting Roy's tie. Everyone but me had their church getup on—I'd been given a rare deferral so I could work on my term paper.

I regretted coming downstairs at all. My head throbbed something awful. I ran my index finger down the page slowly, pretending to read the article as my thoughts drifted back to the scene of the crime.

The windows of the auditorium shatter. The three of us run into the alley across the street. We hunker behind some trash cans and watch our dazed classmates climb from the windows. I have a unique understanding of how disoriented they feel, unable to catch their balance because their equilibrium has been thrown off.

A girl in a pink dress trips as she reaches the terrace; she shrieks in pain as broken glass cushions her fall. I wince at the sight, but don't comment. Neither do Milo or Hana. Lewis still hasn't come out.

Soon, sirens approach. Two cruisers squeal to a dramatic stop in front of the school. A fire truck arrives moments later, and then an ambulance. The red emergency sirens clash with the blue lights of the auditorium, mixing in the yard in a purple sort of haze.

It is through this haze that Lewis finally emerges, stumbling out of the now-open emergency exit. Even at a distance, it's clear he is in pain. But when an EMT approaches him, Ramrod waves him away. He stumbles from group to group, checking on others. We watch until Joe-Joe Brown offers him a lift home. Once Ramrod climbs into Joe-Joe's Bonneville, we feel safe enough to talk.

Well, Milo talks. Hana and I are too discombobulated. My head is aching, and my mind is broken. Hana makes me take off my jacket. She uses it to soak up the blood running down my forehead from an unseen wound.

But Milo is unfazed. The emergency lights flash orbs of color onto his glasses. He watches the aftermath as if a secret dream has been fully realized. He explains that he isn't basking in the pandemonium, but in the damage he's done to Stink. He walks us through it, step by step, as chaos reigns in the street.

He spent weeks setting up the frame. He called the sheriff continuously, and claimed Stink was still tormenting him. Sheriff Milton never took action, but Milo never expected him to. All he wanted to do is provide a consistent narrative.

Milo called the sheriff earlier in the evening to administer one final report—he claimed Stink attacked him in the Royal Atlantis parking lot as he was taking the speakers to be repaired, and then stole the work van to add insult to injury. Now that a local business was involved, Sheriff Milton was forced to take his claim seriously.

Milo tells us he even stole the letterman jacket from Stink's locker and planted it in the van for good measure. Stink chasing

Milo onto the balcony was unplanned, but it actually worked in our favor. With the stolen van in the loading bay, and Stink caught upstairs, Milo confidently calls it an open-and-shut case.

As he says this, two officers lug Stink Wilson from the building and load him into an ambulance. I see the shimmer of handcuffs on his wrists before the door shuts. All of this seems crazy, and impossible. All of this seems too good to be true.

But hey, maybe it wasn't. As I stared down at the Sunday Edition, I allowed myself to accept the possibility that everything might work out.

"I gotta tell you, boy," Dad said, "I'm not sure about your new hairdo."

I'd brushed my bangs down to cover the gash on my forehead.

"It's how college boys wear their hair," Momma said. "I think it's cute."

"It's a little too hippie-dippie for me," Dad groaned.

I handed the newspaper back to him.

"I can't believe what happened last night," I said, as believably as I could.

"It's crazy." He nodded. "And just when I was bustin' your chops for skippin' the dance!"

Momma made herself a cup of coffee and joined us back at the table. Roy sat in her lap, grumpily fidgeting with his bow tie.

"We're goin' by the hospital after church if you'd like to come," she offered.

"Kids are still in the hospital?"

"Oh yeah," Dad nodded, "I spoke to Principal Yonker

earlier. He said it's a miracle more weren't hurt. Doubt it feels like a miracle to the ones laid up, though."

"Why are they still there?" I asked softly.

"Mostly 'cause of their hearing. Adam Wilson got the worst of it, since he was stuck under one of those speakers. But Pam Olson got cut up pretty bad from the glass, and I heard Sergeant Adams has a gash on his forearm. About half a dozen others were hospitalized for this or that."

I couldn't respond. I went to take a sip of orange juice, but thought the better of it once I realized my hand was shaking.

"What's ironic," Dad continued, "is how farfetched it seemed when your hearing disqualified you from the draft. Now who knows how many of your classmates are unfit for service for the *same reason*—all 'cause of loud music."

"Maybe it's a blessing," I said. "Maybe Stink's prank ended up saving the others from being forced to go to war without a choice in the matter."

"Maybe." Dad shrugged. "It's two sides of the same coin, far as I'm concerned."

"What do you mean?" Momma asked.

"Well, like Ronnie said, the kids that are doves will be more than happy if this prank got 'em outta the draft. But some of those boys *want* to serve; a handful are already enlisted. So this damn prank took away *their* choice."

The pain pulsing through my head skipped a beat. *Some of them already enlisted?* Of course they had! Holy shit, how did we not even consider that?!

"Cole Mooney went through hell to earn his Superior Cadet

ribbon in ROTC," Dad continued. "Now he'll be discharged before he laces his boots. Same with Wesson—"

"Doug Wesson?" I asked. He sat a row away from me in French class.

"Mm-hm. Talk about a military family. They've served for generations, back to the War Between the States. He already enlisted with the Delayed Entry Program."

"Oh," I gulped. "Then what, um, what's gonna happen to him now?

"Not sure." Dad shrugged. "I figure they'll examine his hearing today, then they'll need to bring in a Med Corps officer to reevaluate his enlistment status. He and some others will likely be discharged."

I went through the entire student body in my mind, trying to do the math on which kids had likely signed up with the D. E. P. If it was a lot, then the recruiters might get curious. If the military got curious, who knew what hell could be unleashed.

Momma leaned back in her chair.

"Lord almighty," she sighed, "what a complicated world! I dunno if rock-n-roll really *is* the devil's music, but it sure as heck ain't Uncle Sam's."

———

My family was at church, and the dishes were done. But I was still in the kitchen, sitting alone at the table, thinking of what Dad said. I wasn't just worried about the threat of an inquiry, I was worried that I'd taken away my classmates' freedom of choice, just like the draft board—did that make us equitable?

I hadn't even considered it.

Did the Man consider me?

"Shit, Ronnie," I said aloud, "what the hell did you do?"

I stood up with a frustrated moan. My head was still killing me. I walked into the dining room and turned to the foyer to go back to bed, but then something in the window caught my eye—a cruiser was turning onto our street.

It pulled into Milo's driveway and my heartbeat screeched to a stop.

I stuck my nose against the windowpane.

Deputy Wilcox got out. He trotted around to the passenger door, opened it, and helped Milo to his feet. Then Deputy Wilcox wrapped an arm around him and walked him onto the porch. He seemed genuinely concerned for Milo—who was grimacing, flinching, and pulling out every pained expression in the book.

Milo directed the deputy to the porch swing. Deputy Wilcox lowered him as carefully as an ice sculpture. Once Milo was situated, the deputy extended his hand. Milo shook it, and then Wilcox strolled back to his car.

I waited until the cruiser was gone before I went outside.

"You 'bout gave me a heart attack!" I yelled as I ran across the yard.

Milo chuckled as I jogged up onto his porch.

"What were ya doing with that asshole?"

"Who," he asked coyly, "Wilcox? Hell, he's as gentle as a kitten in cotton."

I scoffed as I sat down next to him. The springs creaked above the old wooden swing as we bounced, then steadied.

"Don't worry," Milo said, "everything's cool. Mom drove me to the station while she was on break this morning, is all. I had to make a statement about the van. Wilcox gave me a lift home . . . and man, Mom told off Sheriff Milton big time!"

"I bet she did," I said. "But what did *you* tell him?"

"Same thing I said I would. Adam Wilson cornered me in the parking lot and roughed me up again, then took the van while I was laid out. I said I had *no idea* he took it for any reason but to mess with me. I figured he'd joyride and then drop it somewhere, which is what I told him when I first reported it stolen. As far as the sheriff's concerned, I didn't know about the prom 'til I read the paper this morning."

"And he bought it?"

"Hook, line, and stinker," he grinned. "I mean, what's the alternate theory? That a maimed shrimp like me broke into the school, lugged in all that equipment, and then framed someone to take the fall for the whole thing?"

"Don't ya think that's exactly what Stink's gonna tell 'em?"

"Sure, but it won't matter. Sheriff Milton's floundering, man. He knows I have the film, and he knows his career's toast if any other parents see it. You're gonna have to accept it, Ronnie. We pulled this thing off clean."

I ran my hand through my mop-top, wincing as my palm grazed the wound.

"I dunno about clean," I said. "Some of those kids are already enlisted. Some of them *wanted* to enlist. What if the military looks into it?"

"It won't matter," he scoffed. "Once a doctor declares you 4-F, you're unfit for good. They don't do retests; they have plenty of kids to take those boys' place."

"Oh."

"Did you hear what happened to Stink afterward?" he asked, shifting gears.

"Just that he's in the hospital." I shrugged.

"Wilcox said he tried to attack Sheriff Milton last night when they questioned him. He flipped out so bad, they're thinkin' of transferring him to the loony bin in St. Augustine for evaluation."

"Jesus," I sighed, "that's . . . goddamn, man."

"Don't you *dare* feel sorry for him," Milo snapped. "He's crazy, and he *needs* to be put in the nut house before he kills somebody! He's already hurt so many, it's fucked that this had to happen for adults to take his mental state seriously."

"I know he's dangerous, I know—"

"Then what's with the long face?"

"I just, I dunno. Stink isn't the only one that we put in the hospital last night."

"Minor injuries," Milo said, "everyone's gonna be fine—"

"But what if they're not?" I asked. "Our big anti-draft statement didn't account for the kids that *wanted* to enlist, man. Doesn't that bother you?"

"Didn't account for *who*? Psychos like Marty and Stink?"

"Not just them," I muttered, "good kids, too. Dad said Wesson's from a military family, and Cole, ya know, he's really high up in the ROTC. Both of 'em are still in the hospital, so you know as well as I do that they'll be stamped 4-F. I just hadn't thought about anyone wanting to enlist besides those bullies."

"If you *had* thought of it, would you've called it off?"

"I don't know," I admitted. "I know the war is wrong, and the draft is wrong, and you *know* I know what happened to you and Hana is wrong. What happened to my brother is wrong. But does all that make what we did last night right?"

Milo turned to face me. I'd never seen him look so exasperated.

"There's no equalizer in this world," he said, "no matter how ya square it. So we took away their freedom to get their asses shot off? So what?"

"So," I said, "what if it wasn't ours to take away?"

We sat in silence for a while—it was still the only way to let the subject of Vietnam drop. We rocked on the swing, and the rusty springs above us squeaked and coiled in bullfrog rhythms.

"Hana's leaving soon," Milo said.

"How soon?"

"*Tomorrow* soon. I'm goin' over later to say goodbye. You wanna come?"

"That's OK," I said flatly.

"Come on, man. What's your problem? She said she's not goin' to Vietnam."

"My problem is I don't believe her," I said. "Bruce told Ramrod the same shit until everything got real. She's just as crazy as he was, and you know it. If she gets the option to go write about the war, she'll go. She'll feel like she *has* to go."

"Ease up." He sighed. "We never know *what* she's gonna do. That's why she's the baddest. So suck it up and come with me. You never know which goodbye will be your last goodbye."

"No shit, man. That's why I ain't saying it at all."

———

My term paper was going nowhere. I sat with my throbbing head in my hands, glaring at my desk. Scraps of paper surrounded the typewriter, buried under useless books—*Profiles In Courage, U. S. History, Webster's Dictionary*—plus an unfolded pamphlet of the Constitution and Declaration of Independence.

The more research I did, the less I seemed to get done. Where were all these so-called *courageous* politicians, anyway? The ones I researched didn't think about anything but themselves; there were a few who actually seemed to have their hearts in the right place, but . . .

"Since when is it *courageous* to do your fucking job?" I sneered.

I picked up JFK's stupid book and threw it across my room.

I leaned back in the chair, cracked my knuckles, and stretched my neck.

The watch I didn't deserve said 11:46 p.m.

I groaned and rubbed my tired eyes. It was so late, and I was so far behind.

I got up, I grabbed the bottle of aspirin from my bedside

table, and dropped four of the white pills onto my tongue. I chewed and swallowed the bitterness.

I sat down on my bed. I lay down. I sat back up.

Physically, I was exhausted. Mentally, I was restless. There was no chance of sleep, so I knew that I should keep working on my stupid paper—without the distraction, I'd be unable to avoid thinking of Hana, and I was determined to avoid the urge to run across the street and shout a sappy Romeo and Juliet goodbye.

I had to keep working. I had to keep writing.

I had to take a break.

Stuffy senators and crooked congressmen no longer held my attention.

So I marched up on my mattress and got the stashbox from the ceiling.

I opened it up—all I had left was a roach, two or three tokes, max—but maybe that was enough to downshift my brain and get some productive juices flowing. There was even the improbable possibility it could ease my headache.

I slid the little hope-filled roach into my pocket.

Then I crept downstairs and through the kitchen, like so many nights before. I went into the garage and locked the door behind me. My hand caressed the Bel Air's smooth body, and I let it guide me forward, keeping the other hand outstretched until my fingertips hit the garage door. I took hold of the handle, and lifted it up, hoping for stars.

For once, heaven did not disappoint.

More stars were shining than ever, a billion tiny beacons

calling out from all the black like cosmic candles in the window of the world.

That sparkling sky stoned me before I'd even had a chance to light up.

I was too captivated to notice Hana walking up my driveway.

Once I heard feet on the pavement, I turned back to earth. I took an instinctual step back, thinking she was a stranger. Her short hair made her silhouette look like it belonged to a different person.

"Didn't recognize me, did you?"

"Of course I did," I mumbled. "Shit, you just scared me."

"Milo came by earlier. We went across town to check on Lewis."

"How is he?"

"He's OK." She shrugged. "No one suspects him of anything, at least. He's more laid up than you were, but go figure. The music was way louder this time. But he's a badass, so he'll be fine in a few weeks."

"Yeah," I mumbled.

"You shoulda come with us. But I guess you're still mad over the Hana Hitchens Vietnam Adventure fantasy you've written in your head, huh?"

"Nah," I lied, "I was never mad at you, Hana."

"Perfect," she smiled, "because I need a ride to the airport."

"Tomorrow?"

"No, tonight. I've gotta be at the *Tribune* tomorrow morning. I booked a flight out of Jacksonville at five. That gives us, like, four hours to kill. I figured we could go cruise, and just hang out beforehand . . . plus, I already told my parents you'd take me, so you don't have a choice."

"Even if I wanted to chauffer you, I can't take my dad's car without permission."

She nodded into the garage. I turned.

She meant the 409.

"*No way*," I scoffed. "You know I can't take that."

"Oh yeah, I forgot y'all want it to sit here like an unopened Christmas present for all fuckin' eternity."

"Hana!" I laughed. "You just said *y'all*!"

"No I didn't."

"Yeah you did! Y'all sure did say y'all! Ya hear?"

"*Whatever*," she snapped. "Ugh, I've gotta get the hell outta the South."

She took a step closer. My laughter dried up.

"Come on, take me for a spin. Last chance to dance."

She waited. She took another step closer. She smiled.

The smile twinkled in the starlight. The smile was for me. And suddenly, any consequences I might face for taking my brother's car seemed insignificant.

"Goddammit. Go get your bags."

"Ronnie," she said, "you're real deal rock-n-roll."

She went home to collect her things, and I put the roach between my lips.

My hands shook a little as I lit it. The smoke was harsh, but I kept it in.

I exhaled, turning away from the garage. The next toke was deep enough to suck the remaining life from the roach. When

I exhaled, Hana's silhouette formed in the smoke. I recognized it this time around. She had a suitcase in each hand. I coughed as she lugged them up the drive.

"That's all you're taking?" I asked.

"It's all I brought down here"—she shrugged—"besides my stereo and my records. I told my parents you'd take care of those until they move back, too."

"*Woah*," I said, "I'll give you a ride, but I'm not takin' your records."

I opened the passenger door of the car, and she handed me her bags.

I slid them into the back seat, and then stepped aside for her to get in.

"Of course you are," she said, climbing into the seat.

"*No*," I whispered angrily as I eased the door shut.

I walked around the other side of the car and got in.

"Ronnie, it's not up for debate."

"Damn right, it isn't."

"I know," she said.

"You *better* know," I hissed.

"Are we gonna get outta here, or what?"

"Sure," I said. But I didn't move an inch.

"Well?"

"Roll down your window," I muttered, and began cranking down mine.

"Why?"

"If I start the car in here, it'll wake my parents. If you wanna go joyride, we gotta joy-push first."

I shifted into neutral. She rolled her window down.

The two of us got out.

"You ready?" I asked.

She nodded and gripped the window frame.

Then we pushed the Bel Air out of the garage. Stars beamed off the hood like spotlights on an intergalactic showroom floor. The car rolled slow and steady.

"Right or left?" she asked, once we reached the edge of the driveway.

"Right," I said.

I turned the wheel and we lunged in unison. We pushed that hunk of metal all the way down our sleeping street. We didn't stop until we reached the next block. Then we leaned on the roof of the car to catch our breath.

"OK," I panted, "four hours to kill. Where do ya wanna go?"

"I don't know." She shrugged. "Somewhere on the island I haven't been. Dealer's choice, take me someplace special, someplace close to your heart."

Her words lingered in my mind for a moment.

Then I got back in the car. I pulled down the visor as she slid in beside me. The key dropped into my palm. I slid it into the ignition. I took a deep breath.

"Here goes nothin'," I said, and turned the key.

The 409 engine exploded to life. It roared like a beast stirred from slumber, a cry louder than that of King Kong, Mothra, Godzilla, and Richard Nixon combined.

The Platters were playing on the radio.

They sang "Sea of Love."

Someplace close to your heart, I thought. I knew where to go. Closer to my heart than she could've imagined, directly to the center, right where it was cracked.

———

The graveyard was small, only about ten yards in each direction. A rusty iron fence outlined three corners, but the far end was left open, overlooking the marsh. In the daytime you might glimpse a turtle or alligator, or admire the feminine curve of the mainland arching beyond the divide.

But at night, the marsh life was invisible. It existed only though sound. Bugs, bullfrogs, and unknown noises echoed up at us, muffled only by the Bel Air's radio, playing "Hurdy Gurdy Man," who was singing songs of lo-o-ove.

I parked right against the gate. I left the engine running. The headlights outlined the crooked branches of the live oak that loomed over the boneyard. It looked like a monstrously brittle claw and cast eerie shadows around us. We walked beneath its grasp, and I led Hana to my brother's grave.

It was the third one to left of the overlook.

"That's it," I said, and pointed.

Hana moved her fingers across the letters that were carved into the stone.

BRUCE ADDISON BINGHAM
BROTHER, HERO, SOLDIER, SON
JULY 3RD 1949—AUGUST 21ST 1967

"I put an outfit together for the burial," I told her. "His favorite jeans, his Converse, his letterman jacket. His shades."

"Cool for eternity, huh?" She smiled.

"That was the idea. But he already had on a fancy uniform when they flew his body home. He had a flag folded over his heart."

"The government's full of *ghouls*," she sighed, "spinning tragedies into advertisements for nobility. I can't imagine how hard that was, man."

I touched the cut on my forehead. It still stung like a swarm of wasps. I looked over at Hana. "What if we aren't much better?" I asked.

"This about last night? Milo mentioned you had some regrets."

"I don't regret it," I said, "I just wanna know what you think."

"Well," she said, "I think free will is an American right, at least in principle. But I think *living* is an existential one, and that trumps everything else. So yeah, maybe we fucked some kids outta their right to play soldier, but we protected their right to *exist*. They're free to keep on living, and that's all the justification I need."

With that, she ran a hand through her short hair, and strolled farther down the marsh. I lingered a moment longer, staring at the words on Bruce's grave.

We protected their right to exist, I mused. A sadness crept over my heart. Bruce was gone and the draft was gone and soon

Hana would be gone, too. Would his dream of being a DJ be all I had left? What was a dream without a dreamer?

"Just another ghost." I sighed.

Then I walked to the overlook, searching for Hana. "I'd Rather Go Blind" came on the radio, and Etta James tugged at heartstrings that were already torn and frayed. I found her sitting against a headstone, looking out at the marsh. I sat down beside her. I leaned against the same grave.

"What are you thinking about?" she asked.

"College, and DJing, and . . . I dunno. I just don't know what I should do."

"You're going to college," she assured me. "Don't you think your brother would want you to do your own thing? I mean, *Raspy Ronnie* doesn't exactly seem like a stand-alone celebrity DJ to me."

"I guess. But letting go of it just, it doesn't feel OK. It—" I shuddered, unable to finish the sentence.

She took my hand in hers. Neither of us looked at each other.

"I just don't feel OK," I mumbled.

"Me, either," she said, and then gripped my hand harder, "but we will. We can be OK, Ronnie. We can get out from under it. I have to think we can."

"Yeah," I said, squeezing back, "OK. We can."

I turned my face to the heavens and unfocused my eyes.

The stars became a kaleidoscope of diamonds.

"Maybe free will isn't just an American right," she said, speaking softly. "Maybe it's, like, an existential one, too. Your

brother, all the kids who never got a say in their life or death
. . . maybe they'll get a say in whatever comes after."

"But I thought you believe in reincarnation."

"Yeah," she said, "but what if there's an option? What if we
can choose to take the ride again, or we can go the *other* way—
out into the universal spirit, or whatever the fuck the afterlife
is. Maybe it's like, *Do you wanna go back, or do you wanna go
out?* One last act of free will. No death can be in vain if it's the
start of a new adventure."

I sat very still. I didn't reply. I let the thought sink in.

"It doesn't make it OK," she whispered, "but it gives me
a little hope. If they can choose to live again, then maybe we
can, too."

"Maybe so." I nodded, and kept my eyes fixed on the stars.

"Cry to Me" came on the Bel Air's radio. Solomon Burke's
voice glided over the cemetery on invisible waves. A breeze
picked up off the marsh and sent a rustling through the branches
above us. Hana squeezed my hand tighter.

I turned to her. She smiled.

"Dig that universal spirit, Ronnie. It's groovin' all around."

———

We didn't talk much for the rest of the night. We just drove.

We kept the windows down and the radio turned all the
way up as we pounded the A1A onto Route 17 onto Highway 9,
and then farther—onto unnamed stretches of backroads, sandy
veins zigzagging across the hide of northern Florida. The 409

ran smooth and fearless underneath the stars. It provided us with an unearned sense of protection, as if our problems were deflected as long as we were cradled inside.

I kept one hand on the steering wheel and the other on the gearshift. Hana dangled a cigarette between her fingers and propped her feet on the dash. The radio played a roadhouse jam, "Love Me Two Times" by The Doors.

The clock read 4:33 a.m. in green.

I veered onto Imeson Way. A sign said the airport was coming up ahead. Hana turned the radio down to a whisper.

"Ronnie," she said seriously, "I really need you to take care of my records."

"Don't you get it? The *last* guy who asked me to do that went to Vietnam, and never came back to claim 'em. If you pull the same shit, it'll ruin music forever! Between you and my brother, every song in the world would be a funeral march."

"You're delusional," she scoffed. "I told you fifty times that I'm not going to Vietnam, dipshit! I'm just an intern, Jesus Christ. For a guy hung up on free will, you sure don't have a fuckin' problem trying to deprive me of mine."

"What? You know I don't wanna do that."

"Then you've gotta let me go," she said. "But you've gotta keep my records so I stay on your mind whether I'm in Chicago, or Vietnam, or Timbuk-fuckin-tu. Maybe it's selfish for me to want all that, but I don't really care."

A plane thundered overhead before I could reply.

Both of us shut up.

Farther down the road, the terminal came into view. The

sun wasn't out yet, and Imeson Airport was poorly lit. But I could see the control tower flashing in the dark. I slowed the Bel Air to a crawl. The road veered onto a roundabout that circled the front of the airport.

I pulled up to the front entrance.

Reluctantly, I shifted the car into park. The hum of unseen engines was like the phantom sounds that once haunted my ears.

I turned to her.

"I'll look after your records," I said, "but *only* 'til I come see you in Chicago. And if you're *not* in Chicago, if you're in some war zone, I'm sellin' 'em all."

"What'll you do with the money?"

"Take out an ad in the *Tribune* and tell everyone what a lying, selfish asshole you are."

"Front page?"

"Naturally," I said.

She smiled. "That's fair, I guess."

She reached over and took my hand.

"Nothing can grow in a shadow, Ronnie. Don't forget it while I'm gone."

I nodded. She squeezed my hand once more, then let it drop.

"Need help with your bags?" I asked.

"No," she said, "don't get out. I don't wanna have a weepy crybaby goodbye."

"Shit," I scoffed, "we ain't gonna have a weepy goodbye—"

"Whatever you say, sweaty eyes."

That got both of us laughing. Our giggles tapered off into

a comfortable, comradely silence. Hana looked down at her lap. My eyes stayed fixed on her.

"Hey," she said, "I'm sorry I called you a dipshit."

"It's OK," I said. "Sorry for being one."

Her eyes turned back to me.

"Peace?" I asked.

"Peace."

"We don't have anything to smoke this time."

"Well," she smiled, "then this will have to do."

She leaned over and kissed me. My shoulders eased while the rest of my body simultaneously filled with life. Her lips branded me with her strength, with her courage, with the moment, with *our* moment.

But then, the moment was gone.

Hana got out of the car and onto the pavement before I'd even opened my eyes. They refocused in time to see her walk into the terminal—one bag per hand, both feet rushing forward, strutting fearlessly toward whatever waited for her beyond the coming horizon.

She was gone.

But the heat of the kiss remained.

Burning. Burning.

Now until forever.

Then again after that.

twenty-four

PROFILES IN COURAGE

I stopped for gas at the Texaco just west of O'Neill. I went into the diner to get a coffee, and then headed back onto the A1A toward home. The stars faded back beyond the beyond, and the first tinge of blue brushed across the morning sky. I'd flipped the radio off at the airport, and now I just listened to the engine and the wind and the wheels on the road.

The drive cleared my head. I felt surer of my decision to go to California with Milo. There was no reason I couldn't explore my options out west before fall semester. I would plan on college but keep myself open to other possibilities—if the answer really was blowin' in the wind, maybe I needed to go drift for a while.

I turned off of the highway and veered onto the bridge that stretched over the marsh. Both lanes of traffic were empty. I turned my head to the open window. The air smelled swampy, salty and old.

I couldn't look away from the horizon, or the coming sunrise that preceded itself with a trail of fiery light. I leaned back and dug all the beauty around me.

Then the bridge arched downward, to Cordelia Island.

Before I knew it, I'd merged onto Main Street. It was strange driving through my town as it readied itself for the day; seeing family breakfasts through kitchen windows, shoeless men jogging out for the paper, women in bathrobes taking dogs for a piss. These were my neighbors at their most genuine, just trying to get by, same as everyone else.

Where did their hatred hide in the morning hours, I wondered.

Maybe hate takes more than coffee to roust, or maybe it never sleeps?

I pondered on it pointlessly until I reached my street. Then my thoughts turned to more pressing matters, like how to keep my parents from knowing I took Bruce's car out of the garage. I assumed they were still at the breakfast table, so I figured I could push the car into the garage, the same way I'd taken it out. If I entered through the front door, I could just pretend I'd spent the night at Milo's.

My plan seemed pretty good until I saw Dad standing in the driveway. He was leaning against the open door, sipping a cup of coffee. The sight of him shocked my system; I was unable to react, reassess, or abort. The car kept moving forward, as if the wheels ran on the steel tracks of a terrible rollercoaster ride called GROUNDED FOR LIFE. The car turned into our driveway, coasted to the edge of the garage, and stopped.

The ride was over.

I sat perfectly still, unsure of what to say. Then a Dad-sized shadow spread across the hood. I could smell his aftershave through the window. I cleared my throat and summoned the guts to turn and face him.

"She give ya any trouble?" was all he said.

"Uh, nope," I sputtered. "She ran real good."

He smiled and patted the roof. He didn't look the least bit angry. I was half-convinced I was hallucinating, and I wondered if the lack of sleep had finally caught up with me. I hesitantly unbuckled my seatbelt and got out of the car.

"You look good in that thing," he said, but then his words trailed off and his eyes drifted away. He sighed and shook his head.

"You sore at me?" I finally asked.

"Nah," he said, "just mad at myself, son. Just mad at myself."

He put his hand on my shoulder and he squeezed.

"You oughta take the Bel Air to school today," he said, changing his tone.

"Really?" I stammered.

"Riding with your old man must be gettin' stale," he said, "now come on, speed demon, your eggs are gettin' cold."

———

Country ham. Eggs over easy. Three more cups of coffee.

Zero questions from my parents. They didn't ask where I took the car, who I was with all night, or why. We just sat together as a family and ate a normal sleepy Monday breakfast.

The caffeine didn't hit me until I went upstairs to change for school. I felt exhausted and wide awake all at once, a dazed and jittery zombie. I pulled on a fresh shirt, brushed my hair down, and threw a stick of gum in my mouth. Then I grabbed my backpack and hurried away from my bed's sweet siren song.

I shut the door behind me, but then froze.

The term paper! I never finished it!

I tried to think. I tried to think. I tried to think.

I went back into my room and sat down at my desk. I scanned the notes scattered across it, hoping a quick political narrative would pop out at me. I was sure I'd have to ask for an extension, or partial credit . . . but then I stopped.

"No," I said out loud, "no more politics."

I turned away from the books. I got up and walked back into the hall, then into Bruce's bedroom. I unzipped my backpack and dumped the contents onto the hardwood floor. Then I looked to the shelves and my special vinyl collection.

I put all fifteen 45s in the bag, then hurried downstairs.

I didn't bother closing the door behind me.

I went through the kitchen and kissed Momma goodbye, then shot Roy a smile on my way into the garage. It'd been so long since I'd walked in to find it empty—so I paused for a moment to admire how good the Bel Air looked in the sunlight. The sun made the paint job warble like an eight-cylinder mirage.

"Holy hell!" Milo squealed.

I smiled and continued outside. Milo was standing at the edge of his porch, looking at the car in disbelief. When he spotted me, he trampled down the steps and stumbled across the yard.

"It's alive!" he yelled.

"Yeah," I laughed, "it's alive!"

He tossed his backpack through the open passenger window.

"You not walkin' to school today?"

"Walking's for dogs, baby," he said, in his best Robert Mitchum.

I rolled my eyes. We climbed in.

Then I turned the engine over, revving it up a few times for show.

Milo clapped wildly at the sound of the roar. We backed out of the driveway and headed down the street. Both of us looked over at Hana's house as we passed it, but neither of us said a word. When we reached the next block, Milo boosted himself halfway out the window.

"I wish I had my camera!" he hollered.

"Get back in here, idiot," I snapped, "your glasses are gonna blow off."

"Sorry, dear," he said as he slid back inside.

He turned on the radio. The DJ was doing his thing.

"*. . . gettin' you down? You got a case of those Monday blues? Well don't y'all fret now, 'cause summertime is just around the bend. I'm talkin' sunshine, beach babes, and, heck, maybe even a few Beach Boys.*"

The first bars of "Sloop John B" built under the DJ's introduction.

"Aw, man"—Milo smiled—"I love this song."

"Me too."

We drove past the rubble of the school auditorium. Police tape ran across all three windows. Milo and I gawked at the sight but stayed quiet. Then I pulled into the student lot, which was nearly deserted. The few kids there seemed to recognize the car. I admit, I got a kick out of how they stared.

"Man," Milo said, "we should ditch today."

"You wanna?"

"Yeah, let's go to the beach, or somethin'."

"The beach sounds nice."

"Cool." He added, "We should go get Lewis. There's no way he's here today."

"It doesn't look like many seniors are."

"We may've created a new holiday!"

"Maybe so." I grinned.

I pulled the car back out of the parking lot. But instead of heading toward the beach, I drove around to the front entrance of the building. I stopped under the awning, and then shifted into park.

"Wait here," I said, "I gotta go drop somethin' off first."

I grabbed my backpack.

"Don't leave me out here," Milo whined, "one of my teachers will see me and know I ditched!"

"If anyone hassles you"—I shrugged—"just pretend you can't hear 'em."

Then I got out of the car, leaving the engine rumbling and Milo grumbling. I pushed through the front doors and into the empty concourse of the school. I passed the principal's office. I passed all the trophies, entombed in their glass. I turned down the normally crowded hallway to find nothing but unopened lockers.

I passed by every one of them until I reached Room 112.

Only three of my Government Two classmates were there—kids who likely never found dates to the dance. Mr. Donahue was at his desk, flipping through his attendance sheet.

"Mr. Donahue," I said, as I approached.

He raised his eyes.

"How nice of you to join us, Ronnie," he said.

"Actually, I can't stay."

"Just dropping off your term paper, I take it?"

"Well," I said, "sorta."

I took off my backpack and sat it on his desk. I unzipped it, and then I removed the stack of fifteen 45rpm vinyls. I handed them over to him.

Mr. Donahue looked at the records, confused. Then he noticed one of the letters. He slid the envelope out of the sleeve. He read the name of the sender. He read the return address. He looked back up at me.

"There's fifteen in all," I said, "which is enough to meet your word count. I'm sorry, I conscientiously object to writing about a politician. But if you wanna read about *real* courage, then you can read about my brother. Courage lives in the kids on the front of the lines, and those wild enough to live outside of 'em. But I refuse to waste a second thought on the bastards who pushed 'em there."

Mr. Donahue's eyes turned back to the records.

"Interesting point, Ronnie."

"Well, sir," I rasped, "these are interesting fuckin' times."

Then I walked right out of the classroom. I passed all the

lockers. I passed all the trophy cases, passed each and every name honorable enough to mention.

I felt the rumble of the 409 even before I reached the doors. Milo had the radio cranked to the max, and I could hear Barry McGuire growling out "Eve of Destruction." The drums ricocheted off the walls of the school like a muffled yet jangly echo.

Loud music and loud ideas—the teenage national anthem!

I pushed through the doors of that institution, and I placed a hand over my heart. I wasn't yet sure what it meant to move on, but I was ready to take the ride. It was the end of the world and I was alive and the sun, for once, was shining.

Acknowledgments

My dog Bootsie, who sat vigilantly through every outline, draft, and edit of this novel. Thanks for keeping me on task, baby. Miss you every fucking day.

Librarians and teachers, for the bravery it takes to push subversive ideas.

My readers, for sticking with me. Floored and humbled by your support.

Nat, my brother, for being my eternal creative partner (even when your name isn't on the cover). Couldn't do it without you, bro.

Shannon, my agent, for fighting the good fight and dealing with my crazy ass. Your support, help, input, and advocacy mean more than I can properly say.

Kelsy, my editor, for helping me craft this into something really special.

Everyone at Flux for their openness and support.

Dad, for the help, and your willingness to revisit the war for me.

Mom, for the perpetual (some would say almost nagging) encouragement.

Liz, the real-life Wild One, for the inspiration, partnership, help, and support.

My friends.

My bandmates.

My fans.

My heroes, who don't even know I exist.

Until next time,

Thanks.

ABOUT THE AUTHOR

Rob Rufus is an author, musician, screenwriter, and activist. His literary debut, *Die Young With Me* (Touchstone, 2016) received the American Library Association's Alex Award and was named one of the Best Books of the Year by Hudson Booksellers. It is currently being developed for the screen. Rob lives in East Nashville, Tennessee. You can catch him on the road playing with The Bad Signs or Blacklist Royals, and find out more at www.robrufus.net.